L O V E .

("L'Amour.")

From the French of

M. J. MICHELET,

OF THE FACULTY OF LETTERS, CHIEF IN THE HISTORICAL SECTION OF THE NA
TIONAL ARCHIVES, AUTHOR OF "A HISTORY OF FRANCE," "HISTORY OF
THE ROMAN REPUBLIC," "MEMOIRS OF LUTHER," "INTRO-
DUCTION TO UNIVERSAL HISTORY," "L'INSECTE,"
"L'OISEAU." ETC., ETC.

Translated from the Fourth Paris Edition, by

J. W. PALMER, M.D.

Author of "The New and The Old," "Up and Down the Irrawaddy," etc.

NEW YORK:
Carleton, Publisher, Madison Square.
PARIS: L. HACHETTE ET Cie.
M DCCC LXX.

TRANSLATOR'S PREFACE.

—o—

THIS translation of a remarkable book is presented to the public in
the sincere belief that it will do good—in the hope that it will help
American husbands and wives to perceive, and to feel more deeply,
certain things which, neglected, are often causes of lasting sorrow, in
families that ought to be happy.

The author, eminent as a savant and a historian, by the position he
holds in the world of letters commands beforehand our attention and
respect; and this volume, in which he gives us the result of the observations of a lifetime, deserves our most serious consideration. The
discoveries that have been made during the last half century, in regard
to the physiology of woman, he has turned to the purpose of his work
with stirring earnestness and eloquence. The book itself is a very
bold one—and its boldness is its beauty, for it is the boldness of chas-
tity, of a lofty and a tender morality. Hence I have thought it
judicious to render it without expurgation, and as nearly as possible
in Michelet's own forms of expression.

The intense interest which "L'Amour" has excited in Paris and London since its appearance in January last, seemed to have created a call for its immediate production in this country; and in the necessarily short time allowed by the publishers, it would have been impossible for the whole task to be correctly performed by any one person. Therefore, to my friends FRANK WOOD and B. ELLIS MARTIN, Esqs., of this city, by whom the original hurried draft of this translation was made, I here acknowledge my great indebtedness.

J. W. P.

NEW YORK, *May* 20, 1859.

TABLE OF CONTENTS.

———o———

Introduction.

Table of Contents.

Book First.

CREATION OF THE BELOVED.

Table of Contents.

Book Second.

INITIATION AND COMMUNION.

I.—LOVE IN A COTTAGE.—What influence have you over woman in society? No influence. In solitude? Every influence.—It would be otherwise in a better state of society.—The relative solitude of a tradeswoman, though surrounded by the

Book Third.

THE INCARNATION OF LOVE.

Book Fourth.

THE LANGUISHING OF LOVE.

Book Fifth.

THE REJUVENESCENCE OF LOVE.

Notes and Explanations.

NOTE 1.

A GLANCE AT THE ENSEMBLE OF THIS BOOK.

NOTE 2.

IS THE AUTHOR JUSTIFIED IN BELIEVING THAT WE CAN STILL LOVE!

Official statistics on the decline of marriage, etc.—Although
Europe is diseased, it has still reason to hope.—The decline of

Table of Contents.

Note 3.

WOMAN REINSTATED, AND PROCLAIMED INNOCENT BY SCIENCE.

Note 4.

OF THE SOURCES OF THIS BOOK OF LOVE, AND THE SUPPORT THAT
PHYSIOLOGY LENDS TO MORALITY.

Table of Contents.

LOVE.

———o———

INTRODUCTION.

I.

THE title which would fully express the design of this book, its signification, and its import, would be: Moral Enfranchisement, Effected by True Love.

This question of Love is lodged, immense and obscure, under the depths of human life. It even supports its bases and its lowermost foundations. The Family rests upon Love, and Society upon the family. Hence Love goes before everything.

As the manners are, so is the community. Liberty would be but a word if we preserved the habits of slaves.

Here we seek the Ideal. The ideal which can be realized to-day, not that which we must postpone for a better state of society. It is the reform of Love and of the Family which must precede all others, for it alone can render them possible.

———

One fact is incontestable In the midst of all our

material and intellectual progress, our Moral Sense has degenerated. Everything advances and develops, one thing alone recedes; it is the Soul.

At this truly solemn era, when the net-work of electricity is spread over all the face of the earth, centralizing universal thought, and permitting the world at last to know itself—what sort of soul shall we have to give it? And what if old Europe, from whom it expects everything, should contribute but an impoverished soul?

Europe is old, but she is also young, in this sense that she has, to counterbalance her corruption, the rejuvenescence of genius. It is her task to reform the world by reforming herself. She alone knows, sees, and foresees. Let her but have the will to do it, and all is yet safe.

———

We cannot conceal from ourselves that in these latter times the Inclinations have undergone profound changes. The causes of this are numerous. I will state two only, mental and physical at the same time, which, going straight to the brain and deadening it, tend to paralyse all our moral faculties.

For a century past, the increasing invasion of spirituous liquors and narcotics has been marching irresistibly, with results varying according to the population—here obscuring the mind, hopelessly depraving it—there, penetrating deeper into the physical economy, reaching even the race itself—but everywhere isolating man, giving him, even in his home, a deplorable preference for solitary enjoyment.

No reed to him of society, of love, of family; in their stead, the dreary pleasures of a polygamic life, which,

imposing no responsibility upon the man, not even protecting the woman (as the polygamy of the East does),
is therefore more destructive, indefinite, limitless, stimu-
lating and enervating continually.

Marriages are steadily on the decrease (*vide* the
official reports). And, what is not less serious, the
woman is not married until very late. In Paris, where
she is precocious, and marriageable at an early age, she
does not become a wife before her twenty-fifth year.
Hence, eight or ten years of waiting, most frequently
of misery, sometimes of disease in consequence. Marriage
is not even binding enough to warrant desertion.

An inhuman state of things is that where love is but
a war upon the woman, profiting by her misery, debasing
her; and, when debased, casting her off to starve.

Each century is characterized by its great malady.
The thirteenth was that of leprosy; the fourteenth, of
the plague; the sixteenth, of syphilis; the nineteenth is
stricken at the two extremities of nervous life—the
intellect and the affections—as shown in the man by the
enervated, vacillating, paralytic brain; in the woman by
the painfully ulcerated matrix.

The punishment is this : this suffering woman will
bring forth, from her pain-torn womb, but a sickly infant,
who, if he lives, will always seek, to counteract his
natural enervation, a fatal relief in alcoholic and narcotic
stimulants. Let us accept the painful supposition that
uch a man reproduces his kind : he will have from a
more diseased woman a still more enervated child.
Rather let us have death for the remedy and the radical
cure

1*

It has been fully felt from the commencement cf the century that this question of love is the essential question, which is being discussed under the very foundations of society. Where love is established and powerful, everything is strong, solid, and fruitful.

The illustrious Utopians who, on so many other subjects (on that of education, for example), have thrown much and vivid light, have not been so fortunate on the subject of love. Here they have shown, I will venture to say, but little independence of mind. Their theories, bold in form, are not the less, in substance, subservient to fact, timidly predicated on the manners of the times. They found polygamy, and they bowed down before it, creating polygamic Utopias for the future.

Without any great philosophic research, in order to find the true law for this matter, they might have consulted History simply, and Natural History.

In History, races of men are powerful in mind and body, exactly in the ratio of their monogamic life.

In Natural History, the superior animals tend towards the married state, and attain it, at least for a time. And it is from this fact, in great measure, that they are superior.

It is said that the love of animals is inconstant and variable, that mobility in pleasure is with them a state of nature. I see, however, that, from the time there is any possible stability, or regular means of living, temporary marriages at least are contracted between them; entered into not merely for the love of generation, but from actual affection. I have remarked this a hundred times, but particularly in Switzerland in a couple of finches. The female having died, the male abandoned

himself to despair, and left the young to perish. Evidently it was love, and not paternal love alone, which
had bound the male finch to his nest. When *she* was
dead, all was over.

Increasing scarcity of food as the season advances
obliges many of the species to dissolve their temporary
marriages. Then the pair must needs separate, to ex
tend the radius of their purveying search ; and they can
no longer return to the same nest at night. Thus they
are divorced by hunger, not by mutual consent. The
little industrious habits that an established union always
engenders are interrupted, annulled.

But for this they would remain together. It is not
pleasure alone which keeps them so, for the fructifying
female communicates none. It is the true instinct of
society, of life in common ; the delight of feeling near
you, all day, one little soul devoted to yourself, which
leans upon you, calls upon you, feels the want of you,
never confounds you (finch or nightingale, as you may
be) with another of the same species, listens to your
song alone, and often replies to it by low and plaintive
cries—in a whisper, so to speak (that she may be heard
by but one), from her heart to yours.

———

In our day the question of love has been profoundly
considered. Writers of genius, one in immortal romances, another under a theoretical form, eloquent,
acrimonious, and austere, have forcibly agitated it. For
reasons which will be understood, I refrain from examining their books; our points of discussion will appear
plainly enough in my own. I will permit myself to say,
however, despite my admiration and sympathetic re-

spect, that on neither side has the gist of the matter been satisfactorily penetrated.

Its two faces, the one physiological, the other moral, yet remain veiled.

The discussion continues without any one knowing, or deigning to remark, that it bears upon more than one point where the supreme authority, that of facts, has pronounced its verdict, and settled the matter beyond all cavil. The object of love, woman, in her essential mystery long unknown, unrecognised, was revealed by a series of discoveries, dating from 1827 to 1847. We now know this sacred being, who, precisely in what the Middle Ages characterized as impurity, was in reality the saint of the saints of nature.

The innate fickleness of woman is known; and not less her constancy, which marks with such fatal durability all union and marriage.

How can we speak of love without saying a word of this?

————

Still another essential thing: love is not, as people say, or would have you believe, a crisis, a drama in one act. If it were but this, an accident so transitory would hardly be worth our attention. It would be only one of those ephemeral, superficial maladies, of which we strive to rid ourselves at as little cost as possible.

But, very fortunately, love (and here I mean faithful love, fixed only upon one object) is a succession, often a long one, of very different passions, which feed and renew our lives. Leaving those *blasés* classes who have need of tragedies, of abrupt changes of scene, I perceive that love still continues the same, at times all a life long,

with different degrees of intensity, and exterior varia-
tions which do not alter the substance. Granted, that
the flame only burns on condition of its changing, going
up or down, intensifying, varying in form and in color.
But nature has provided for this. Woman ceaselessly
alters her aspects; one single woman contains a thousand
of them. And the imagination of man changes also its
points of view. On the ground-work, generally solid
and tenacious, of habit, circumstances construct changes
which modify and renew the affection. Take, not the
exception (the refined, romantic world), but the rule
(the majority, the homes of working men, which form
nearly the whole); you see there that the man, older
than the wife by seven, ten years perhaps, and having
seen besides much more of life, is much superior at first
to his young companion in experience, and loves her
somewhat as his daughter. She overtakes him or passes
him very soon; maternity, the wisdom of economy,
augmenting her importance, she counts for as much as
he does, and she is loved like a sister. But when work
has worn the man down, the sober and serious wife, the
good genius of the house, is loved by him as a mother.
She cares for him, provides for him; he reposes upon
her, and often allows himself to be like a child to her,
feeling that he possesses in her a good nurse and a
visible providence.

See to what is reduced, *among little folks*, that great
and terrible question of the superiority of one sex over
the other, a question so irritating when it comes to concern the *upper classes*. It is, above all, a question of
age. You will see it solved, the day after the marriage, to the man's profit, when the wife is yet a young

girl—solved later to the advantage of the woman.
When, on Saturday night, the man brings home his
week's salary, and she puts aside the necessary portion
to feed and clothe the children, she leaves for her husband enough for his little indulgences; and she forgets
no one but herself.

————

If love is but a crisis, we can also define the Loire an
inundation.

But you must remember that that river, in its course
of two hundred leagues, in its various and multiplied
offices, as a great thoroughfare, irrigating the earth,
refreshing the air, etc., has thousands and thousands of
means of influence.   It is doing it injustice to view it
solely in that violent aspect which you may think most
dramatic.   Let us leave then its accidental drama, which
really is but secondary.   Let us rather look upon it in
the regular epopee of its great life as a river, in its salutary
and prolific characteristics, which are none the less poetic.

In love, the dramatic moment is interesting, without
doubt.   But it is that of the fatal violence to which you
can be but a passive looker-on, where you have but very
little influence.   It is like the torrent which you observe at its narrowest point, foaming and furious.   You
must take it in the totality and continuity of its course.
Higher up it was a peaceful brook, farther down it becomes a mighty river, but a calm one.

Love is a power easily disciplined.   It gives, as does
all other natural strength, a foothold for the will, for
the art which, say what you will to the contrary, very
easily creates it, and as easily modifies it by its surroundings, exterior circumstances, and habits.

How shall the man, older, more experienced and en
lightened, initiate the young woman ?

How shall the developed woman, arrived at her apogee
of grace and power, retain, retake the heart of the man,
help him when he is weary, renew his youth, give him
wings to soar above the miseries of life and of labor ?

What influence has man over woman, woman over
man ?

This is a science, an art. We give here the clue;
others will go deeper.

To sum up:

Hitherto Love has been regarded only in its least instructive phase.

One of its forms, an inevitable and profound one, that
of its relations to Natural History, has an immense influence upon its moral development. This has been
neglected.

It has likewise a free and voluntary character, where
Moral Philosophy acts upon it, and which also has been
neglected.

This book is a first attempt to fill these two vacuums

II.

So long as the inevitable and invariable side of love
was not turned to the light, we did not know precisely
where its liberty, its own spontaneous and variable
action, commenced. Woman was an enigma. Still we

could prattle about her eternally, give the *pro* and the *con*—nothing more.

One alone stepped forward, among these speech-makers, and put an end to the discussion· one who understands it thoroughly—the sister of Love: Death.

These two powers, apparently in opposition, cannot go on without each other. They contend with equal strength. Love does not kill Death, Death does not kill Love. At the bottom of all this, they understand each other wonderfully. Each of them explains the other.

Observe, that death was needed (in order to catch the yet lukewarm life)—death in its sudden and cruel form, violent death. It is death, after all, which has taught us the most. It was the hangman's victims who revealed to us the mysteries of digestion; and suicidal women those of physical love and generation.

A place, too, had to be found where violent death was common, where suicide ever afforded to observation an immense number of women of all ages, the greater part of them in their crises of suffering; some at that monthly period when they are exalted by nature; others, *enceintes*, hoping to die with their infants; and veritable virgins, poor, bruised flowers, who despaired of ever being loved.

I have not the exact figures for Paris. But the place in Paris where they expose the bodies of those who do not die in their beds, La Morgue, receives fifty a year. This makes five hundred in ten years! An enormous number, when you consider their natural timidity and their extreme fear of death.

In what month are these violent deaths of women

most common? In the beautiful months, when they feel their desertion most cruelly; in the blooming months, when women love most. For it is an essential fact that love, generation, is most sought by man in the holidays of winter and in the banquets which follow them; by woman in the season of flowers, under the purest influences of reviving nature, of the sunshine, and of spring. Then can they least' support their painful isolation, their inconsolable misery, and they prefer to die.

The statistics do not show this. They class the greater part of those who die thus, in the exaltation of love, under the head of lunatics.

From the commencement of the century, Science has been progressing towards the great revelation. Geoffroy Saint-Hilaire and Jerres created embryogeny. Baër (1827) commenced ovology, and was followed by Messrs. Négrier and Coste. In 1842, a master, Pouchet de Rouen, reduced the whole science to a formula, and by a book of genius set it up for the future in proportions of daring grandeur.

We have noted little beyond the inferior mammalia; woman herself very little. The ingenious and learned Coste and his able assistant Gerbe (an anatomic artist), had the glory and the good fortune to discern all the truth. For nearly ten years (from the creation of the professorship of ovology to the publication of the incomparable atlas which completes these revelations), they read death itself, and hundreds of women disclosed to them the supreme mystery of love and of pain.

What is the total result of this solemn inquest?
What comes of this great and cruel wreck of woman,
of this funereal alluvium deposited each year by isolation, abandonment, betrayal, despair?

What comes of this wreck is a great truth, changing
infinitely the ideas that were entertained of woman.

That which the Middle Ages insulted and degraded,
and called impurity, is precisely her holiest crisis; what
constitutes her an eminently poetic and religious object.
Love had always believed this, and love was right. The
stupid Science of the time was wrong.

But woman labors under a great fatality. Nature
favors man. She gives woman to him, feeble, loving,
depending on the constant need of being loved and protected. She loves in advance him to whom God seems
to lead her. To distrust, resist, stop herself in this
descent, she must have much more strength of mind
than we ever need, and ten times more virtue. What a
duty for us? Nature confides her innocent daughter
to the magnanimity of man.

———

But there is yet something of greater importance.
Facts, coming from another source (*v. Lucas*, vol. ii.,
p. 60), commence to prove that the union of love,
whither the man betakes himself so lightly, is for the
woman much more profound and definitive than has
ever been believed. She gives herself up, entirely and
irrevocably. The phenomenon observed in the inferior
female animals is found, less regularly indeed, but still
is found, in woman. Fecundation transforms her in a
lasting manner. The widow frequently bears to her
second husband children which resemble her first.

This is a great and terrible fact. The conclusion is
overwhelming for the heart of man. . What I has Nature
done so much for him, favored-him to this degree? He,
too, who makes the laws, has favored himself, armed
himself against a poor, weak creature whom suffering has
delivered up to him! With this double advantage how
gentle he should be towards the woman, how tender in
his protection!

The vital flux and reflux, the profound renewing that
she suffers with so much pain, makes her the gentlest,
the most modifiable of beings. As soon as you love her,
envelop her, isolate her from bad influences. Every folly
of woman is born of the stupidity of man.

With what perfect harmony, with what astonishing
regularity, is composed the great movement of life and
of ideas! The details come all confused, it seems, and
quite by chance. Stand off, and look at the ensemble;
you are more than surprised, transfixed with admiration,
by the singular appropriateness with which pieces quite
unlike, and apparently disconnected, knowing not each
other, fit together and arrange themselves, to build up
the eternal poem.

During this period of twenty years, when the physical
dependance of the woman was so forcibly demonstrated
by Science, her free personality not less strongly burst
upon Literature. To that law of nature which subjects
her to pain, makes her a suffering creature, she replies
" No, I too am a soul."

Behold her then revealed, both in her destiny and in
her personality. By as much as on the one hand she
commands our pity, on the other she compels our admi·

ration and respect. On both sides an unexpected happi
ness is opened to us, that of increased love, an infinite
prospect into depths of love.

Who will deny this new power with which she has
burst forth ? The great prose-writer of the century is a
woman, Madame Sand. Its most impassioned poet is a
woman, Madame Valmore. The greatest success of the
age is that of a woman's book, Mrs. Stowe's novel—the
gospel of liberty for a race, translated into all tongues.

If the first words of the woman seem rebellious, wh:
can mistake the cries of pain which come from that poor
invalid, in the agitation of her awakening ? Care for
her, and love her . . . Ah ! but the proudest of her
sex would gladly give all the glories of the world for a
moment of true love ! The book that woman longs to
write in, the only book, is man's heart—to write there in
letters of fire, never to be effaced.

Literary demonstrations have much exaggerated the
changes that have taken place. All this agitation is on
the surface. Woman is what she was. As recent science
explains her to us, with love's wound bleeding in her
always, softened by suffering, glad to rest upon some one,
such she was, such she remains. Wherever she is alone,
where the world does not spoil her, she is a good and
docile creature, willingly submitting to our habits, which
are often very offensive to her, subduing man's rude
will, civilizing him and ennobling him.

Women and children form an aristocracy of charming-
ness and grace. The bondage of business debases man,
and often renders him coarse and avaricious. Woman's
bondage is simply that of nature ; it is nothing but her

weakness, her suffering; and these render her touching and poetic.

Correggio never tired of painting very young children, at the period when the lacteal life, the physical and helpless life, being passed, the first ray of their littl freedom appeared. It is then revealed, with unspeakable grace, in their pretty motions. The child is pleasing because he feels himself free and much beloved, because he knows instinctively that he can do everything that he pleases, and that he will always be loved the more for it. The mother is not less delightful in this first transport: "Ah! how active he is! and how strong too! . . . he can beat me already!" These are her exclamations. She is happy; she adores him in his resistings, in his charming rebellions. . . . Does he love his mother the less for that? She knows too well the contrary. If he sees her looking at all sorry, he throws himself in her arms again.

Why was not the man to the woman, at the first outbreak of her individuality, what the mother is to the child?

For a long time she seemed dumb, said nothing.

See, on the Indian stage, the sadness of the lover when he cannot obtain a word from that beautiful mouth. How does he know that he is loved? and is it a person or a thing that loves him? "In the name of those you love, will you never speak to me? . . . . Oh, my God! how shall I know? . . . ." This silence, this eternal ignorance of the consent accorded, and of the thought hidden, is, in reality, a true divorce. It is the cause of that sadness so often described, of that fury of which Lucretia speaks, of that despair even in the midst of pleasure.

At last she has spoken ! . . . . O joy, it is a living creature ! From the overwhelming darkness her freedom is now rescued. . . . She can hate. . . So much the better, for then she can also love. I wished her thus. This first quick, strong outbreak delights me, does not frighten me. Let us be friends, beautiful Clorinda. Heaven keep me from ever crossing swords with you. I would much prefer being wounded ! . . . But, alas! you are so already. Stern nature wished you to be always wounded, that we might always have an opportunity to cure you.

————

To speak frankly, between us men (but let it not come to the ears of the women), we have made ourselves very ridiculous by getting angry, and scolding. The duel was all a mock one.

They have not used the warlike words which have been uttered in their name. Where they have not obliging female friends to teach them the arts of war, they are peaceable, gentle, and ask for nothing but to be loved.

But this is their utmost wish, and for it they spare nothing. A lady (Madame de Gasparin), in a book mystically beautiful, eloquent, tender as it is solemn, declares to us that their happiness is in obeying, and that they desire the man to be the stronger, that they love those who command, and do not dislike the rigor of the command.

This lady, who believes that she follows the Apostle, but leaves him far behind in the spring of her young heart, assures us that a passive and patient obedience does not suffice for woman; that she wishes to obey for iove's sake, actively, obey even in advance of the possible desire, the divined thought, and without ever crying enough, until she sees the satisfied nod of the beloved object.

A true and profound revelation this. It is much more man's indifference than his tyranny that torments woman, much more her not having occasion to obey enough than performing the simple act of obedience. It is of this she complains.

No barriers, no external protection are wanted here. They serve, justly remarks this autnor, only to make mischief between husband and wife, and to render the woman miserable. Nothing remains between him and her. She goes to him strong in her weakness, in her defenceless bosom, in her heart that beats for him alone.

This is woman's warfare. The most valiant would be conquered. Who now will have the hardihood to discuss whether she is higher or lower than man? She is both at once. He is to her as the sky is to the earth; he is above, beneath, and all about her. We were born in her. We live by her. We are encompassed by her. We breathe her into our lungs; she is the atmosphere, the element of our heart.

III.

On three occasions in twenty-five years the idea of this book, of the profound social need to which it should respond, presented itself to me in all its gravity.

The first time, in 1836, before a raging literary flood had swept over us, I desired to write this history. I was then in the flower of middle-age. But the necessary treatises were not yet published. I wrote a few venture-some pages on middle-aged women, and there fortunately stopped.

In 1844, the confidence of youth, and I dare say, the sympathy of every one, surrounded me, in my professor's chair of History and Moral Philosophy. I then saw and knew many things. I became acquainted with the public morals. I felt the necessity of a serious book on Love.

In 1849, when social tragedies broke the hearts of men and women, till the very air was chilled with horror, it seemed as though the blood had all abandoned our veins. In presence of this phenomenon, which imminently threatened an extinction of every kind of life, I appealed to what little of animal warmth still remained to us; I invoked, to the succor of law, the renovation of morals, a purifying of love and of the family.

The occasion of 1844 deserves to be remembered.

In gathering together my recollections, and looking over my numerous letters of that time, I see that the singular confidence the public manifested in me arose from the feeling that I was a man abiding in solitude, a stranger to all classes, removed from the quarrels of the day, shut up in thought.

This isolation, however, was not without its draw backs. In the first place my remarks were not pertinent to the times. Like a near-sighted man, I ran against walls and posts without number. Though I made many trials, I invented old things, which had long before been discovered and known. In return, I myself remained young. I was worth more than my writings, more than my discourses. I brought to this teaching of philosophy and history a soul as yet entire, a great freshness of mind—under forms often subtle, a true simplicity of heart—in fact, at the very height of the contest, a certain peaceful spirit.

Whence came this? From the fact that, well preserved for my age, knowing man not at all (and books but little), I hated no one. My battles were those of an idea against an idea.

This touched the public. They had never met so ignorant a man; that is to say, one who knew so little of what was the town-talk.

Knowing nothing of the theories that had been promulgated, nor of the hackneyed solutions which would have helped me to answer, I was obliged to depend upon myself, to draw from myself, and, having nothing else, to share with the public my life.

This was what they wanted, and they came to me. Many revealed themselves to me, did not fear to show their hidden wounds, to bring to me their bleeding hearts. Men, always defiantly closed against the mockery of the world, opened themselves willingly to me; I never laughed. Ladies, brilliant and worldly, and for that the more unhappy; others pious, studious, austere— ay! even nuns—ignored the fictitious barriers of worldly propriety and opinion, as we do when we are lying ill. Singular, but very precious correspondences these, which I have preserved with the care and respect that they deserve.

I had not gone to the world ; the world had come
to me. From it I obtained much information. ʻSecrets
of our nature, to which I should never have penetrated,
were revealed to me in an instant. I learned more of
them in a few years than the monotonous spectacle of
society's drawing-rooms would ever have taught me. I
. saw to the very bottom of men's hearts. But, to reply
to their appeal, I was obliged also to explore carefully
my own, to seek there resources and strength. I cannot boast of having felt no emotion from the habitual
contact of so many disordered minds. But even that
helped me. The impression I received from them, a
real and profound one, was often of itself a remedy.
More than one felt himself comforted by the sympathy
that he found in me. Failing in other means, I had, in
my own emotions, an art without artifice, a moral
homœopathy.

I did not blush at being a man.

A country physician, whom I did not know, wrote
me one day, that death had taken from him his betrothed whom he was to marry in a week, and that he
was in despair. He asked nothing, wanted nothing,
except to say to a man whose heart he believed in, " I
am in despair." *

What could be said, what replied to this? what
phrases to find, alas! what consolation to offer, for so
terrible a catastrophe? I wished to write to him im-
mediately, however, and I began to do my best. In
the midst of this labor, which I felt was worse than use
less, interrupting myself to read his letter once more, I
experienced such a shock of inconsolable sorrow that
. the pen dropped from my hand. . . . . For it was not

a letter, it was the thing itself, so naïf, so bitter. I saw the whole scene. And my paper was moistened with tears, my letter effaced. But, such as it was, illegible as it was, I sealed it up, and sent it to him.

———

It was my heart, nothing less, that I gave to these people. In return, what did they give me?

At a still early hour of the day, as I am closeted at work, an impetuous young man rushes past the servant at the door, reaches my room, knocks, enters.

"Sir," said he to me, "excuse my abrupt entrance. You will not be vexed, I know, for I am the bearer of news. The proprietors of certain cafés, disreputable houses, and ball-gardens, complain of the effect of your teachings. Their establishments, they say, are losing terribly. The young men have taken to serious conver sation, and forget their former habits. . . . . In short, they make love elsewhere. . . . . These balls are in danger of dying out. All who, until now, have earned their living by providing amusement for students, re-gard themselves as menaced with a moral revolution, which will ruin them without fail."

I took his hand, and said to him: "If what you tell me is true, I declare to you that it will be a victory and a triumph for me. I desire no other success. When young men become thoughtful, liberty is saved. Let such a result follow our teachings, and I will carry it, Sir as the crown of my life's efforts, to the grave."

He went away. And, left alone, I said to myself: "I, in return, shall sooner or later make them a present. I will write them the book of enfranchisement from moral servitude, the Book of True Love."

I was very far, at this time, from suspecting the gravity and the difficulty of this grand and profound subject. I was, above all, ignorant of the unforeseen and fresh renewals that love undergoes from age to age. The past weighed me down; the future oppressed me I was in danger of remaining what I had been until then, an erudite artist.

I wished to liberate the age, and it was the age which was giving liberty to me. These transparent and confiding young minds, which laid themselves open to my gaze, revealed to me many things. They have furnished, without knowing it, a considerable part of the great array of facts from which, little by little, this book has grown.

But nothing has been of more service to me than the friendship of those to whom everything is told—I mean physicians. I have been intimately acquainted with several of the most illustrious of this century. I have been, for ten years, more than the friend, I may say the brother, of an eminent physiologist, who carried with him into the natural sciences an exquisite sense of moral things.

I learned much from him on many subjects, but especially of love.

One thing struck me in this very delicate and gifted man, the systematic perfection of his domestic life. He had a wife, comely but graceful, ignorant but charming (a native of Savoy). He had found means to engage her in his ideas, his researches, and his discoveries.

He worked with no display of instruments, no laboratory, near her and by his fireside—inventing such a reduced and convenient apparatus as to carry on in a common room experiments, often complicated, which, on a large scale, would have taken him away from home and from his wife, and thus broken up this union and harmony of minds.

A great trial came upon him. His wife, in consequence of a family malady, became insane, and continued so for a year or two. He kept her with him, and continued his labors in the midst of this harrowing distraction.

Her madness was mild enough, but she talked continually. She dreamed wide awake. She was troubled with vain fears. She interlarded all conversation with queer speeches, and hardly permitted you to follow the thread of an idea. Her husband's patience never failed him. One day I expressed my admiration of his conduct. He said to me : " In an asylum, where they would treat her harshly, where they would not put up with her little whims, she would become entirely mad, and would never recover. But well treated, not being startled or frightened, seeing only a friendly face, hearing only connected and sensible words, she will be cured at last, without any other remedy." And so, in fact, it did really happen.

I do not believe that a more remarkable example of affection can anywhere be found. Young men in their first transports for a young and pretty mistress, who has nothing but roses for them, think themselves very far advanced in love. " They would give their life for her." I dare say. Life itself is often easy to give, and to give it is but the affair of an instant ; but the persevering gentleness of a well-tried patience, which endures for years the pains of continued interruption, the tranquil

endurance which ceaselessly rectifies, reassures, strength
ens a poor, wandering, and diseased mind, possessed by
evil dreams, is perhaps a proof of the greatest, of the
highest love.

What surprised me more than all was the obedience
that he obtained from her as to matters she could not
understand. A result of the complete harmony and perfect moral development in which she had lived. With
a body very much impaired, a mind utterly bewildered,
something still remained in her, surviving all the rest—companionship and the necessity of pleasing; in a word, Love

I felt assured by this fact, and by others analogous to
it, that between the prescribed world of physiologists,
and the world, more or less free, wherein moralists abide,
is a mixed sphere, which I may call that of voluntary
fatality, that is to say, of habits indulged, and free at
first, which, through love, become at last a happy necessity and a second nature.

It is the great work of love to create this.

————

A very illustrious writer, who has recently treated
these questions, thinks that woman should obey, and
believes that she will obey, by the sole fact of her inferior nature.

The lady, of whom I have previously spoken, in her
beautiful book, does not consider woman inferior, but
still believes in her obeying. Equal? and obeying?
How can these words ever go together? She does no
sufficiently explain. She vaguely refers to Christian sentiments, to the Bible, to the grace of God.

This is a point more difficult of solution than most
people think.

The man should have over the young woman, and the aged woman over the man, a great, a very great ascendancy. But to obtain it, to establish between them the true unanimity, to insure, above all, the keeping alive, the *crescendo*, of this unity of hearts, habit is necessary, a harmony of ways.

And there is a method which leads to this.

The common framework of life has much to do with it, as well as all the forms of mental and material communication. I would say, if the phrase had not already been spoiled in trashy books, that the *art of love* is needed.

I understand the art of love thoroughly. The first steps are far too easy. But, I believe that this art aiding nature, the latter accords to the soul, at every age, and even until death, what I call (in Book v.) the rejuvenescences of love.

I believe that I have effectually suppressed old women. They will no longer be met with.

———

Must I say a word about the arrangement of this work?

It is an insignificant matter, in a book so important in itself, and on a subject, in reality, so new. I have supposed that the reader (interested in the subject, for every man is) would not care much for the style. And I have, accordingly, thought nothing of it.

No literary pretensions here; I have gone on as best I could, "running, swimming, climbing, flying" (to use Milton's words). At times I address myself to all, to the public; often to one alone; often, too, I convey the precept under a narrative form.

For this purpose I have imagined a young couple, whom I marry, and whose life I constantly folLow.

Yet this is not a novel. I have not that kind of talent. Besides, the romantic form would have presented the inconvenience of individualizing too much.

My two lovers are anonymous.

Characters with names (like the *Emile* and *Sophie* of Rousseau) do the ideas harm. The reader occupies himself with precisely the useless part of the biography, of the *mise en scène;* he forgets the useful parts, the groundwork and basis of the book. I have preferred to retain the liberty to leave at times this couple, either to speak of the vices of the age, or to state, in my own name, some grave truth, where I feel the need of strongly expressing my convictions and asserting my belief.

Is this to say that my young man, who turns up at all parts of the book, does not exist? Not at all; he does exist. The strongest proof of this is that I am going to speak to him.

————•◦————

IV.

If you have been to the museum of the Louvre you may have seen, among the statues there, *The Deliverance of Andromeda.*

This group has been very ill used, having stood under the trees at Versailles for one hundred and fifty years, where it was several times whitewashed, and, moreover, outrageously defaced by barbarians, who have destr;yed its most delicate beauties. No matter; reconstruct it in your mind's eye, chaste, glowing, breathing, as it came from the feverish hands of Puget. This great artist, in whom dwelt the suffering soul of a depraved age, born in Provence, and having constantly before his eyes the galley-hells of Louis XIV., has, all his life long, sculptured unfortunate prisoners: such as Milo, taken in a tree and devoured by a lion; the pitifully broken-down At lases of Toulon, and the young Andromeda.

Perseus has just killed the monster who was on the point of devouring her. With unspeakable joy he removes with one finger the heavy iron chains by which the young girl was suspended. Unconscious and nearly dead, she does not know where she is. She does not know who delivers her. She cannot stand, being paralysed by the rude fretting of the chains, and, above all, by fear. She seems thoroughly exhausted. This state of extreme weakness and passive self-abandonment is so much the better for her deliverer. For, after all, she is not dead; her little heart still beats, and for whom it is easy to imagine. With closed eyelids she rests her whole weight upon him. Though closed also, her pretty, quivering lips seem to say: "Take me in your arms and let me rest upon you. I am yours, take care of me. I give myself to you; be my providence, do with me whatsoever you will."

A charmingly impassioned work is this, though absurd n one feature (an additional sign of passion). The artist has been so anxious to excite our pity for Andromeda, that he has made her scarce taller than a child, though she has the form of a woman. She seems of a different race from her preserver, who is a very tall young man—tall, but not large—a feeble Hercules of the declining days of Rome, easily imagined in the effeminate reign of Louis XIV., but one that would never have been conceived by the robust mind of antiquity.

And yet this admirable man has attained his object. He produces a marvellous effect of love and pity. Whoever gazes upon this statue cannot refrain from exclaiming with emotion, "Oh! how lucky is Perseus! Would I had been there to rescue the little darling!"

Fortunate is he who rescues a woman, who frees her from the physical-fatalism in which she is held by nature, from the weakness imposed upon her by seclusion, from so much misery, so many drawbacks! Happy he who instructs her, elevates her, strengthens her, and makes her his own! For in delivering her, he also delivers himself.

In this mutual deliverance man must, of course, take the initiative. He is stronger, in better health (especially in not having to endure the great malady of maternity). He has a solid education. He is favored by the laws. He has the best occupations to himself, and earns much more than woman. He is his own master; if not suited in one place, he can go to another. Poor Andromeda, alas! must die on her rock; if she were clever enough to free herself and get away from it, we would say: "She is an adventurer."

But once delivered by you, dear Perseus, from what will she not rescue you in return? Let us enumerate.

From the servitude of your base passions: If your

home is a happy one, you will not go under the smoky lamps of a ball-garden in quest of love, nor to the street for intoxication.

The servitude of weakness : You will not drag your self feebly along, like your pitiful comrade—that young old man, so pale, debased and broken-down, whom the women ridicule. True love will preserve you from this, and concentrate your strength.

The servitude of melancholy : He who is strong and does a man's work, he who in going out to his daily toil leaves at home a beloved creature who loves and thinks of him alone, is by that very fact inspired with cheerfulness, and he is happy all the day.

The servitude of money : Receive for a truth this exact mathematical maxim :—*Two persons spend less than one.*

I see many bachelors who remain such from sheer fright at the expensiveness of matrimony, and yet spend infinitely more than a married man after all. They live very dearly at the *cafés* and restaurants, and at the theatres. Havana cigars, smoked all day, are to their solitude an extravagant necessity.

Why do they smoke? "To forget," they say. Nothing can be more disastrous. *We should never forget.* Woe to him who forgets evils, for he never seeks their antidotes. The man, the citizen who forgets, ruins not only himself but his country. A blessed thing is it to have by your hearth-stone a reliable and loving woman, to whom you can open your heart, with whom you can suffer. She will prevent you from either dreaming or forgetting. We must all suffer, and love, and think. In that is the true life of man.

Some men call themselves bachelors. But are they really so? I have long sought, but I have not yet found that mythical being. I have discovered that everybody is married; some by temporary marriages only, it is true, —secret and shameful these, lasting sometimes for months, sometimes for a week, and often only for an hour. These marriages of hourly duration, which are the utter degra dation of the woman, are not effected at a less cost to the man. It is easier to feed a whale than a *Dame aux Camellias.*

If the wife has no female friends whose rivalry incites her to extravagance in dress, she spends almost nothing. She reduces all your expenses to such a degree that the formula given above is no longer correct. We must not say "two persons," but *"four persons spend less than one."* She supports the two children besides.

When the marriage is judicious, entered into with forethought, when the family does not increase too rapidly, the wife, far from being a hindrance to liberty of action, is, on the contrary, its natural and essential element. Why is it that "the Englishman emigrates so easily, and to so much advantage for England herself?" Because his wife follows him. Except in sickly climates (like India) the Englishwoman, we may say, has sown the whole earth with solid English colonies. It is the strength of the Family which with them has made the power and the grandeur of the nation.

———

Young man, if you have a good wife and a good trade, you are free; I mean by that, that you can go abroad or stay at home, as you please.

If you go, for a time at least (for I cannot conceive

of any one leaving France forever), having a world of love and freedom with you, you will feel great confi- dence in your own abilities. You will see which way the wind blows, and will say, "The whole earth is mine."

If you stay, freed (by love) from vice and extrava- gance, you can laugh at the hosts of uneasy millionaires and despise the legions who bow themselves to fate. You will say, "Let them wear out their lives in amass- ing riches. I love, and in that I have found mine."

———

With an occupation and a wife comes the first acces- sion of freedom. After that come others.

I say an occupation, not a luxurious art. Have an art besides, if you will; and if you have, so much the better. But first, you want an art which is useful to all. Whoever loves and wishes to support his wife, does not indulge his personal pride in this matter, nor does he lose time in seeking the ·exact line between Art and Trade—a line which is, in reality, fictitious. Who does not see that the majority of trades, if you can analyse them, are legitimate branches of an art? Those of the bootmaker and the tailor, for instance, come very near that of the sculptor. If I may so express myself: for one tailor who understands, copies, and improves upon nature, I would give three classic sculptors.

———

Think of all this, dear friend (whether you are a stu- dent at college, or a young workman elsewhere, matters not). Begin now, in your days of rest, to reflect, to prepare and mark out your future life. Make the most of this time; and, if by chance this book fall into your hands, read a few pages and think. The book has among other faults, that of being extremely brief. The subject will be resumed by others hereafter, and better handled. When the one who writes this, down deep under the sod shall rest from his labors, one more able than he will take from his imperfect sketch a chapter, and make of it, perhaps, a great, exhaustive, and immortal book. But as all this is to be done with one and the same element (the same in you as in me, love and the heart of man), you can already, even on these dry data, compose for yourself in advance the book of life.

Think of it on Sunday evenings, when the noisy troupe of your thoughtless comrades hammer at your door and say: " Hallo! what are you doing? Are you a bear? Come! we are waiting for you. We are going to la Chartreuse, to la Chaumière, to the Lilas. We are going to take Amanda, Louise, and Jeannette with us."

Answer them thus: " I have something to do now. By-and-by."

If you say that, I assure you that between the two sickly flowers which you are training on your window-sill, languishing in the smoke of Paris, a third will appear, a flower, and yet a woman—the slight and misty image of your future bride.

She is rather young yet. She is perhaps but thirteen years old; you are twenty. She must have time to grow. Still, young as she is, if you devote much of your thought to her, she will guard you better than either your father or your mother. For the little one is very strict; she does not countenance follies of any sort. If any come into your head, she will manage to

ι γ without speaking to you: "No, my love; do not
g ι; stay and work for me."

I give you this charming vision for a guardian and for
a Mentor, for a preceptor and a governor. When she
is seventeen or eighteen years old, the relations between
you will change. As a wife, she will come into your
house, and think it very proper and very pleasant for
you to become master in your turn.

You will then thank God, whose inventive kindness
has made woman for you—woman, the miracle of divine
contradiction.

This book will explain her to you by facts, not by
hypotheses. She changes, and does not change. She
is inconstant and faithful. She goes on, the lights and
shades of her gracefulness undergoing a ceaseless change.
She whom you loved in the morning is not the same
woman at night. An Alsatian nun, it is said, forgot
herself for three hundred years in listening to the notes
of the nightingale. But whoever could listen to, and
look at, a woman in all her metamorphoses, would be
always astonished, might be pleased or offended, but
never tired. One alone would occupy him two thousand years.

And yet, with all this self-renewing power, such is the
force of love, its happy certainty, that the woman is so
thoroughly impregnated and imbued with the beloved
object, that she becomes herself a part of him.

So that, as they grow in years, she gains in womanly
grace. But her solid foundation is of man.

Then, if this book be reliable, and if following it step
by step, you keep your wife free from exterior influences,

and faithful to her nature, I can here boldly pronounce the phrase which sums up the whole matter: "Do not fear that you will tire of her, for she will ceaselessly change. Do not fear to confide in her, for she will never change."

BOOK FIRST.

———o———

CREATION OF THE BELOVED.

I.

WOMAN.

THE object of love, woman, is a being who stands quite alone, and is much more unlike man than would at first appear; even more than differing from, opposed to him, but pleasingly opposed, in a playful and harmonic contest, which constitutes the great charm of this world.

In herself alone, she presents to us another opposition, a struggle of contrary qualities. Elevated by her beauty, her natural poetry, her quick intuition, and divining faculty, she is not the less held down by nature in the bonds of weakness and suffering. Every month she wings her flight upward, our poor dear Sybil, and, every month, nature admonishes her by pain, and by a painful crisis returns her to the hands of love.

She does nothing as we do. She thinks, speaks, and acts differently. Her tastes are different from our tastes. Her blood even does not flow in her veins as ours does, at times it rushes through them like a foaming mountain torrent. She does not respire as we do. Making provision for pregnancy and the future ascension of the lower organs, nature has so constructed her that she breathes, for the most part, by the four upper ribs. From this necessity, results woman's greatest beauty, the gently undulating bosom, which expresses all her sentiments by a mute eloquence.

She does not eat like us—neither as much, nor of the same dishes. Why? Chiefly, because she does not digest as we do. Her digestion is every moment troubled by one thing: she yearns with her very bowels The deep cup of love (which is called the pelvis) is a sea of varying emotions, hindering the regularity of the nutritive functions.

These internal peculiarities are translated externally by one still more striking. Woman has a language peculiar to herself.

Insects and fish are mute. The bird sings, and would articulate. Man has a distinct tongue, well-defined and explicit words, and a clear tone of voice. But woman, above the man's voice and the bird's song, has a magic language, with which she intermingles this voice or this song : it is the sigh, the impassioned breath.

This is an incalculable power. Though it may but just make itself felt, the heart is at once moved. Her bosom heaves; she cannot speak; and we are won over in advance to everything she wishes. What manly harangue could produce such effect as a woman's silence ?

————◄◆————

II.

WOMAN AN INVALID.

OFTEN, seated pensively by the sea-shore, I have watched the first movement, beginning silently, then

palpably increasing until it became fearful, which surged
the flood back upon the beach. I have been over
whelmed, absorbed by the potent electricity which
danced on the legion of spark-crested waves.

But with how much more of emotion, with what
religious and tender respect, have I noted the first signs,
light, delicate, and concealed, then violent and painful,
of the nervous impressions which periodically announce
the flux and reflux of that other ocean, woman !

Besides, these signs are so evident that, even to the
eyes of a stranger, they are manifest at the first glance.
With some, who seem strong (but who at this time are
so much the more weak), a visible agitation, like a tempest, or the approach of a severe illness, commences. In
others, who, being more severely attacked, look pale
and embarrassed, you can divine something like the
destructive agencies of an undermining torrent. In the
more common case, the milder influence seems the most
salutary ; the woman grows younger and renews herself, but always at the cost of suffering, at the cost of
that mental uneasiness,- which singularly affects her
temper, enfeebles her will, and makes quite a new and
different person of her, even to him who for a long time
has known her best.

The most vulgar woman, at this period, is not without
poetry. Long in advance of, and often at the middle of,
the lunar month, she gives touching indications of her
approaching transformation. Already the wave is coming and the tide rising.

She is agitated or pensive. She has no confidence in
herself. By turns, she sheds tears and heaves sighs.
Then treat her tenderly, speak to her with extreme con-

sideration, care for her, treat her with attentions, yet
abstain from importunity, lest she be made aware of
them. Hers is a very defenceless state. She bears
within her a power greater than herself, and formidable
as a god. She astonishes you with singular speeches,
sometimes eloquent, and scarcely to be expected from
her. But (except when you have the brutality to irritate her) an increase of tenderness, of love even, overpowers all else. The warmth of the blood quickens the
impulses of the heart.

"Is this a physical and fatal love?" you ask. Yes
and no. Things pass in an inextricable confusion, and
the whole remains an enigma.

She loves, she suffers, and needs the support of a loving arm. This, more than anything else, has strengthened love in the human race—firmly established matri-
monial union.

It has often been said, that it was the helplessness of
the child which, prolonging the cares of education, had
created the Family. True, the child does retain the
mother, but the man is kept at his fireside by the
mother herself, by his tenderness for his wife, and the
happiness he experiences in protecting her.

Higher, and yet lower, than man; humiliated by
nature, the weight of whose hand she feels heavily upon
her; but, at the same time, elevated by dreams, presentiments, and superior intuitions, that man could never
have, she has fascinated him, innocently bewitched
him forever. He remains enchanted. And this is
Society.

An imperious power, a charming tyranny, has prevented his stirring from her side. This ever-renewing crisis, this mystery of love and pain, from month to month, has kept him there. She has deprived him of the power of motion by a single sentence: "I love you still the more when I am sick!"

When she has not the care and oversight of an indul· gent mother to humor and spoil her, she requires a kind husband, whom she can abuse in her service. She im· plores him, she calls upon him, right or wrong. She is excited, timid, cold, has had bad dreams—what not? There will be a storm this evening or to-night; already she feels it coming: "*Do* give me your hand. . . . I do not feel safe."

"But I must go to my work," you answer.

"Return, then, as quickly as you can. I cannot do without you to-day."

They are called capricious. Nothing could be more untrue. They are, on the contrary, very regular, and submissive to the laws of nature. Knowing the state of the atmosphere, the date of the month, and, finally, the influence of these two things on a third, of which I shall speak hereafter, they are able to predict with more certainty than the ancient augurs. You can tell, almost to a certainty, what the woman's humor will be— sad or gay; what turn her thoughts, her desires, her dreams will take.

Of themselves they are very kind, gentle, and consi-derate to him upon whom they depend for support. Their sharpness, and little fits of anger, are nearly always the results of suffering. That man is a great fool who takes any notice of these. He should rather, at such times, care for her, attend to her, and sympathize with her the more.

Presently, they are themselves again; then they regret these sad moments, excuse themselves often with tears, throw their arms around your neck, and say: "You know it is not my fault."

Is this a transitory state, then? Not at all. Wherever woman does not blot out her sex by excessive labor (like our hardy peasant women, who, at an early age, make men of themselves), wherever she remains a woman, she is generally ailing at least one week out of four.

But the week that precedes that of the crisis is also a troublesome one. And into the eight or ten days which follow this week of pain, is prolonged a languor and a weakness, which formerly could not be defined, but which is now known to be the cicatrization of an interior wound, the real cause of all this tragedy. So that, in reality, 15 or 20 days out of 28 (we may say nearly always) woman is not only an invalid, but a wounded one. She ceaselessly suffers from love's eternal wound.

⸻

Shakspeare has said: "Pity, under the guise of a little child."

Women will say the poet has said well. At the word "child" their whole heart opens, and is moved to pity.

But, we men, who know more of the truth in this matter, would say that children, so gay and thoughtless, favored by nature in a hundred ways, powerful in their youthful growth and increasing age, know but little pain or sorrow, and do not form the universal symbol of Pity.

Do you ask who the unhappy, really unhappy person, and true image of Pity, is? It is woman, who, in winter, at a certain period of the month, suffering, and fear ful of certain prosaic accidents, which often come at the same time, is obliged to display an unfelt gaiety at a ball, in a careless and unsympathizing throng.

Alas! where is her mother then? or rather her loving husband, who protects her, works for her, and permits her to remain at night in her comfortable room, by the fire? On such days he should make her retire early, and still keeping watch, would receive for his reward her last whispered word ere she fell asleep: "My God, to you I give my heart, to you and to my husband!"

III.

WOMAN SHOULD WORK BUT LITTLE.

REAL workmen, who know that a good start is always important, often all-important, also know that a job which is often interrupted does not amount to much in the end. Woman, so often interrupted by sickness, is a very bad worker. Her changeable constitution, the constant renewing which forms the basis of her existence, does not permit her to apply herself long to any one thing. To keep her seated in her chair all day would be in the highest degree cruel.

She is not at all adapted for work, when in full health. How much less then when she is *enceinte*, in that great travail of pain, which man so often thoughtlessly entails upon her? During the first four months, when the

child, still floating about in embryo, agitates her, like
the rollings of a vessel in a storm—during the five months
of absorption, when he feeds upon his mother and lives
on her blood—finally in the three months, at least, neces-
saiy to heal her poor, torn viscera, what would you have
her do ? After this horrible toil, when she has given
away the best part of herself, her blood, her marrow,
and her very life, are you going to put her to work ?

All that the economists and people of that sort have
said about woman's fitness for labor, applies to but one
exceptional country, imperceptible on the map of the
world, forming but a little black spot on that of Europe.
They have left the rest of the world out of consideration !

In all countries, and in all times, woman has been and
is now occupied only with domestic labors, which, among
savages (where the warrior reserves himself for the
greater fatigues of the chase), includes a little agricul-
ture or gardening.

And it is in doing little or nothing that woman pro
duces the two greatest treasures of this world. What
are they? The child, the man, the beauty and the
strength of race. What else ? The flower of man, the
flower of arts, of gentleness, and of humanity, which
we call Civilization. All this has come, from the beginning, of the delicate, kind, and patient culture that
woman, in her functions as a wife and a mother, has
given us.

Woman is no more idle than we are, though she acts
in a very different manner. I know some who work
twelve hours a day, and yet do not know that they are
working. One of the most industrious of these once

said to me modestly: " I live like a princess. He does
the work and supports me. Women are good for
nothing."

This "nothing" means a light, slow, interrupted and
voluntary work, always having in view those whom she
loves, her husband or her child. This work, which does
not absorb her mind, is like the woof to the web of her
thoughts. She weaves upon it the household matters
which the man, engaged in his business, had not thought
about; often, too, serious dreams about the future of her
children; and sometimes a higher and more universal
poetry of humanity and charity.

Some one asked the illustrious and charming Mrs.
Stowe under what circumstances she had written *Uncle
Tom's Cabin*. " While I was keeping the pot boiling,"
she replied.

Woman's work must always partake of love, for she
is fit for nothing else. What is her natural aim, her
mission? First, to love; second, to love but one;
third, to love always.

And we may add: to love always to the same degree,
without ever tiring. When the world does not come, to
unsettle her, and change her, woman is more faithful
than man. She loves very equally, in a continued course
which is stopped by nothing, which flows on like a rivulet
or a river—like a certain beautiful and solitary spring in
the Black Forest, of which, passing by there in July
1841, I asked what her name was. She answered:
'I call myself, *Forever*."

————————

IV.

THE MAN SHOULD EARN ENOUGH FOR BOTH.

Your poor little wife is yet asleep. It would be a great pity to wake her, for you see by the expression of her face that her dream is a pleasant one. It is of love; so it must be of you. It is only five o'clock. Besides, it is well that she should lie abed, especially at this time of the month, and sleep a little later in the morning. Now, if we could only find out the meaning of that smile upon her lips! What is she thinking about, or what does she wish?

"I do not know." Then I will tell you: "I am wholly thine, and in thee I live."

This is very simple, and yet it has a world of meaning. A complete revelation, the whole formula of nature, the marriage creed itself, is contained in those words.

"My love," she says, "I am not strong, nor good for much else but to love and care for you. I have not your muscular arms, and, if I devote myself too long to a complicated piece of work, the blood rushes to my head, and I have a ringing in my ears. I cannot invent anything; I cannot take the lead in anything. Why? Because I always wait for you, and look entirely through your eyes.

"In you alone reside the impulse, the energy, and also the patient and inventive power which leads to execution. Then you shall be the creator, and make me a nest with your talents and your strength.

"A nest! ay, and more than a nest—a harmonic world a world of order, and kindness, and peace; a city of refuge, where I shall see no more suffering, where I shall have nothing more to wish for, where the felicity of all shall crown my own. For of what use, you know, would this place of refuge be, if I were the only happy person in it? If I were an object of pity there, I should almost hate my happiness."

Now that she has spoken, let us try to formulize her thought, or rather her law; yes, for it is the law of Love.

"In the name and on behalf of Woman, ruler over all the earth, Man is commanded to transform the World, to make it the abode of justice, peace, and happiness, and to reproduce Heaven here below."

"And what will she give me in return?" Herself. In proportion to your heroism, will her heart be enlarged to you. Make, you, a paradise for others; she knows how to make yours.

It is the paradise of marriage that the man shall work for the woman; that he alone shall support her, take pleasure in enduring fatigue for her sake, and spare her the hardships of labor, and rude contact with the world.

He returns home in the evening, harassed, suffering from toil, mental or bodily, from the weariness of worldly things, from the baseness of men. But in his reception at home there is such an infinite kindness, a calm so intense, that he hardly believes in the cruel realities he has gone through all the day. "No," he says, "that could not have been; it was but an ugly dream. There is but one *real* thing in the world, and that is *you !*"

This is woman's mission (more important than gene ration even), to renew the heart of man. Protected and nourished by the man; she in turn nourishes him with love.

In Love is her true sphere of labor, the only labor that it is essential she should perform. It was that she should reserve herself entirely for this, that nature made her so incapable of performing the ruder sorts of earthly toil.

Man's business it is to earn money, her's to spend it: that is to say, to regulate the household expenditures, better than man would.

This renders him indifferent to all enjoyment that is bought, and makes it seem to him insipid. Why should he go elsewhere in quest of pleasure? What pleasure is there apart from the woman whom he loves ?

It is well said in Eastern law, that "the wife is the household." And better still said the Eastern poet: "A wife is a fortune."

Our western experience enables us to add: "Especially when she is poor."

Then, though she has nothing, she brings you every thing.

V.

SHOULD THE BELOVED BE RICH OR POOR ?

SHE should be gentle, trusting, willing to be guided, and above all, fresh in heart.

All the rest is of trifling consideration.

To commence with that which most affects people now-a-days, money, I must say that I have never seen a rich bride who was in any way tractable. It is not long before she begins to display inordinate pretensions, and claim the right of spending her marriage-portion, and even more. So that the man who thought his fortune made, soon finds himself reduced to poverty, and obliged to plunge into the quicksands of speculation.

Twelve years ago, I set up this axiom, which every day acquires additional verification. "If you wish to ruin yourself, marry a rich wife."

There is even a greater danger than of losing your fortune, it is that of losing your former self, of changing the habits which have made you what you are, which have given you all your force and originality. In what is called a good marriage, you become something like a hanger-on to a woman, a sort of prince-consort, or queen's husband, as it were.

A beautiful, a very beautiful widow, all amiability and goodness, said to some one: " Sir, I have fifty thousand livres a year, and quiet and unworldly habits. I love you and will obey you. . . . You are my old friend; tell me if I have a fault." " You have but one, madame; you are rich."

" Is it then a crime to be rich ?"

No. All that is here meant to be conveyed is, that the woman who marries a man poorer than herself is rarely willing to be guided by him. She will not adopt his ideas, his ways of living, and his habits; she will impose her own upon him. If she do not succeed in turning the man into a woman, disputes will arise. The sweet and imperceptible blending of two lives into one will not take place. The grafting of the wife upon the husband will be impossible; there will be no marriage, in fact. On the contrary, when the wife is the poorer of the two, she is rich in amiability. She loves and trusts; and these are not trifles. But are these all ? No; a third something is wanted, and this she cannot always give. She must *understand* the man whom she loves.

When there is too great a distance between the two, of position and education, when there are many social barriers to be surmounted to bring our couple together, the danger is imminent. In such a case much more time, tact, and patience will be required than a business man has always at his disposal. At some time or other you may see a young country girl, well-born, and a perfect flower of beauty, goodness, and virtue, exquisitely pure, loving, gentle, and obedient. Make love to her, marry her, and you are sadly surprised when you realize the difficulty of making yourself understood by her. She does her best; she listens to your words and desires to profit by them; she gives herself wholly up to you. And yet all this does not help the matter. She has not the power of concentrating her attention. Her excess of blood troubles her, too; country people, when taken away from their rude toil, are painfully overcharged with blood. She feels all this, only too well. She weeps, and is vexed with herself " for being so stupid." She is not stupid at all. She is even very intelligent about things coming within the province of her capabili- ties. The fault is not hers, but yours—you who believed that the few initiative steps could be so easily taken.

This young country girl could and should have mar- ried a thriving mechanic of the neighboring city. And the daughter who would have come of this marriage, already one degree finer, in point of class, than her mother, and also the recipient of a better education, might have married a man of letters; she could at once have followed and understood him in everything with- out difficulty. It would have been a marriage of minds also.

Will it always be thus? No; quite the contrary, I hope. Classes, as well as races, are continually changing. All old barriers will fall before the omnipotent vindica- tor, the grand-master of equality, Love.

VI.

SHOULD YOU CHOOSE A FRENCH WOMAN?

It is not enough to love, nor even to understand each other. You must give back something in return for what is given, sparkle for sparkle, thought for thought On this account, so far as nationality goes, I should pre fer the French woman to all others in the world.

The German woman is all love and gentleness, full of child-like purity, which transports one to Paradise. The English woman, chaste, exclusive, thoughtful, and absorbed in her home affections, so loyal, so firm, and so gentle, is the ideal of a wife. The passion of the Spaniard bites deep into the heart; and the Italian, in her beauty and softness, her warm imagination, often with her touching frankness, renders resistance impossible, and you are enraptured, conquered.

However, if you desire a wife whose soul shall respond to your own by the sympathy of intellect as well as love—who shall renew your heart by a charming vivacity and gaiety, a helping wit, womanly words or bird-like songs—you must choose a Frenchwoman.

One thing to be remembered is, that they are very precocious. A French girl at fifteen is as well developed, as to her person and her passions, as an English girl is at eighteen. This is to be attributed to her Catholic education, and confession, which is so instrumental in the forcing of young girls. Music, which is cultivated so assiduously

among us, has also a great influence. The English girl is
likewise instructed in it, but for her it is only a task. The
Italian and the German women love music for its own
sake. But, for the French woman, it is Love in the form
of art. When love comes, music is quite dismissed; the
piano, to which she devoted so much time, is utterly for
gotten.

———

Generally speaking, the young French girl has neither
the dazzling complexion, nor the visible purity, the touching and virginal charm, of the German girl. With us,
both sexes, for a season, are visited with a certain barrenness. Our children are precocious, have ardent,
scorching blood in their veins. We are not born young
in France, but we become so afterwards. The French
woman is wonderfully beautified by marriage, while the
Northern virgin loses by it, and often fades.

You risk very little in marrying a plain woman in
France. She is most frequently so simply for want of
love. When she is loved, she becomes quite another
person; you would scarcely recognise her.

———

VII.

WOMAN REQUIRES STABILITY AND COM-
PLETENESS IN LOVE.

WOMAN takes hardly any interest in the vain discussions which are carried on in her name at the present
day. She troubles herself very little about the famous

inconsistent debate, whether she is superior or inferior to man. The theory of the case is, with her, quite a secondary consideration. Wherever she proves herself thoughtful, clever, and prudent, there she is mistress; she manages the household, directs the business, keeps the money, arranges everything.

Will she obey? At this question you fancy she will resist. Not at all; she merely laughs and shakes her head. She knows perfectly, in her own heart, that the better she obeys the surer she is to govern.

What is it, after all, that woman desires most profoundly? What is her most secret wish—the indistinct yet instinctive thought which follows her, without her being able to account for it, into all places and at all times—the thought which fully explains her apparent contradictions, her prudence and her folly, her fidelity and her inconstancy?

She wishes to be loved, without doubt; but that answer does not by any means fathom the uttermost depths of her desires.

She wishes sensual pleasure. Yes, but in a very small degree. In her capacity of invalid she is prudent and abstinent, more loving yet purer than we are.

Then she desires most to reign at home, to be the mistress of the house, mistress in her bed, mistress by her fireside, at her table, in all her little world. "This," says the ancient Persian, and says Voltaire in his Tales, "is what pleases woman above every other thing." That, to be sure, is true; but it may be explained by a deeper sentiment, to which the three preceding considerations are in a great measure related.

The secret, essential, capital, and fundamental idea is,

that every woman feels herself to be a powerful centre
of love and attraction, around which everything should
revolve. She wants man to envelop her with an insatiable desire—a never-ending curiosity. She has a confused consciousness that her nature affords an infinity of
discovery; that she possesses the power of fully satisfy-
ing the persevering love which would pursue this endless
search—that she would surprise it for ever by a thousand
unexpected visions of grace and passion.

This obstinacy of love, this effort of ardent curiosity,
which seeks the infinite in a single being, implies a
thoroughly pure, exclusive, and monogamic home-circle.
Nothing is less genial than a harem; it is the abode of a
caterpillar-love, which crawls from rose to rose, spoiling
the edges of the petals without ever reaching the cup.

Woman, in all history, is the mortal enemy of poly
gamy. She wishes for the love of one only; but it
must be real love—an eager, restless passion, which, like
a flame, burns on and must burn on. She never par
dons the chosen possessor who examines so little into
the value of his treasure as to stupidly think, the day
after the wedding, that he has no more to discover.

Hence come the deplorable attempts of a creature
naturally very faithful, and who would have always
remained so, to find elsewhere a soul which desires to
know more of her own, to dive deeper into it and discover a greater happiness. In this she never succeeds.
The lover, like the husband, only skims over the surface
of the deep cup, and neither of them knows that the
treasure lies at the bottom.

Man has desire; woman love. He has invented hundreds of creeds, and founded polygamic institutions

He wished to gratify his sensuality, and have his name
live longer in the land; so he first sought pleasure, and
then perpetuity by a numerous family. Woman has
wished for nothing but to love, to give herself to one,
and to belong to him for ever.

How great is love in woman! and great, too, her
resistance to the polygamic impurity which men sought
to thrust upon her as a duty! In the Mahabharat of
India, she wishes to love but one; she is punished for it;
she dies. In the Zend-Avesta of the Persians, sum-
moned by the Magi to tell what woman most desires, she
asks for a veil, and covering her face therewith, says:
"To be loved, to be studied by her husband, and to be
mistress of the house." This beautiful answer displeases
her judges; she is stricken down, and dies. But her
soul, winging its flight to heaven, exclaims: "I am
pure and undefiled."

One very remarkable thing, in these ancient revelations
of woman's heart, is that love always appears, but the
thought of generation never.

In love she sees but love, her lover, her husband; the
child will come by and by. It is man who troubles himself about the perpetuation of his race.

A young and thoughtful lady (Madame de Gasparin)
has had the courage to touch upon this delicate point,
and to reveal woman's secret: " *The object of marriage
is marriage;* the child is but an auxiliary. Conjugal
love requires more self-sacrifice, more virtue, than maternal love; for the child is but a continuation of the mother;
in loving it the mother loves herself."

She has said this simply, innocently, boldly. She did not

ask for a veil like the Persian matron, feeling herself sufficiently protected by her virtue, and that noble maiden hood which the wife never loses.

A very pure avowal is the above, and one which in reality pleads for the interests of the child—one also which the child, could he speak before he is born, would make himself. What the child has most to wish for, is the preliminary unity of those from whom he is to spring. If they are in perfect communion of heart, he may come; his home is ready, a soft nest is open to receive him. If, at his advent, he found divorce threatening the marriage of his parents, he would perish morally, and perhaps physically. So, every question of family, education, etc., is subordinate to a previous consideration—that of love, and the mutual identification of the two who love, and who, little by little, come to form but one.

———

This is woman's thought, divested of all hypocrisy, and in its sacred gravity put in opposition to the idea, obtaining in the Middle Ages, that the sole end of marriage was procreation, forgetting that the mother, before being a mother, is the wife and the companion of man.

This argues profound ignorance. They did not know that woman, even she who has no child, is prolific in a hundred different ways. She is so to her husband, into whose nature even the simplest woman instils, imperceptibly, sentiments, thoughts, and habits in the end. At all times, when fatigued, and having exhausted or lost his mental vigor, man takes in a new supply from woman, from her soothing presence, her chaste bosom.

She is his daughter, in that he finds in her both youth

and freshness. She is his sister, in that she takes the
lead on the roughest road, and, weak herself, supports
him. She is his mother, since she ever throws her mantle
about him. In his darker moments, when he is in trouble, and seeks in vain his star in the heavens, he looks
towards woman, and behold! that star is in *her* eyes!

———

We must not let the present state of morals, the
public vertigo, and unchecked whirlwind of licence which
we have now before our eyes, deceive us as to the essence
of things; we must not stop at certain women, or classes,
r times. We must look at the eternal woman.

In all history she is the element of stability. Common
sense sufficiently explains the reason of this. It is not
only because she is the mother, the embodiment of the
family and the household, but because she brings into
the co-partnership a disproportionate share, which becomes enormous when compared to that of the man.
She enters into it entirely, and without the possibility of
withdrawal. The simplest one among them fully understands that any change is to her disadvantage, that in
changing she rapidly lowers herself; that, in going from
the first man to the second, she loses a hundred per cent.
What is it then when she leaves him for a third? What
will it be when she reaches the tenth? Alas! . . . .

When the parts are transposed, when the woman
grows fickle and calls for change, which is her degrada-
tion and her ruin, we must consider it a case of disordered
mind, a hideous symptom of misery and despair. This per-
version of woman's nature condemns her less than it does
him who causes the evil—for the crime is really man's.

The astonishing aspect of restlessness and agitation

which we now behold in their mania for dress, results less from real frivolity than from rivalry and vanity; frequently also from chagrin at their youth and beauty slipping away, and their consequent desire to renovate themselves every morning.

These surprising changes of decoration are very frequently the caprices of an ailing heart, which wants to retain a love, and finds it difficult to do so. Some of the most faithful among them, in order to retain their lovers, work incessantly at disguising and varying themselves. They would do precisely the same in the midst of the greatest solitude, in a desert, or an Alpine hut, if they lived there with "him."

Do they employ the right means to attain their end? I think not. The impressions received upon the heart are rather unsettled than strengthened by this continual change. You are tempted to say to them: "My love, do not change so rapidly. Why force my faithful heart into a permanent infidelity? Yesterday you were so lovely! I had already begun to be fascinated by that beautiful woman. And to day where is she? Already disappeared. . . . . Ah! how I regret her absence! Give her back to me. Do not force me to love change so."

Dress is a great symbol. There should be some novelty, but nothing violent; above all, never so complete a novelty as to cause love to lose its reckoning. A slight accessory to the costume gracefully varies it, and suffices for all change. A flower more or less, a ribbon, a bit of lace, a mere nothing, often enchants us, and the whole portrait becomes transfigured. This changeless change goes to the heart and silently says: "Always different, and always the same."

The follies and passing epidemics of luxury and fashion do not at all, so far as we are concerned, affect what we have, in the universality of time and place, set down as the essential law of woman's heart, and of the depths of her nature.

What she wants is not love merely, but the fixity, the passionate perseverance, the unlimited eagerness and curiosity, the endless intensity of love.

She wants this and she has a right to it; for to such ardent researches she could reply for ever, with the fresh and inexhaustible eloquence (improvisation) of unlooked for happiness.

———

Two speeches of a comedy, which may have been regarded as trifles, appear to me to merit attention. They are these.

LADY.—Will your master really love me?

VALET.—Ah! Madam, he has sworn that as fast as you renew your attractions he will renew his love.

But the lady might have replied: "And why shouldn't he?" If he is faithful—not stupidly faithful, with a monotonous constancy, but with an inventive love—insatiably curious to better understand the woman he loves, the latter, rich as the sea, liberal as the electric machine is of its sparks, can surpass all his expectations. In her is the bright rainbow of the graces of attachment, of the desires which embellish, or the refusals which attract. What limits are there to her power? None, but those of Nature, and she is Nature's self.

———

VIII.

YOU MUST CREATE YOUR WIFE—SHE HER-SELF DESIRES NOTHING BETTER.

THE girl of eighteen will be willingly the daughter—that is to say, the docile spouse—of the man of twenty-eight or thirty.

She trusts to him in everything, easily believes that he knows more than she, and all the world besides—more than her father and mother (whom she quits with tears, but without inconsolable sorrow). She believes everything he tells her, and confiding her body and soul to him, she is very far from discussing any differences of opinion which may in reality separate them; uncon-sciously, also, she even yields him her faith.

She believes that she is beginning—she wishes to begin —a totally new life, which shall have nothing in common with her former life. She desires to be born again, with him and of him. "Let this day," she says, "be the first of my days. Your creed is my creed. Your people shall be my people, and your God my God."

This is an admirable moment for the man, in which he can exercise a most powerful influence. His be the task to make that influence an enduring one.

He should do as she wishes, and take her at her word; he should re-make, re-new, re-model, *re-create* her.

Deliver her, therefore, from her insignificance, from all that hinders her from becoming an intellectual being from all evil precedents, from any faults of education or association she may have.

It is her interest, moreover, and the interest of your love. Do you know why she wishes to be renewed by you? Because she intuitively knows that you will love her the more, and with an ever increasing love, if you make her yours and a part of yourself.

Take her, then, as she offers herself, to your heart, and in your arms, like a loving little child.

———

She feels—she knows by the power of feminine intuition—that love, in these modern times, loves not *what it finds*, but *what it makes*.

We are workmen, creators, manufacturers, the true sons of Prometheus. We do not want a ready-made Pandora; we prefer to make one for ourselves.

This is proof that these latter days, which we believe to be cold and heartless, are like to produce instances of a force of love, of a revival of ardor and passion, unknown to by-gone ages.

Old-time passion for a monotonous ideal was almost still-born at the outset; it soon became indifferent to what was not its own work. But our modern passion for a progressive being, for a living, loving creation, which we fashion ourselves, hour by hour, for a beauty which is truly our own, which increases in proportion to our own power, is the source of an inexhaustible flame. So it will be in all cases, whether light or serious, so always, so everywhere. It will be like the immense sheets of flame which smoulder beneath the surface of certain provinces of China; you have but to strike the ground at any point, dig a little hole, and the **flame bursts forth.**

IX.

AM I FIT TO CREATE A WOMAN?

THIS is the timid objection that more than one will make. Such men, though vain otherwise, here confess their weakness. The difficulty, the importance of the work, overpowers them.

To love her a little, seems to them all very well; to enjoy her for a single night, very well also; but the assiduous and persevering culture of her soul intimidates them; they draw back in dismay.

"I am not prepared for that," they say. "Already impaired by the life I have led, by a rigorous bringing-up, and by the violent reaction in the course of pleasure which followed it, I do not feel worthy to take this maiden in hand, to mould this young loving heart, which calls me to be its creator, its earthly god. Have I enough intelligence, alas! enough of love even? Have I retained the faculty of love?"

But you must not despise nor distrust yourself thus; with will and perseverance you can accomplish great things yet, both in life and in love. This ill-spent past which haunts you, was not love. You are not yet able to conceive of the true love. The faculty slumbers in you, but it still exists; it was reserved for you by God. Even the prostitute is susceptible of it. The deeper the abyss, the more ardent Heaven's desire to lift you up from it.

If you were to live with your young bride, seeking

in her nothing but the gratification of passion, your heart would soon fail you ; ennui would come between you and her. But with you such a thing is impossible ; see how confidingly she gives herself up to you, in order to become part of yourself! This work of transformation, this sweet blending of your natures, will preserve in your union the ardor of its first day, will even increase that ardor. How can you help loving her more, when you feel yourself better and purer in her? when ceaselessly from her pure heart are reflected the rays of your primitive nature, of the beautiful young light which shone over your cradle, which had become overcast in you, but which she, your guardian angel, reflects upon you again more beautiful than before?

Do not then, when she comes to you of her own accord, do not be so foolish as to hesitate and say (with cowardly and culpable humility) : "I am not worthy." You have no right to say so. There is no middle-course, no mediocrity in marriage. He who does not take firm and powerful possession of his wife, is neither respected nor beloved by her. He wearies her; and between weariness and hate, with women, there is but a step. She lives apart from him, her minor self at least; and not only she, but the children, the whole family, become estranged.

———

You ask what right you have thus to take possession of her. I will tell you :

The first and principal title to your claim is the deepfelt happiness which, on contracting marriage, she herself feels in being able to say, "I am yours."

She feels free, provided that you are her master. Freed from what, do you ask ? Freed from her mother who, though loving her all the while, treats her up to twenty years of age, and would treat her up to thirty, exactly like a little girl. French mothers are terrible. They adore their daughters, but they wage continual war against them, eclipsing them by the brilliancy, the charm, and the force of their own individuality. They are much more graceful, often prettier even, and always younger, much younger, than their daughters. So long as the daughter is under the control of her mother, she has the mortification of hearing the men say every night among themselves: "The little one is not so bad, but she does not compare with her mother."

Rich or poor, the mother diets herself and her daughter altogether too much. But the mother, who is all grace, wit, and sparkle, has no need of bloom. With the daughter, it is different; low diet keeps her pale, sickly, and a little thin. The poor young girl too often prolongs the "ungrateful age," up to the very day of her wedding. Then at last, happy in you, she assumes a graceful outline; she will owe her beauty to you; if you are careful of her, if you tenderly but firmly wrap her up in your love, your young rose will blossom, fresher and more lovely than in her melancholy youth.

To become beautiful, and through love—what happiness! I dare not attempt to describe to you the excess of her gratitude. To be beautiful is Heaven; and to woman, it is everything. If she but know that it is to you she owes so great an advantage, she will readily yield on every other point; she will be delighted to feel that you are the master; she will like you to decide everything, and in general, to save her the trouble of having a will of her own.

She will cheerfully grant, what is the truth, that you are her guardian angel; that your ten or twelve additional years, your experience of the world, have taught you a thousand things from which you can preserve her, a thousand dangers to which her youth and the semi captivity of her girlhood would have blinded her, and into which, most likely, she would have rushed headlong.

Take an example: Though the daughter has often desired to be freed from her mother's authority, she nevertheless is grieved at the moment of parting. "Why not all live together, my dear?" she asks of her husband. And the wish often comes from her very heart. The husband knows, better than she, that nothing could be more fatal to the happiness of all, that a life of discord and trouble would be the result.

"But," she continues, "if I could only have my nurse, who loves me so, who is so clever, my Julia! There is none who can dress me as well as she!" Here again, it is the husband who guards her from a danger. He succeeds in not having her bring to their new home the cunning and compliant *femme de chambre*, who humors the wife, and would be the real rival of the husband, flattering him openly, and secretly influencing the wife against him, the dangerous confidante of her little griefs, and gradually becoming the mistress, the true mistress, of the house. Fortunately the young man foresees all this, and induces his bride to dispense with the alluring viper.

These are very important points, on which there is often some little disagreement. Sometimes she even turns aside to weep, though acknowledging the while that, after all, you have more experience, that you are undoubtedly right.

If you carry your point in these matters, you are sure of all the rest. In business, where the interests of both are concerned, in matters of opinion, she readily acknowledges that you know and see more and better than she does—above all, that your habits of mind are very different, stronger, and more serious.

The mere fact of having an occupation, a speciality, is a great advantage to the man. He must have passed through a previous course of moral gymnastics, must have overcome the stiffness of his joints, broken, trained, and strengthened his active faculties. It is in conquering a trade that we conquer ourselves. Herein we especially learn that, to succeed, to bring any undertaking to an end, perseverance is required ; and not only that, but conscientiousness, a firm desire to do right, and an incalculable precision. Women would be capable enough of this precision, yet they seldom possess it, because their wills are not strong enough.

You must know, too, that, being young, the woman is easily fatigued, often troubled by an excess of blood.

Those modest and charming roses, so often visible on her cheeks, are an ornament; but an obstacle, nevertheless. They render her incapable of continued application. And this beloved woman, if you permitted it, would be only too willing to throw herself upon you, and say: "Think for both of us," like a child, who, tired after a dozen steps, wants his mother to carry him. But you must not allow this. You must help and sustain the indolent beauty, without relieving her of the necessity of walking.

4

It is now or never, my friend, that you will have an opportunity of knowing whether you are a man of good sense or not. This cherished child-wife unwittingly propounds to you the most trying problem. How will you give up the scholastic pursuits in which you have been educated? How can you bring these rigid exact sciences, in their pure crystal state, back to life, and make flowers of the diamonds, to give to your child?

This is a great and beautiful problem. How difficult! and yet for you how useful! Without it you would never have known that you fully comprehended, that you were master of all this learning deposited in you, but not assimilated with you, not infused into your being. But, henceforth, you will know this perfectly, when science becomes so mingled with the hottest blood in your veins, and passes, burning its way, through your heart, and your love.

I have placed myself out of the possibility of all dispute. My heart is too full of this to allow me to turn aside and reply, to those who seek, plausibly enough, to discourage you by saying that modern science, having as yet but little unity, cannot thus be brought down to a vital simplicity, in which it can be transmitted to the uneducated woman, to a child.

A word here will suffice :

Modern reason has but two component parts :

The science of life, which is that of love, and teaches us of the universal life—our common parentage, and the fraternity of man.

The science of justice, which is the highest charity, and impartial love. This is fraternity also.

Are these two separate things then? No; there is

out one. These two great churches of God, which we have been building for the last three hundred years, unite at the top; they have a common spire, and blend in one near heaven.

The more Law has ennobled and humanized itsel', the more have the brotherhood of Justice gone forth to meet the brotherhood of Nature, and of Medicine, the science of life, of love and of mercy. (See notes.)

This is modern science, common and uniform to both sexes. You penetrate to it by justice and truth, order and harmony. And *she*, your young pupil, is conscious of it through mercy and gentleness. Both of you through love.

_____

Young man, you wish to be loved, do you not? Well! for that you must be *a man*. I mean that, above the necessary devotion to the details of business, you must preserve a reverence for humanity at large, the love of all. It is thus that you will be worthy of being loved yourself—great, noble, and having power over the woman, who is herself but love and life.

If you are studying law, for example, go on Sunday . evening to the church of Nature; I mean to the *Jardin des Plantes*. Let your friend, the young medical student, take you to the dissecting table, and teach you what death is.

And if you are a physician, pause occasionally in your career. You are seeing too much pain. Learn the social causes of it. Inform yourself, in your spare moments, of the great therapeutics of Equity and Civil Order, which would empty these hospitals, of that Justice which would cure by the diffusion of happiness.

On this ground, my friend, you are sure to be under
stood, for your wife is all pity, affection, and trust.

And what delight does she take in believing you when
you come to her with your heart full of so many new,
refreshing, and touching truths! What a striking contrast is here offered. Your maiden, your bride of sixteen
summers, your fresh and blooming rose, presents to you
the effects of a Byzantian education—a mind, old and
decayed, wrinkled with the ideas of the Middle Ages.
You, on the contrary, the man of modern times, fresh in
intellect, in learning, in conceptions, go to her new and
strong, in the dazzling heyday of youth. Here is work
for the incredible power of love; and what happiness
will it not procure you!

By an innocent error, caused by her affection and
gratitude, she ascribes and credits to you all that has
been effected by the increased intelligence of the age.
She loves you for Linnæus, and for the mystery of flowers. She loves you for the stars in heaven, as they were
first seen by Galileo. She loves in you even the science of
Death, which has taught us the profound secret of love,
and, in opposition to the barbarous impiety of the Gothic
times, has told us: "Woman is pure."

Be resigned to this, my friend. It is from you that
everything comes. You have the credit of everything.
It is you who have made all living things, all science.
She, indeed, dares not think thus, but her Love thinks it
for her; for, being her creator, you are also the creator
of the world; the world and God are both lost in you.

BOOK SECOND.

——o——

INITIATION AND COMMUNION.

1.

LOVE IN A COTTAGE.

Lovers' follies are worthy of attention. Wise men should not despise the sayings of fools. Lunatics at times have uttered oracles.

Listen to this young man who for the first time, in May, is walking with his timid and affianced bride in the country. The parents follow behind, but not too near. The lover seems to appeal to all nature, to heaven, and to earth, to share with him his great joy. But heaven, and earth, and, I must add, even his betrothed, all seem to disappear in a new transport. What is it that he has seen? A rustic cottage.

"Ah!" he exclaims, "that is the desire of my heart! Small and solitary, it is the very home I have dreamed of for you and me. Here, why may we not live together, ramble thus together, escape from society and its impure associations, and seal this Paradise of ours with mystery, and forgetfulness of the world!"

. . . .

Young man, you are not so silly after all. That common laborer's cottage is undoubtedly too rude a dwelling-place for your delicate companion; but your instinct at least reveals to you one thing that many others do not learn until long afterward, and then to their bitter cost:

" Do not sow seed by the roadside.
Do not plant trees in the torrent.
Do not love amid the crowded haunts of men. "

What influence can you have over a woman in society ?
None at all.

In solitude ? Every influence.

Besides, it is not she, perhaps, whom you must guard
thus, but yourself. The more solitary she is, the more
you live with her, the more your hearts are blended.
But so soon as she has any society, even the best, that
of her mother, her sister, or a female friend for instance,
you feel less fear in leaving her, and the bond between
you is in danger of being loosened. "Her mother is
with her," you say; "I will go and see my friends. She
is with her sister; I can pay such and such a visit now."
Then you will be sucked again into the vortex of society;
you will undoubtedly love her still, but with continued
diminution. Do you imagine that coming home every
night, fatigued, exhausted, and abstracted, you will find
the same woman, and the same love awaiting you ?

"Then, according to you, marriage should be the life
of a recluse, of a captive ? The woman shut up at home
alone; the man hardly going out at all, and then only
to attend to his business ? This is not life; it is an anti-
cipated death. Let us make our wills before marriage ;
the nuptial couch is a sepulchre. No more friends, no
more country. Good-bye to the citizen. Love and the
home-circle are going to exterminate patriotism."

This is *not* what I mean. I hope for quite a different society, pure, free, and strong, where the table of manly companionship shall reserve its place of honor for the wife, the mother, and the maiden; where, at public festivals, we shall see our charming women seated, crowned with flowers, on the stand with the magistrates. Woman, queen over the multitude, the delicate yet strict arbiter of public morals, will be the most delightful feature of future communities.

All this is yet far distant perhaps. Let me then, in the meantime, speak of possible and practical things, those which alone we need now.

The solitude that I would wish for woman is not immurement in the house of the jealous old Arnolphe, who keeps continual watch and ward over Agnes, the body of Agnes at least, while stifling her heart and suffering her mind to stagnate.

In the first place I would wish Agnes to have a husband, of an age suitable to her own. I have before given the proportion: twenty-eight years in the man to eighteen in the woman. To depart from this rule there will need to be very special affinities between you, very singular and very rare, too; these may be found, but seldom are.

I wish Agnes to have complete liberty. If woman is born feeble, and subservient to suffering, love is her edemption, marriage her successful enfranchisement. Herein she becomes equal to the man, often superior in the end

> ' And her height, pry'thee?"
> " Just as high as my heart."—SHAKSPEARE.

4*

Solitude, besides, is entirely relative. Love is a tLing
so mighty that it prevails over all circumstances. It can
live solitary even in the greatest crowd. It is pure and
wholesome even when it rages most fiercely. To it a
palace, a garret, a throne, a shop, are all one. Remem
ber, however, that it does not wage successful wai
against the troubles of this world except when it is aided
by an honest heart, industrious habits, and a succession of
labors which beneficially occupy every hour of one's life

Who has not seen, in the darkest and dreariest corner
of Paris (*Rue des Lombards*, if my memory serves me
right), a beautiful woman, born very wealthy, who,
despite her finished education and her great fortune,
passes her life in a counting-house ? There, in a little
glass-panelled office, she writes and keeps accounts, gives
orders to·and oversees a score of clerks. This woman
is alone among so many men, not as an employee, but as
mistress. Her young husband is away all day, conduct-
ing the outside business of the house. In the evening
they meet again. Madame shuts her books, sends away
her clerks, and goes up-stairs to her husband. No union
is stronger than this, no marriage happier. The husband adores rather than loves his wife. That dismal
shop is the same to them as a rustic cottage.

––––––

If, however, you will permit me to form a wish for
you, it is that your young wife, that poetic creature who
has enslaved your heart, shall be less occupied with
invoices and bills payable, and that you, yourself, be not
exiled from her all the day long. The union, in the case
cited, is strong and beautiful; but is it enduring ? Is it
not something like the partnership of two men of busi-

ness? Is there true blending of hearts between two persons who are engrossed in business? Even in bed, as the chaste and worthy spouse sinks back upon her pil-low, she murmurs between two sighs : "Do not forget, my love, that to-morrow is the thirty-first."

Love is undoubtedly a flame, a desire, a heaven, which can be found everywhere. But, it is also something which requires cultivation. Time and meditation are needed, in order to know and understand each other, and gradually, day by day, penetrate one step further into the mysteries of the soul.

When I meditate and devise happiness for others (which I often do), I wish for those who love, and would love always, even in the thickest of the crowd, a mea-sure of solitude—solitude which alone initiates one in the art of love—a few quiet years at least, to permit the blending of their mutually-strengthened hearts, before they return again to the world and to the battle of life.

I see in my mind's eye this little solitary house—not exactly the laborer's cottage that you had set your heart upon, but not much larger even than that—two floors only, three rooms on each. No servant, or at the most an honest country girl, who will be treated by her mistress as a child, and who will spare her the heaviest part of the work. I would have this house at some dis-tance from the city, whither you go to your daily business, so situated that it may receive all the warmth of the sun, with a large orchard, and a small flower-garden where your wife may work a little ; above all, plenty of water, and, if possible, springs.

Yours be the task to plan, order, and arrange all this, even in its least details. Do not depend upon the women of the family, who will pretend that they understand these arrangements much better than you.

You alone, whom it concerns so deeply, should prepare the comfortable and charming cage to tempt your little bird, to make her wish to be caught, to live as your captive in order to become at last your queen.

Ask counsel of the bee. She tells you: "I put the same egg in two different cells—the royal cell, and the working cell. Two very different bees come from these different cradles."

As the nest is, so is the bird. Our surroundings, circumstances, and habits make us what we are. This nest of true love is a beautiful subject. But I do not wish to spoil it by forestalling it here. I do not wish to show the house while it is yet empty. How different will it be on the day, the happy day, when some one (I do not say who) comes to invest it with the charm of her presence, illuminate it with her beautiful eyes.

But if it has been partly, a very little, planned by affection, it will be so well constructed, so ingeniously and artfully disposed, that her young heart will be taken captive in every part of it ; and the arranging and managing of it will add to her affection the discipline of order, so powerful in its gentleness, and will deliver her wholly up to love.

II.

MARRIAGE.

" You are my brother, father, my revered mother;
You my dear lover, my young husband are."

[Iliad.]

THIS speech is spoken not alone by Andromache, but comes from the mouth of every woman at the time of her great transition.

First, it is spoken from her heart, by an impulse of nature, as it were.

She utters it also from a true and just appreciation of her situation. She well knows that he is now her all in all, her sole protector; and she pays no attention to the ceremonies by which the Church and the Law seem to protect her.

In reality, the force of this serious act is shown in that she gives herself away without any precautionary reserve, with no chance of withdrawal. If love is not there to receive her, if she does not fall into kind hands, all legal precautions will but aggravate her situation. All these paper barriers will be in vain; and not only that—by hardening and irritating him to whom she belongs, they will put her in still greater peril. A foolish thing this, to institute a preliminary war in marriage, and to believe that the interference of the law can be called in at all hours of the night or day, and keep watch even over the bed. From him who possesses woman by the divine right of cohabitation, and who can impose upon her the pains of labor and the perils of maternity, there is absolutely no appeal. She has no other security but his love.

Ceremony, solemnity, and publicity are doubtless ex cellent in their way. But the foundation of the matter is in the heart. As the Roman jurisconsult said, "Mar riage is *consent,*" an act of the will, a freedom which is voluntarily relinquished—a mutual exchange of hearts; but also a sacrifice of the weaker party, who, in giving herself over to the stronger, body and soul, with no stipulation whatever, risks everything for the future.

This is a very unequal contract, and neither the laws of the Church nor the laws of the State have yet seriously attempted to modify its nature. Both, in reality, are very hard upon woman.

The church is openly against her, owing her a grudge for the sin of Eve. It considers her a temptation incarnate, and closely in league with the devil. It permits marriage though it prefers celibacy, as the life of purity; for woman is impure. This doctrine is so thoroughly that of the Middle Ages, that those who wish to renew the spirit of the latter, contend (against the teachings of chemistry) that in her sacred crisis the blood of woman is unclean. So much for physiology and law! When woman is so far abased as this, what is she fit for but to be a submissive servant to the purer being, man? She is the body; he is the mind.

The civil law is not less harsh. It declares woman to be a minor all her life long, and pronounces upon her an eternal interdiction. Man is constituted her guardian when it comes to the crimes that she may com‧ mit, the penalties that she may endure, she is treated as a perfectly responsible person, of the full age, and dealt with very severely. There exists moreover the same contradiction in all the old barbarian laws. "She is given to man as a chattel, punished as a responsible person."

"But the family at least," you say, "is on her side, and will really protect her."

I don't see that. I have known many theoretical friends of freedom, who, when it came to this point, forgot all their previous enthusiasm over this precious attribute, and married their daughters, in spite of themselves, to rich old men, whom they could not endure.

It is never dreamed that the feeble creature will, in this matter, attempt a siege against her father, her mother, and her whole family. She will yield to them, and allow herself to be urged onward to the fatal day, which she reaches wholly unprepared.

Every mother practises a sort of self-delusion; she will say, most emphatically, "Oh! how I love my daughter!" And yet what does she do for her? She does not prepare her for marriage, either mentally or physically.

For one thing are mothers deserving of praise; they generally keep better watch over the daughter's virtue than men believe. They wish her to arrive at marriage as a virgin, ignorant of everything, if possible; and to have the husband delighted at finding her so like a little girl in simplicity. And, in fact, this does astonish him (he who has seen only abandoned women) to such a degree that he thinks she is playing the hypocrite.

This ignorance is, however, very natural when the girl is under the care of a jealous and watchful mother, and especially if she have no young female friends to instruct her. But there is danger in this total igno- rance, by the mere fact of which the innocent maiden is exposed to more than one risk. The mother should enlighten her, and put her on her guard, as soon as she becomes a woman. At all events, it is her sacred duty to perfectly initiate her daughter before marriage, so that she may know well beforehand to what she is going to consent, what it is that she is to undergo.

No compact can be voluntary or worth anything if the conditions are not previously known.

Does she know in the morning what she promises for the evening? Is she, then, a person whose inclinations have been consulted? or a mere thing, silently handed over to her master? Does she know, above all, the exorbitant right that the husband is about to assume, in constituting himself (on doubtful authority) the judge of her past morals, of her proper conduct, her purity and her virtue?

She is not better prepared physically than mentally. Too much thought is given to the wedding dress, not enough to the maiden. Father, mother, friends, and even her betrothed, all busied with a thousand trifling preparations, neglect the very person who is the object of them all.

What is her condition at this moment of agitation, on the eve of such a trial?

In the first place, she passes a restless night. Fatuity would have you believe that it is caused by impatience;

generally it is for quite the contrary reason. This most desired thing, now that it draws near, inspires her with fear and sadness, especially when it comes to the complete putting aside of all her former habits, when she finds herself on the threshold of such a vast and unknown future.

It is very natural that she should be restless and agitated, should have at times a little fever, that the circulation of her blood should be irregular or very rapid, the nutritive function slow, and difficult of accomplishment. This should all be thought of long beforehand; but every one is thinking of something else. Often, when the time finally comes, the maiden is very ill from fright, and in a state of painful plethora, which requires kind and gentle treatment.

Young man, read this all alone, and not with that thoughtless comrade whom I see behind you, mocking over your shoulder. If you read alone, you will read to some purpose. You will feel the responses of your own heart. And the holiness of Nature will touch you.

This book treats of religion, of truth, and of purity. If you find it a subject of amusement and ridicule, I do not doubt that you would laugh over your mother's coffin.

In marriage your happiness is immense, but how serious also! Respect it. Consider the sacred gravity of the adoption you are about to make, the infinite love that is expected of you by her who comes to you alone, and with boundless confidence.

Yes, alone, my friend. For you have seen that the Church affords her no protection, neither does the Law

And the family, alas, has not taken much pains to comfort her on this painful day. The family does not sustain her, but brings her to you, gives her to you—to the chances of your judgment.

But I trust in you for her sake. And I am sure that, were all else in the world to fail, you would be to her that all—country and priest, and mother; and that she would find in you the guaranty of this triple pontificate.

This is her whole thought, faith, and hope, when she tremblingly advances, so beautiful in her pallor, robed in fresh garments. She knows that she is no longer in her own house, and not yet in yours. She hovers between two worlds.

Where is she going, and what is required of her? She hardly knows. She does not know much of anything, except that she gives herself away in all the devotedness of her heart.

She has the bliss of thinking that she is henceforward in your hands. Will this be well or ill for her? and how will you treat her? are questions which concern you, not her.

In holding back nothing from you, in coming to you alone and without protection, in loving you and abandoning herself to your love, lies all her defence and security.

Said Christopher Columbus, when he drew near to the unknown world:

"Let heaven and earth pray and weep for me."

III.

THE WEDDING.

THE hour has come. Her mother sheds a few tears, and leaves her. But I shall not leave her yet. I have something to tell you which even her mother does not know.

Do not be impatient and angry with me. Not for my sake is it, that I ask you to stay a moment. She has entered without fear, she loves you so! She has that modest assurance which is the gift of purity. But still, she is very much agitated; it is human nature Her poor little heart beats so violently that you can see its throbbing. A moment, I pray you; let us leave her to recover a little, and breathe.

What I have to say to you is this:

I make and institute you her protector against your-self.

Yes, against yourself. Do not attempt to deny it; at this moment, you are her enemy.

A gentle, respectful, and loving enemy, it is true; but no less an enemy for all that. Let us cut short the insipid things that a man of the world would say about what the good breeding of gentlemen prompts them to do on such occasions. I know that when the greater part of them reach marriage, their ardor has been spent in the life they have led, in a great, too great, experience of pleasure. But even for those who are the most *blasé*, it is a matter of *amour propre*, of vain impatience. This

may have endless consequences. Hence, I believe her«
in that quotation from Natural History, which, though
it may sound harsh, is very comprehensive: "The male
animal is very fierce"—a verdict unhappily confirmed
by medicine and surgery, which are too often consulted
as to the consequences; and by those who, when cool,
are indignant at the impious fury which can sully so
sacred a moment.

———

There is another very serious thing, and one of grave
importance:

Are you aware that, in this moment of agitation, you
are divided between two conflicting thoughts? You do
not understand either yourself or her. This white
statue on whom you gaze so fondly, who is so touching,
so love-inspiring, who, fearing to appear afraid, forces a
pallid smile to her quivering lips—you flatter yourself
that you understand perfectly; and yet she remains to
you an enigma.

This bride of yours is the modern woman, made up
of a soul and a mind. The antique woman was a body
only. Marriage, in those times being but a means of
generation, a man chose for his wife a large rosy girl
(red and beautiful are synonymous terms in barbarian
languages). The woman was required to have plenty
of blood, and to be ready to shed it. Great stress was
laid upon this particular. The sacrament of marriage
was a baptism of blood.

In modern marriage, which is in the highest degree
the blending of souls, the soul is the essential thing.
The woman that the modern man imagines for himself
is a delicate and etherial being, altogether different from

that ruddy girl of former times. She is the embodiment
of nervous life. Her blood is all movement and action.
It is shown in her quick imagination, her ever-working
brain; in her sickly and morbid nervous grace; in her
excited, often brilliant speech; above all, in that deep
look of love which sometimes overwhelms and enchants
you, sometimes agitates, but oftenest touches your heart
and makes you weep.

This is what we really love, what we dream about,
what we pursue and desire. And yet, when it comes to
marriage, oddly enough, we forget all that, and expect
to find a woman of hardy race, a robust country girl,
who, when overfed and indolent, especially in the city,
has an abundant supply of the red fountain of life.

The increase of nervous strength and the decline of
that of the blood, begun a long time ago, is also a fact
of these times. If the illustrious Broussais should return to the earth, where would he find in our generation
(I mean among the cultivated classes) the torrents of
blood that he drew, not without success, from the veins
of the gentlemen of his times? Since then there has
been a fundamental change; whether for good or evil, I
leave to be decided. But, one thing is certain, and that
is, that man has become refined, and delights more in
mental pleasures. An uninterrupted succession of great
works and discoveries has distinguished these last thirty
years.

Everything has changed—woman with the rest. She
has read these works, and informed herself after a manner of their teachings. She has lived on our thoughts.
The young girl tries to conceal this, but who cannot
read it in her eyes, in her often too expressive face, in

her easily-offended delicacy? Your betrothed feared
nothing more than to possess the vulgar charms to
which to-day you attach so much importance. You
spoke so gloriously of pure love that she would be
transparent if she could. She thought that you desired
here on earth an aërial being, and that in your eyes she
lacked nothing but wings.

Besides, those who have the least cause to fear this
trial, who come to it more than pure, innocent, ignorant
of everything, are often those who disturb and alarm you
the most. So far does man lose his wits on that day,
less through love than distrust and pride, that the touching shame, the nervous excitement, and little fears of
the woman, so natural at this time, are at once inter-
preted in the most sinister manner. The man is a prey
to various mortifying conjectures.

"Undoubtedly," he says, " she fears this trial. She
puts off as long as she can a confession which she is
afraid to make."

She does not understand this at first; but, if at last
she discovers the burden of his thoughts, her agony and
indignation may be imagined. She is choked by it; her
eyes refuse to shed tears now. She who loved him so,
and who would have told him everything, if there had
indeed been anything to tell, to be thus distrustfully
treated, thus wronged! It is enough to make her hate
him for ever!

The man should remember that, if he judges the woman
he judges him also, at this time. She is profoundly sensi
tive and loving then, but so much the more vulnerable. She
receives in the deepest depths of her heart a shaft which
either kills her love, or assures it an eternal existence.

Oh! what a strange, astonishing, inhuman change has taken place in the man! He who protested his love to her so vehemently, has now no mercy upon her. He does not see in her face what is often the fact, that she is really very ill from emotion. From the beginning she has had much difficulty in breathing. Afterwards, the nervous flood has mounted higher and higher, and sometimes bursts forth in a fearful tempest. Sometimes again, it is worse still; nausea comes on; the most tem perate woman is completely disordered. Her situation is horrible, her agitation excessive.

Have pity on her! be kind and gentle to her. Appreciate her situation, care for her, re-assure her. Let her know that you are not her enemy; on the contrary, a most devoted friend, entirely at her service. Be discreet, full of tact, understanding and respecting her situation. And encourage her to the utmost.

Tell her this:

"I am thine, I am a part of thee. I suffer in thee. Take me as thy mother and thy nurse. Confide wholly in me. Thou art my wife and my child also."

This is a very precious time, when he who constitutes himself a mother and a nurse, repairs the wrongs of the lover. When the mind is calm, the body soon becomes calm also, and, the nervous tempest gradually dying away, feminine good-nature and docility begin to speak for you; it pains and alarms her to see you looking sad. And though she may not yet have entirely recovered from her timidity, she will grant, through tenderness or sweet feebleness, such charming favors as would not otherwise have been vouchsafed to you. Watched

over by you, she will go to sleep in confidence. On her
awaking you will lose nothing.

———————•+———————

IV.

THE AWAKENING.—THE YOUNG MISTRESS
OF THE HOUSE.

On awaking the next morning, what ecstasy for the
young bridegroom—yesterday alone, to-day doubled, as
he contemplates (scarce believing his eyes the while)
that charming face, that beautiful and defenceless person
reposing there under his care; it is too much for human
nature, and the proudest are touched. No language,
not even tears, can avail him then; sometimes the heart
overflows with gratitude, and thanks the goodness of
Nature and God. Sometimes, too, pride prompts him
to an animal thought, and he can scarce restrain himself
from exclaiming, "I own her! I am her master! It is
really so ; she is mine, mine!"

But this blind impulse of triumph is succeeded by a
nobler sentiment, the deep necessity he feels to give
something in return to the one who has brought him
an infinity of bliss. Heaven and earth, his own life,
seem not enough to offer her. His very heart seems to
leap from his breast to give itself to her. "Take me,"
he says, "accept me; my soul, my whole being, my
thoughts, my will, for ever!"

The ancient laws have here taken advantage of the
occasion, and conjured man to consecrate this hour, and

perpetuate it—to ease his heart by insuring his wife's destiny. This was called the *morning gift*.

"Though a man should give his life for love, he would not think he had made a sacrifice."

———

And I also, young man, shall stop you here; I, your master, am going to ask a gift of you.

Are you rich? Have you lands, forests, palaces? Well, keep them. She is above all that. What I ask for her is your word only, your promise to honor and respect your wife, never to be to her again what you were for a moment last night. Let her youth, her weakness, and her gentle obedience, be as sacred to you as the commands of your aged father. You should blush at having been harsh and violent, against your own nature; and to whom? to her! At having entertained the unworthy thought that you were strong, and she weak. Strong against her, who gives herself to you, trusts in you—strong against love, against God!

———

Day breaks; and so, fatigued, she has fallen asleep again upon her pillow. How pale and enfeebled she is! It is evident that she has suffered severely. That harsh conflict was too much for her. And what a cruel disappointment to find a hard and imperious master in the adored lover! He says to himself: "I am angry with myself. I have been a fool. I have defeated myself. Before this violence I was sure of her heart and of her will. Will she forget it? forgive it? What if she should cease to love me?"

He knows very little about her if he doubts her. She awakes, opens her eyes with a half smile, sad and gentle

5

at the same time; looks about her to see where she is; and then, like a timid child, hides her face for a moment. Is she really very angry? No; a little ashamed rather. Ashamed of what? Of having suffered; and it seems as if she would ask pardon for the harm that has been done her. She has need of quiet and of love, and she makes peace herself, by putting her little hand in his, with a sigh and these words: "My love!"

Who could resist that? He does not attempt to: tears fill his eyes. She sees them, and kisses them away; then languidly administers this mild reproach, which is in itself a caress of love: "How impetuous you are! there is no resisting you. Oh! you are truly my master; and yet I love you. But I am very unwell. May I get up?"

She is slow, a little heavy and lazy this morning—she who is usually so light and active. The young matron rises, however, with careful chasteness, but soon takes possession of an easy chair in which she lies back, weak and overpowered by lassitude. At her first glance in the mirror, she exclaims: "Heavens! how ugly I am!" This you strongly deny, but she still repeats it.

To make her appear at the breakfast-table before a mixed audience of jocose friends of your own, jealous lady-friends of hers, inquisitive sisters and brothers, would be barbarous. Spare her this exhibition.

How grateful she will be to you if you prevent this, and secure her solitude and repose. Her mother even will be *de trop* at such a time. Happy as the daughter might be to see her, she does not care to answer questions; for the secret is henceforth the property of two She cannot be a good and confiding daughter without telling too much about her husband

"No," you say to her, "fear nothing of this; be calm
and rest yourself; nobody shall come to you; eat this
warm and light breakfast that I have had prepared for
you; it will give you strength. Then, I shall have the
pleasure of showing you your house and your garden."

Now, if you have married wealthily, is the time I
pity you. It is so hard to satisfy a rich woman. The
prettiest things you show her barely raise a smile; and
the smile itself often means, "Not so bad, but I have
seen better."

She on the contrary who is only rich in beauty, mind,
and virtue, who with this great marriage-portion modestly thinks that she has brought nothing with her,
who, from a somewhat poor condition of life, passes to
an easier, freer, and more comfortable one, is full of hap
piness, charming in her artless joy and astonishment, in
the pleasure that she takes in seeing, touching, and
adapting herself to everything, and saying the while :
"And this is really our home !"

And again she adds: "What a nice house! Everything has been thought of. It almost makes one believe
that it was all arranged beforehand, for a woman."

Do you imagine that what charms and touches the
feminine heart must be something costly and luxurious ?
Not at all. What pleases them most is that act of yours
which puts everything in the hands of the mistress of
the house, permits her to arrange, take care of, and
keep things in that order and cleanliness that woman so
.oves. It is then that she feels they are hers, and takes
possession of them. They like large cupboards, deep
drawers, good oaken closets to keep linen in, and little out-of-the-way hiding places,—they all like these ;

but especially those who have nothing to hide in them.

Different kinds of furniture, seats of all heights, some ven as low as a child's chair, they want, and should have. The sedentary woman needs to vary her working postures; these are but the liberties of the voluntary captive.

Have good carpets too, as cheap as you please, but thick, doubled, tripled even, with some soft lining; have them laid in all parts of the house, even on the stairs; for they are the delight of a woman's little foot, which delicately appreciates their gentle resistance, their velvet charm and soft elasticity. This is a great advantage, she has less cause to sit near the fire.

Have no stoves, but open fireplaces. Stove and headache are synonymous. Have wood to burn: it is more cheerful and healthy than coal. The imperceptible dust that comes from coal does the man, who comes and goes, but little harm, but is very injurious to the woman, who goes out much less than he, and whose lungs after a time become filled with it.

A happy moment is it for her when you put the keys in her hand. To let her have all the money, and the power to spend it, is a certain means to make her economical, if she is alone, and left to her natural discretion. From that moment all childish longings are checked. When anything tempts her, she says, " I can buy it, but I will wait till to-morrow." And to-morrow she thinks no more about it.

Let us not forget that the best of young women often comes to you from an extravagant mother, who has humored her every caprice; or a despotic mother, who, forbidding her to meddle in household affairs, has left her in ignorance of the real value of things, and the relative worth of money. You must instruct her, teach her how to defend herself against the tricks of trade, the dishonesty of servants, etc.

Although you give over to her the minor matters of the household, she will want you to retain the management of its higher interests, to regulate the more important receipts and expenditures. They do not like men who abdicate too much. By a charming contradiction they wish to be the mistresses, but have the man still master; that is to say, strong, and worthy of them. They often take pleasure, even in womanly things, in consulting him, and having him command and decide. It is a sensuality of love for them to obey, to feel that they are possessed by some one who wraps round them his loving strength, and who sometimes gently makes them feel the spur.

We shall return to the house; let us go now into the garden.

And to begin: can you not at a little cost, with a few pillars and a light zinc roof, build her a little open gallery or winter portico between the house and the garden, where she can work, and walk in the sun? another for summer, where she can sew, embroider, or read in the shade, before a purling fountain? Such a place of helter costs but little, and yet is very necessary in our changeable climate.

How changed are all things here! How charming his solitary garden has become through her! With what a soft sunlight she has illuminated, bewitched it! Things have cast off their *thingly* qualities, and are invested with spirits as it were, expressly to receive and bless her. Not a wall nor a stone that is not softened at sight of her. The flowers, with all their corollas opened wide, admire and contemplate her; and the grass even grows fresher at having been touched by her foot.

She too is fascinated, delighted with the place. Now that she is here she wishes to remain for ever. She would never ask for the end of such a sweet enchantment. Lost in her thought of love, she lets you talk on without answering, absorbing the gentle moisture like the turf around the fountain. Her expressive mouth, though it utters no word, is full of eloquence, her gently heaving bosom still more eloquent. She walks, leaning upon your arm, and little by little letting herself down, until, clasping her hands, she suspends herself to you, and becomes almost heavy. This is doubtless through tenderness, from fatigue also, and from the heat of the day. The dear child lets herself go thus, partly carried by you; saying, with a sigh: "Ah! how happy I am with you!"

V.

NARROWING THE HOME CIRCLE

LOVE creates love, and augments it. The secret of loving each other much, is to occupy ourselves much, one with the other, to live much together, the closest d most that we can.

" And what if they get tired of one another? ' you exclaim; " it will have the contrary effect; they will hate instead of love." Granted, if the alternation of solitude and society, a restless, unprofitable, and constantly vary. .ng life, prevents the mind from assuming a proper balance. But not if a contented life, varied only by love and labor, excludes all vain attractions, and binds the pair closer and closer together in that constant communion, where they think, live, and are happy, each through the other.

In Zurich, in the olden time, when a quarrelsome couple applied for a divorce, the magistrate never listened to them. Before deciding upon the case, he locked them up for three days in the same room, with one bed, one table, one plate, and one tumbler. Their food was passed into them by attendants who neither saw nor spoke to them. When they came out, at the end of the three days, neither of them wanted to be divorced.

———

The mere arrangement of our modern apartments is enough to hinder a real union. The multitude of little rooms divides the household, breaks up the family, isolates the married pair. Furthermore, the putting of one story upon another, in the great unhealthy barracks in which we crowd ourselves, brings us continually in contact with strangers.

The husband will work by himself, and the wife will suffer from ennui by herself, or occupy herself in useless talk with women whom she knows too little about. One must have a study, the other a *boudoir* (significant word); two bed-chambers, so that they can at all hours ignore and avoid each other, defend themselves against

each other if need be. The dining-room and the parlor
bring them together momentarily, but their visitors and
guests occupy their attention and divert them from each
other ; they are relieved of the necessity of speaking to
each other, almost of seeing each other. I would
advise such spouses to prudently put bolts on the doors
of their respective chambers, for mutual assurance.

Why apply for divorce? A marriage like that
amounts to the same thing. Those separate apartments
effect it sufficiently.

And when you really love, how can you help envying
my neighbor the carpenter, who has but one room in
all? So that while he is sawing and planing, his wife,
who is a washerwoman, sings at her ironing-table all the
day long. Often have I forgotten myself in listening to
her fine voice, which is strong and vibratory, fresh and
clear. Sometimes she sings a little too loud, and dis-
turbs me at my work ; but that does not hinder me from
saying: " Sing on, sing on, you poor little lark !"

" All very well for a carpenter," you say. " But my
labors are of a higher order, have a more important
object. I am a thinker. Every distraction withdraws
me from my profound meditations." Too profound, sir—
often hollow. Your works, those of these times at least,
are for the most part barren; witty, I grant you—but
with so little life in them, so unfeeling, so rarely *humane*.
The author, at every moment, loses sight of the worlds
of heart and of good sense.

A really human work, a powerful and living thought,
one with a body to it, is not disturbed so easily. Its
powerful impetus carries it along, and assimilates and

appropriates to itself all that might otherwise have diverted it from its course. How much easier is this, then, if what you call distraction is in reality from the very bottom of your heart, love and the beloved one! But both these are one and the same thing. Can she take you from work, or work take you from her? Neither. On the subject which seems the most remote even, she exercises an influence, by the warmth of love which she infuses into it.

———

I am always pleased with Dutch pictures. I find in them continually that charming promiscuousness of the man's study and the woman's housewifery, where the former is ennobled, the latter inspired with new ardor and increased in fruitfulness. Everybody has seen at the Louvre (and also in the exquisite description given in *la Foi Nouvelle*) the *Saint Joseph* of Rembrandt. But I am not the less struck with its microscopical philosophy, a picture of study familiarized with the family. In the faint light of the declining sun, near a window on which is spread a large open book, is an old man, who has ceased reading and is engaged in meditation, brooding over his thoughts. His eyes are shut, it seems; and yet he sees everything. He sees the servant poking the fire. He sees his wife (scarcely distinguishable in the picture) coming down the winding staircase. These pleasing images, you may be sure, are blended with the pleasant nature of his thoughts. Behind him is a closet cellar, containing a little generous wine, with which he sometimes refreshes himself. Such is the complete picture of a man who has gone through life, and is now living on its vintage.

5*

If that book is the Bible, I am sure that the good man will take the best and highest sense of it. His is the intellect to understand the sayings of Tobias, Ruth, and the patriarchs. He will not lose himself in vain and unprofitable analysis, and will not care to inform himself, as others do, of the sex of the angels. The same man, in the cell of a convent, would have made commentaries like those of Scotus, and Thomas Aquinas, upon the Bible; refining, subtilizing, and in fact reducing every thing to barrenness. Here, it is quite the contrary. And why? Because the household, the family and affection, bring him ever back to the real. All that touches the heart in this chronicle of remote times, is re-made and renewed in him; he sees it again through the medium of his heart.

A charming thing to observe, which I have often remarked with pleasure among my more studious friends, is the infinite delicacy of the young wife, who in a restricted space comes and goes, and moves round the student, without in the least disturbing him. Any other person would have put him out; but "she," he says, "is nobody." In fact, she is himself, his second and his better soul.

She holds her breath, and steps on tiptoe. She glides along the floor. She has such respect for work! In this you can see what a gentle and quick-sighted creature woman is; above all things affectionate, and feeling in constant need of the beloved object. If he allows her she will remain in the room sewing or embroidering. If not, a thousand occasions or a thousand necessities will occur to her as pretexts to come into the room.—

" What is he doing now ? How far has he got? Per
haps he is working too hard ? He will make himself
sick."—All this passes through her mind.

There are many studies to which unwittingly she im.
parts more than she can take away. Do you think that
the charming electricity she communicates in passing
you, lightly touching you with her dress, goes for nothing with the artist and the author, if with our tire
some and uncongenial work is opportunely mingled that
perfume of the flower of love which revives everything?
So in old Italian pictures do we see in a death's head a
hundred-leaved rose ; and death itself seems to enjoy it.

And how happy he is to feel that she is there. He
pretends not to see her. He remains bent over his work,
as if absorbed in it. But his heart gains the upper hand,
and he exclaims :

" My darling, my charming rosebud, do not muffle
your steps. Your movements are harmony, your voice
a melody which enchants my ear. Your presence sheds
its influence upon my work ; it will be adorned with
your grace, and glow with the flame of my palpitating
heart.

" Without seeing you, I guessed you were here by
the increased ardor of my work, by the light which
overspread my spirit."

A thousand years from now they will say: " His is
yet a live book, all warmth and affection." And the
reason of it all—she was beside you when you wrote it

VII.

THE TABLE—DIET.

In order that such a great change in life may not be harmful to the young woman, everything must be thought of and arranged beforehand; her girlish diet should be slightly and slowly changed. Care should be taken not to let her pass abruptly from the fruit and vegetable feasts, which most girls prefer, to the stronger food of man. She would be ill, if this were neglected. Nothing is more senseless than the custom we adopt from the English—that of keeping an indolent and sedentary woman on a heavy meat diet, scarce necessary to a hearty workman, or active man of business. The woman can only stand such irritating diet by adding to it the greater irritation of spirituous liquors. By this course she becomes faded, used-up, and red-faced, at a very early age; it leads to the extermination of all beauty, and, in the end, a serious decline in the race itself.

You must preserve to your young wife all the habits of her girlhood, modifying them little by little; and see that, from the first day, she finds in her new house everything that she had in her mother's. You have thought of these, I am sure, for I know your good heart. You have learned long beforehand from her mother, her nurse, or perhaps the family physician, all about her physical constitution, and how it is to be treated. To prepare her nest properly for her you should know everything, her habits, her usual state of health, her

.lttle indispositions, all her womanly peculiarities. This should not spring from an empty curiosity, but fiom an absolute necessity. You should even, without exercising undue inquisitiveness, go back a little into the history of her family, into its *blood* inheritances, and know something of the diseases to which it is subject. Her health will depend on your knowing this, as will also your own diet, for you will surely choose such dishes as agree with her and preserve her strength.

Many women of the high classes reach marriage in a state of great debility (their blood being too much thinned out)—sickly from their birth, or in consequence of unwholesome diet. He who receives into his house such a frail flower as this, too often finds that she is not able to endure the labors of love. Before having a child from her you must strengthen the poor creature herself, bring her to woman's full estate. You must be her mother in order to be her husband.

One great fault in mothers and nurses is that they wish the child to eat until he is in danger of making himself ill. If it goes so far as an indigestion, they are delighted and say: "He is improving." I have seen the strange spectacle of doting mothers absolutely begging, nay, forcing their sons to eat and drink to excess, manifesting at each mouthful the delight and pleasure that they themselves felt from it. They really made gluttons and sensualists of themselves, for their sons' sake. Love has similar effects. Dining one day with a very quiet friend, I noticed, at dessert, that he had become quite affected · somewhat as a gastronomer might be if served with his choice bit. But here there was no cause nor

pretext for anything of the kind. I looked across the
table and saw his young wife eating a favorite fruit.
My friend looked at this fruit, blushed, and became agi
tated. I understood it all then. He himself made no
secret of it. "I felt her pleasure so sensibly," he said,
" that I could not contain myself. I love her, and everything that she feels, I feel myself, in a greater degree."

But these impulses of your nature are too strong, and
she must not see them. She would be disturbed by
them. Such physical identity of appetite and faculties
would be harmful to the weaker of the two. Her flame
would be lost in yours. Be calm, then, I pray you;
practise moderation and prudence; be gentle with her,
not precipitate.

———

A very profound communion is this of the table, especially where there are but two in the family, when
domestics interfere but little, or none at all.

Man nourishes woman, brings every day, like the
bird in the fable, the bread to his lone love. And
woman nourishes man. She prepares and cooks his food
according to his needs, to his physical condition, to his
known temperament; part of herself goes with it;
with the food is mingled the perfume of her beloved
hand.

Hence, these two are fed by each other. Each of
them feels with delight that not an atom in their respective beings belongs to one of them alone; but that day
by day, everything is renewed, revived by the beloved
object. Of this law of the stomach, which we consider
low and base, nature has made one of the gentlest
bonds, a high poesy of the heart, wherein union becomes

unity. Who shall say that their natures are n.t more blended by this calm and gentle communion than by the crisis even, and the transport of love? In mutual alimentation, as in generation, an equal interchange, a transmutation of substances, is effected.

Behold them then at the table, seated opposite each other, and eating together for the first time. You are delighted to be where you can feed your eyes upon her. She, during your short absence, has thought of you, and wished to beautify herself for your sake; she has adorned herself, and yet with how little? With a flower from the garden, which she has set in her hair.

This single day has profited her. She is another person now. The smiling girl has become an impressive woman. Her smile now is that of modest gravity, and she is *Madam* already.

She has not much appetite. A few vegetables, a little fruit, some milk, is what she likes. Your carnivorous diet has no attractions for her. She has a horror of death, a horror of blood—very natural this, since she herself is the flower of life. It is especially for this that she needs that country girl of whom I have spoken. She would gladly prepare your food, but this bloody meat is too repulsive to her. She is also too delicate for the heavy work, which is nothing at all to the robust pea sant woman, who, in addition, can cultivate the garden.

Cookery is a medicine, the best kind of medicine, a preventive. Hence, it should be the duty of the wife, who alone knows just what her husband needs, how hard he has worked, and his expenditure of vital strength. In all that is proper, not repugnant to her, all that does not deface her pretty hand, in all that may be *touched* by her hand (and let us add, necessarily mingled with the emanations of the person), it is desirable and charming that she should be the only performer. .Certain pies, cakes, and puddings can be made only by one whom we love and cherish.

Pure as she is, she is not the less possessed of the sentiment and the power of divining what affords you pleasure. She knows your gastronomic weakness perfectly, and how well you relish everything that has been touched by her hand. She has forestalled your thought. The thing that you like best, that thing she has prepared for you. This dish which you so affect has been prepared by her hands; she has touched it with her mouth, consecrated it with her lips. She brings it to you with a smile:

" Eat this, my dear, for I have tasted it."

VII.

YOU SHOULD WAIT ON EACH OTHER.

I do not write for the rich, who complicate their lives at will with a thousand tiresome and dangerous inutilities, who live in the continual presence of their servants (for "servants" read "enemies"), who eat, sleep, and love beneath those malevolent and scoffing eyes. They have no intimacy, no privacy, no home.

And unfortunately I cannot write for those who have

no time to themselves, no liberty; who are crushed and overpowered by the fatalities of circumstance, those whose incessant labor controls and pushes forward the hours. What advice can we give to people who are not free to follow it? I write for those who are at liberty to regulate their own lives, for the poor but not indigent man who works at home, and for those who are voluntarily poor—that is to say for people of fortune who are sensible enough to live plainly, without servants, and to have something which can really be called a home.

The saying that "a third person spoils company" is essentially true of the married state.

A quiet country girl, however, for the "hired help," does not break up the *tête-à-tête*.

If you are so fortunate as to have a little house by yourselves, she will have her kitchen and laundry on the ground floor, and seldom come up-stairs.

The girl is not entirely alone; her mistress goes down to see her, especially during your absence, and gives her good advice, such as she can readily understand. She will teach her to read, and train her in good habits.

She has also the garden to herself, as well as the cat, the dog, and the chickens, with which she holds daily talks, as when she was on her own place.

This honest creature, however honest she may be, is not the less a woman, and consequently curious. Hence, in going up to her bed-room, at the top of the house, she will not fail to put her eye to the key-hole, and listen to what is said. A double door and a little ante-chamber should be between your apartment and the staircase up which she passes, goes and comes, listens and observes.

"But how," asks my lady, "will this gawky country girl take the place of my Julie, my femme de chambre, who is so clever, and knows how to do everything?"

Clever? Why, you are as clever as she. Come, my lazy beauty, you do yourself injustice. In making a tasteful toilet, I have full confidence in your delicate hands. Woman, in this particular, has an inexhaustible fund of dexterity and invention.

And, if you absolutely need a femme de chambre for other and more delicate attentions, I will present you one who is fairly dying for the place; who has a hundred times more zeal than Mademoiselle Julie, Mademoiselle Lisette, and all the illustrious disciples of the art; who, moreover, is not malicious; who will tell nothing to your disadvantage to your neighbors; who will not make sport of you to her lover; who will not make faces behind your back when you speak to her. "But where is this treasure?" you ask. "I will engage her at once; she is just what I want." "She is beside you."

Behold your subject, O queen! who beseeches you to take him into your service; he will regard it as an exaltation if you raise him to the dignity of a titled valet de chambre, to the feudal position of chamberlain, head lackey, or master-butler of your house—leech in ordinary (as to hygiene at least), for his zeal knows no bounds. All these court offices he will fill gratis, and in addition to his masculine duties will perform those of woman also, feeling proud and honored, Madame, if your majesty will accept his very humble service.

"But he has too much other business," you say, "he has no time for this. I should be ashamed to employ him, for my own sake, in such an unprofitable

manner. I must confess, too, that all these little womanly things require to be done *idly*, slowly, and with
very little expedition. All should progress slowly, and
be diversified with gossip. The man who is really a
man is too impetuous, he wants to hurry everything,
and get to the end of it. We should have accomplished
nothing in the end. All his attentions would be turned
into caresses. My toilet would be more disordered than
improved."

Let us have secret for secret, Madame, confession for
confession. You must know then that the busiest of
men has abundance of time, a superfluity even, so soon
as his real pleasure is concerned. Some Roman, whose
name I have forgotten, either a general, or a magistrate,
or a courtier, or a king of the world, as Roman kings
were in those days, found time enough every morning
to be present when his son was in the hands of his
nurses, noted what was done for his physical education,
saw him washed, dressed, etc., etc. Henri IV. with all
his affairs of state, did not fail for a single day to have
a minute account written, and rendered him, of all the
new-born Dauphin's actions—having it set down hour by
hour, by a skilful physician, how the child had eaten,
slept, digested, etc. The great men of our day, much
more occupied than the emperors and consuls of Rome,
more occupied than Henri IV., find time to exercise
their brisk loquacity four hours a day at the Bourse, the
Palais de Justice, at the cafés, and six hours of the night
at the play (to which they never listen). No, decidedly
it is not time that is wanting.

It is not wanting for the useless and foolish questions of the day, from which we always come away

yawning, no wiser than before. It is only wanting when our happiness is concerned.

Now here is a man who says that he will be perfectly happy if you accord him an hour of which you can make but one disposition. You are his child, his Dauphin, his play even, his opera, his charming and divine comedy.

Yes, *Divine.* I will not retract that. I judge it so by the devotion with which he presides at these things which you think small and futile. You laugh; he does not. The day that you admit him to your dressing-room, you will find him moved, affected with a true religious feeling. Never did pious oriental, after a long pilgrimage, enter his holy pagoda in a more appropriate state of mind. He is inquiring, but above all tender, full of respectful desire—admiring, adoring. You need entertain no fear of him. What servant, however devoted, ever regarded you with such partial eyes? Do you think that Julie, whom you regret, so flattering and favoring, has not (I say it in a whisper) remarked some little fault on your most beautiful person, that she has not sometimes laughed in her sleeve?

He, on the contrary, has eyes so predisposed, that he sees nothing but what is lovely, superlatively beautiful. What looks he casts upon you! how loving, how caressing! And all this is pure. There is nothing so pure as true love.

Montaigne says somewhere that the sight of healthy people communicates health and cures disease. I shall change this but a little, to say that it is the look of love which bears happiness with it, and brings beauty into blossom. From this results that charming refulgence

which a woman so soon assumes. The reason is that she
has been visited with this look.

Sacred object that you are, you need fear nothing.
You yourself are his religion, and, if you keep you
heart worthy and pure, will always be. Never in hi
eyes of burning love, and yet of respect, can you descend
from your divinity. You will not lose your altar. You
will be adored for ever.

" Alas !" she says to herself, for she would never dare
to whisper it to other ears, " how can I be always
adored ?   And is it not the natural result of such a close
intimacy that, never being able for a moment to escape
the attention of the one who loves, of his tender uneasiness, you will at last show him the more vulgar and
inferior aspects of your life.   Who can be sure of being
poetic every day? of not being brought down by
relentless nature from his high ideal of love to common
prose ?"

These are but girlish fancies, and spring from her
perfect ignorance of the real state of things. Those who
understand love, know very well that it is not here that
the honeymoon first begins to wane. None of these
simple and harmless things ever affect the man.

If you wish to know how woman really descends from
poetry to prose, I will tell you.

It is not in showing herself a woman, in artlessly confessing what she is, what we all are, mortal, human ; but
in showing herself to be cold and vain, in letting his
eyes, so blind to certain things, and so sharpsighted for
others, discover her moral infirmity.

People think it is satiety which so soon kills love ; but
they do not appear to know that satiety often comes

not from too complete possession, but from too little from a feeling that the woman's inner self will not be reached, her soul not attained; that she is empty, vain, and frivolous; that all quest would discover nothing in her.

This girl, yesterday so adorned, so coquettishly dressed to the very hour of her marriage, as seen to-day, a wife at her toilet, seems totally changed in this particular. She scarcely takes proper care of herself. But the wedding guests are invited; there is to be a great ball this evening. No sooner does she think of that than, as if to prepare for a second marriage, she becomes active, pains-taking, and difficult to please.

Love, so fascinated, so blind a moment ago, here takes another view of the matter. It translates this negligence of every day into, "I am dressed well enough for my husband." And this adornment for the ball into, "I long to please other people, above all."

Well, this cools his ardor, and satiety sets in. She is vulgar, frivolous; the ideal here is torn down, and will never be set up again.

The impression is just the contrary, if the earnest observer remarks a nice attention to the toilet of which he is to be the sole spectator, a loving coquetry of dress for the hours when they shall be alone together. "Nothing for others," he says, "and everything for me." This is what is meant in these matters. Not a word is spoken, but that which would give rise to the words is but the more deeply felt. Love here feels itself upon solid ground, and it will take deep, strong root. You need fear nothing for Love's ideal; it will continue to flourish upon both the poetic and the real.

But why distinguish them? When one loves, they are one and the same thing. O frigid generation, timid and weak woman, ignorant of your true powers, how little do you know that love is of a robust constitution, and laughs at such things! how little it in reality cares about that which is the subject of such grave alarm with you!

In true married life, everything is poetry, and in the person who is loved everything is noble.

The proudest of men does with a good grace whatever he can do for the woman he loves. And she, queen of the house, whatever she may do, does everything royally.

They are servants, one to the other, but with this distinction: she is the servant in all things of love and usefulness, connected with themselves and the household; he waits upon her *herself*, in showing her personal attentions.

These are humble functions, but of great grace and favor. Do you remember on this point the good old feudal rule? The rank of the several dignities was determined by the opportunities they afforded to approach, and to serve, the royal person, not by affairs of state then, but by those which concerned the individual.

VIII.

HYGIENE,

YOUTH of a loving and a faithful heart, understand well from the beginning, that your most sacred duty is to profit first by the artless faith of your young wife; by her eighteen years, by the bountiful supply of docility she brings you; to take entire possession of her, mentally and physically, taking her body and her soul—her soul to fertilize, to illumine, to enlarge it—her body, to strengthen, to prepare it for the great trial it soon must undergo—I mean the sharp pains of maternity.

Your moral responsibility is far greater than you have ever dreamed of or imagined. The life of the heart, and the life of the body, are to be so blended in you, that the lightest matters between you will become vastly weighty, or delightful, or sad. No detail is to be scorned, no trifle neglected. Everything is of immense importance to your future.

––––––

Make haste to be her master. For, in a little while, I predict that she will be your mistress, at least by habit; and she will hold you firmly on all sides. Yes, the more gentle, the more docile, ay, the more humble, the woman is, the more she entwines herself, the more she clings and holds fast to you. All this by seemingly slight, invisible, weak bonds, yet possessing an unheard of strength. At first, it is a thread, light and graceful, like the "*Threads of the Virgin*," which fly in the wind, and yet are fastened with so much strength. In the second stage they are like the tendrils of the vine, whose prehensile fingers, though of infinite delicacy, already clasp tightly. In the third stage, my friend, it will be the strength of the ivy, which so clings to and twines around the oak it has once seized upon, that it incorporates itself with it; that it even pierces it; the pruning knife cannot separate it; no means of disengaging the one, except by cutting to the heart of the other.

. Well, all this is as nothing to the worth of a woman who, in solitude, imbued by you, imbues you; who, cherished by you, cherishes you; who holds you by the house, by the fireside, by the bed, by the children; finally, by all your feelings in common; who takes possession of you by her boundless compliance and docility, who submits to your whims, and who, for the joy of one moment, returns an eternity of pure love.

"So much the better," say you, "that she should take possession of me! This does not frighten me at all. It is what I desire." That is well; but, thus warned, you should early make yourself master of this young and potent influence, which, in a few years, without art, without artifice, by the force of love alone, will conquer and absorb you.

This absorption will be the greatest misfortune for both of you, if you have not imbued her with your soul —that is the modern soul. For such as you are, young man, and however corrupted by experience, you are still a great deal more than she, the repository of truth. The poor creature, alas, is in utter darkness! She has learnt, strictly speaking, only those things which she must unlearn. Her good heart, her maidenly nature, her charmingness, will serve only to ruin you both, with your child and your future, if from this day you do not assert the authority of science and of knowledge. It is not in vain that for three centuries human genius has stored up in your hand (your strong masculine hand), the treasure of certainty. Avail yourself of it to day or never, my friend; for it is your salvation. Great heaven! What will become of you if you see her ere long, relapsed into the past, become your innocent adversary, waging on you a war, not of words, but of tears and sighs. I pray you do not lose her—hold fast to her. For your life, and for her life, moral and physical, remain master (she desires it, she prefers it); subdue her. Inclose her in yourself, in your constant, unchanging, clear-sighted thought.

———

You should not lose sight of the fact that you will shortly (who knows? it may be in nine months) have to undergo the rudest trial to which nature is subjected. I say *you*, for at that moment you will suffer as much as she; the tortures of inaction and of impotence make a man feel at such times more than the agony of death. Then, though you should weep tears of blood, you could do nothing. Your strength, the impulses of your heart, your vows, your anxiety, your useless terror, will avail her nothing. You must foresee, you must provide for it from this moment, in these yet quiet days; and have present, beforehand, the chances and the perils of that terrible day.

This should render you attentive to, and careful of everything. The indifferent attentions of a physician, who comes at intervals, often thinking of other matters, will not suffice for you. Rather do I put my trust in your clear-sightedness, in the intuition of love, in its fixed and powerful look, riveted on the beloved object, from which nothing can distract it, which it sees through and through !

But the woman physically is a being all ductile, of a strange mobility. One is almost dazzled by looking at her ; symptoms so varied are mingled and confused. Distrust your memory. Nothing will sustain you better than keeping a little journal of her physical life. If this was done by order of Henry IV., for Louis XIII., if the most prosaic incidents of the life of that disagreeable king, were noted day by day, why should you not do it for your sweet wife, all poetry, all purity, and who holds your life dependent on her fragile young life ?

You must not worry or beset her with these details. It is not necessary for her to see too much of the burning anxiety of your love, ever uneasy, and often without a cause. That would deprive her of much serenity. Do this for yourself, to remind you, to guide you ; this fixed foundation of experience and observation will soon assist you to foresee, almost always correctly, what she will be to-morrow, or even for days ahead, in health and disposition—a great, a very great advantage. You will bear much better with her caprices (which are only sufferings). You will ask for nothing but at the proper time, at the very moment, perhaps, that she herself was thinking of it.

Interested to this extent in the details of her physical life, you should by a gentle, incessant, patient progress, entirely surround her, take possession of her, little by little. But no precipitation. Nothing should be more sacred, more skilfully managed, than the modesty of a young wife. They are complained of too soon, and as a general thing, wrongfully. There is no coldness, no affectation in them. But the most loving, the most devoted, is at times nervous to a point of real suffering. They are like birds of a superior and delicate organization. A nightingale, which I have lost, loved me very much, but he could not bear to have me approach him, he trembled at being touched.

Still an intimate life creates almost inevitable embarrassments. The familiarity refused to the lover, to the tender friend, to the most kindly observer, is granted to persons less worthy, less trusty. When Madame de Gasparin advised the lady not to allow herself to be seen in what she called "the sad reality of unadorned nature," she did not fully feel that the favor forbidden to the husband would be granted to the *femme-de-chambre*. "Is this a trifle?" Not at all: it is the beginning, the opportunity, of a certain relative intimacy, more dangerous than would be believed, and fatal to your union.

To the pure all things are pure. To treat this delicate point frankly, we must say that it is better that this familiarity, which will come sooner or later, should not come through the freedom and unrestraint between an old married couple, but shortly after marriage, between lovers. And this all artlessly, all simply. You risk but little by it. Love, then exalted, accepts everything, adores everything, of the loved object, grateful for every step towards confidence. This is the right moment to break through those little barriers which must be broken down in the end, and at a less favorable epoch.

A month will not pass without the opportunity   If she is ill, must the husband be driven out and the mothei called in ?   Is it necessary, in so simple a matter, one which concerns pure hygiene alone, that the latter should send for a physician, a stranger, to whom the young wife must painfully confess those little mysteries which she does not tell even to her husband ?   Often, in case of *delay*, she confides in her silly old nurse, or some foolish "good wife," who, to relieve her, advises dangerous stimulants.

Now who should concern himself in this, if not he who has so much interest in it ?   This crisis, which is (a thing proved) only that crisis of love which furthers fecundation, comes from love itself.   Thus, contrary to the gross and barbarous prejudice which would sequester the woman at such a time, no one who loved could ever conceive that she was then an object of estrangement. He has always thought her very pure.   So interesting at this time, so tender and so confiding, her languor signifiantly says : " I suffer, and it is for you."

___

She needs an attentive, confident guardian, who knows everything, who can aid her in everything.   For she is so exposed !   If she takes cold, there is an end to all. If she has a fright, or is aggrieved, if she weeps, there also is an end of it.   If she digests badly, all is perilled. What she dare not tell, you must have a presentiment of, must be able to conjecture.   She is so afraid of displeasing !   They are unhappily deeply imbued with that old idea of a so-styled impurity, now contradicted by science.   It is the first duty of love to enlighten them on this point.

Poor martyrs to modesty! The smallest matters often seem grave to them, and terrify them. A little while after marriage, the young wife is looking very red, her head is heavy, her eyes blood-shot. "What is the matter?" "Nothing." She dare not tell you. This lasts a week. Then she appears feeble and pale. Another week. But she is still silent. You know she is not *enceinte.* "Call the doctor," says the mother. It is very easy to understand, without a doctor, that a new diet, perhaps a little too rich, has troubled her, producing at first a feeling of fullness, then the contrary effect—inflation and weakness. A slight aperient will set all right again. Let the physician order it, and she modestly bows her head, and is resigned. If it is the husband who begs and supplicates, she blushes, and becomes indignant. "Good heavens! she has committed no excess; she has not been a glutton." You must be gentle, patient, discreet, and not urgent. Let all be within her reach; she will timidly, in secret, do what you desire. Happy in reality not to be compelled to submit to the interrogations, to the solemn inquest, of the physician.

———

He who is truly loving, who loves for her, and not for himself, envelops her in himself, but without weighing upon her. She does not feel the weight of the air which she breathes; and why? Because it is both within and without. It is the same with love. She who has it in her heart finds it only very sweet to feel it around her, to find it in everything, as if it were her inevitable atmosphere, the element of her respiration. It will become necessary to her; and if this envelopment, which you may think persecution, is withdrawn from her a single moment, she will be very unhappy.

As to the rest, in these first months your cares will not be very heavy. Almost always the physical life, benignantly influenced by hope and by happiness, assumes the most charming aspects. Your drooping flower raises itself with an unexpected brilliancy and grace. That she were a little stronger is all that can be desired; and even this must not be desired impatiently.

Let her live a country life, work a little, perspire a little (a very little in the beginning). Let her go to and fro in the large garden, not remaining seated too long. Let her bathe herself in the sunned water, otherwise cold. Let her, too, often, all alone, at her ease, in security, bathe out of doors. It will be an advantage if her white skin assume a healthy brown tone. Plants kept in the shade are emaciated and pale. Our clothing unfortunately keeps us in the same condition, by separating us from the father of life, the sun.

IX.

OF INTELLECTUAL FECUNDATION

" The child should not come before his cradle has been suitably prepared."

Which means that it is not desirable that the union should be too soon fruitful, but that the young wife, who must herself be the first cradle of the child, should previously strengthen herself for the emotions of her new situation.

She must have a respite between the two dramas of her life. Marriage, which appeared to you so agreeable an incident, was to her a trial, and too often a trial lasting even until now. Leave her alone, that she may breathe. Let her have an interval of calm, in which, feeling no longer the thorns of the beginning, and not yet the agitation of pregnancy, this sweet creature of suffering may enjoy herself also, and taste a moment of tranquillity— an interval, moreover, very necessary, infinitely precious, in which your moral union, scarcely commenced, will be really formed; in which your wife, intimately associated in your thought, brooding over it in her imagination, will prepare, unconsciously, the new being which shall be, which is, only that thought in the bosom of the dear dreamer in whom your love will be incarnated.

That union you think you already have. You believe you possess your wife, and are assimilated with her. Far from it !

Possess ? It is not for one night (or for several, often still very painful) that you can have the satisfaction of employing this word—not even for that dazzling state in which love plunges her, causing her, first of all, to admit the ideas of her lover, however new they may be, and thoughtlessly to believe all that he says to her.

In reality, matters do not progress so fast. Coming together from two opposite worlds (she is almost always educated by her mother in retrograde opinions), you cannot fuse in a moment. The old-fashioned things on which she has been nourished, from which she seems emancipated, may re-appear one day to divide you. Your pride says, no. She, at heart more tender, loving her love so much, wishing so much to preserve it, she insists with a happy instinct on entering in, still more, without reserve, and without retreat.

"I work by your side, and I see you work. But this is not enough for me. What you are doing is an enigma to me, and I wish to understand it. I feel that during these hours, although present, I must be forgotten, and that I am almost always exiled from your thoughts . . . . This is very hard. Ah, that I might share your toil, that I might aid you! I should be so happy!

"But I am incapable of it! Far from comprehending your ideas, I can scarce unravel my own. When you urge me to open my heart to you, I cannot express myself. Then you complain, and call me cold. Ah, you are wrong! I know not what hindrance, what shackle, remains to me of the past. Is it because I lack intelligence, or are my teeth locked together? I cannot speak—speak to me, you who can; free me from myself, instruct me, put a soul in me."

This is nearly what the intelligent young wife says. She wishes very earnestly to be associated with him, and this in two ways, if she can.

His technical, special life, of art, of science, or of business, will not be repulsive to her. (One will set herself to work to dissect! Another to copy, or to calculate astronomical tables!)

But it is above all the highest life of her husband, his

more general ideas, which she desires to comprehend and appropriate to herself. She asks for his trust and his faith.

This, then, is your docile pupil. Happy situation! Charming kindness of nature! Her young mind complains only of not being sufficiently mastered, of not belonging sufficiently to you. She devotes her mind and heart to any pursuit that you may choose. She aspires only to give herself to you, to belong to you still more entirely.

———

Nothing is more delightful than to teach a woman. She forms a perfect contrast to the perverseness and insubordination that a child often offers. Call him to his lessons, he runs off as fast as he can; she anticipates the hour, she is attentive, happy, eager for your teachings, believing in, full of deference and respect for the learning of him whom she loves. So that even when she is not yours, your loved one, the delight of your heart and eyes, by her amiability alone she is a model pupil.

Mark well, that she is pleased by this thing, at assuming this rôle of pupil which makes her so young. She is as much delighted to receive these lessons as your caresses, as anything else, since all comes from you. She is sensitive to the gentle encouragement, the praise, by which you stimulate her; sensitive also to reproaches. She does not dislike to be scolded; but if you are very severe, if you call her "Madame," she becomes agitated, and almost weeps. She throws herself in the arms of the master. That ends the lesson.

"That is enough for to-day. We will read no more."

In these charming tasks there is but one thing to be regretted. Do you wish me to tell you what it is?

It is that often she has not paid attention, she has not understood at all, or has conceived an entirely different matter.

Not that she may not be very intelligent, often very intellectual. But she is infinitely more so for knowledge that she derives intuitively, than for what is imparted to her.

Strange truly, that a being so receptive by nature, and made for fecundation, should with difficulty receive the fecundation of the mind, even when lending herself entirely to it!

The odd title of a Spanish book of the sixteenth century has often set me a-dreaming: "The Seven Fortifications of the Soul's Castle."

Seven? It is not enough. Those enclosures are infinitely numerous. You force one or two of them, and believe that all is done, the place is carried. . . . Not at all. Other ramparts are behind which must be surmounted. But the peculiarity is, that here is a place wishing nothing but to surrender itself, to open its gates. The mind of the woman who loves much, and feels that she is loved, burns to surrender itself without reserve, and to become entirely subordinate. It drives no hard bargain for itself. It wishes to yield, and it cannot.

The obstacle is not in the least in her will.

It is in her education;

It is in her woman's nature;

And, above all, in your awkwardness.

If the education of the boy is severe, that of the girl has almost always been negative and barren. I do not speak of the worldly ones, who are spoiled, and fine ladies at fifteen. But the education of those who are modestly reared is, by a vexatious contrariety, almost like that of a plant cultivated in a cellar. They come from it sad and awkward, with but little address. Time is required to give them courage, buoyancy, confidence in themselves. Grace will return to them through loving and being loved. With grace, too, the intellect will be quickened. They become susceptible of mental germination, of being mentally impregnated.

But how shall the seeds be sown?

It is very seldom that a man knows the course of instruction precisely suited to a being so delicate and so different from himself.

Either he sermonizes, makes long speeches, and fatigues her, not seeing that she in no wise follows his processes of deduction, and that she tries in vain to listen to him.

Or it may be that, more modest, he keeps himself back, and thinks to act on her by reading, by books,—not knowing that a book truly adapted to a woman has never yet been written.

There is not one entirely suited to a young woman. You must choose from the best that which is most fitted for her. This will vary infinitely, according to character and circumstances.

Reading, too varied and not discreet, has deplorable effects upon women.

They are in nowise prepared, either by constitutic n or by education, to receive all sorts of indigestible nourish. ment. Nature, reserving them for things more elevated and more delicate, has not given them that brutal strength of digestion, which crushes and overcomes iron, stones, poison; which takes only the good from them, and lives, like Mithridates, continually poisoned.

And when I speak of poisons, I do not even think of immoral things. Her purity will repel them. I speak of a world of things unwholesome from their very nul· lity—vulgar things, useless things, which weary the mind.

The man is condemned to the daily fatigue of pro· digious inquiry, to exhaust the world of details, to learn everything, to sound everything, even in the most muddy stream of experience; but it does not follow from that, that he should drag into it the sacred being who guards the very heavens for him.

Oh, for a book worthy of woman! Where shall I find it? A holy book, a tender book, but one which shall not be enervating! A book to strengthen without hardening, without blunting her, which will not trouble her with idle dreams! a book which will not lead her into the sadness and weariness of the Real, into the thorns of contradiction and discord—a book full of the peace of God!

Spare me here your elaborate discussions on the equality of the sexes. Woman is not only our equal, but in many respects our superior. Sooner or later she will know everything. The question to decide here, is whether she should know all in her first season of love?

Oh! how much she would lose by it! Youth, freshness, and poetry. Does she wish, at the first blow, to give up all these? Is she in such haste to be old?

There are things upon things to learn. But at every age the woman should know something different from the man. It is less learning that she needs, than the essence of learning and its living elixir.

We by no means deny that a young woman can read and inform herself of everything, can go through all the trials to which the man's mind is subjected, and still remain pure. We merely maintain that her intellect, withered by reading, wearied by novels, living habitually on the stimulation of the play-house, on the aqua-fortis of criminal trials, will not be corrupted perhaps, but vulgarized, made common-place, like the curb-stone in the street. This curb-stone is a good stone. You have only to break it to see that it is white within. This does not prevent it from being sadly soiled outside, in every respect as dirty as the street gutter by which it is splashed.

Is this, Madame, your idea of her who should be man's temple, the altar of his heart, whence he daily rekindles the flame of pure love?

––––––

Oh, let us give all to woman! I withhold but one thing—one single reservation:

Give her all that will leave her her freshness and her purity, her charm of young wife-hood, that rathe flower of youth and of moral virginity. Leave her that, I pray you, and as long as possible. What shall be given her in exchange for it? What treasure of human wisdom shall console her for being no longer a dream of Heaven?

This will pass away, swiftly enough, and to-morrow it
will be over. She will always be good and beautiful,
virtuous and accomplished; I have no objection. There
s wanting only a certain thing, a breath, which a breath
will carry away. And what is that? The *velvet-down*
of the soul.

You have, hundreds of times, noticed and admired on
the odorous peach (which makes the very roses jealous),
a fine, delicate down:—Well, it is not that! That is
still too material; that silky down is palpable, may be
touched.

I speak of another thing, which may not be handled,
of a certain glaze (a light rime, like the white glimmer
of the hoar-frost), in which is enfolded the deep violet
hues of a savory fruit. Do not touch it, hold it at a distance; for the softest breath already impairs its bloom.

This is the only thing to which I can compare the internal virginity which the young wife preserves in the
sanctuary of her heart; the velvet down which surrounds
that heart, so pure, so good, so loving!

Is this velvet down a flower, a grace, a charm
of beauty, of imagination, which intoxicates one's
thoughts? It is much more. It guards and covers
what will be the strongest support of man, a fruit of
tenderness, of infinite bounty, a fruit of youth and of
inexhaustible brightness.

The man shall pass through the misfortunes, the
crosses of existence; he shall pass over the deserts, the
sterility of the world, the stones, the flints, the rocks,
on which his feet often bleed! But every evening he
shall drink life from this delicious fruit, all full of the

dew of heaven. Every morning, at day-break, he shall
awake re-youthed.

It is this that we must preserve.

X.

OF MORAL INCUBATION.

I ONCE heard this conversation between a young
couple. They lived in the country; he had returned
from the city where he had been arranging his business:
"Oh, how long you have been! I have been looking so
for you!"—"I've brought you this."—"Thank you;
tell me about yourself."—"Our business is in such a
condition."—"That is good; tell me about yourself."—
"I was told so and so; I met such a person."—"Yes,
but tell me about yourself."

Such is the artless heart of the young wife, at least in
the beginning. She is not occupied with the news. The
bustle of the world, the infinity of little events, which
appear important to us, and are forgotten to-morrow,
are matters of indifference to her; and if you speak to
her of them, she cannot listen. She pretends to do it
for a while, out of respect for you; but she cannot keep
it up long. Her mind is elsewhere, and she gazes on
vacancy. She lives out of the present, in the eternity of
her love.

She undoubtedly wishes to acquire a science, a single

one, to know one thing; what? The heart of her husband.

But this may be immense. A man's heart, strictly
speaking, can contain a world. Since she desires no
other food, be it your task to expand that heart, that all
great and good things may be therein. Thenceforward
she will accept all with avidity.

"The lady of Fayal ate one, and said: 'I find it so
good, that I will eat nothing else.'"

The complete responsibility for the development of
woman rests to-day on him whom she loves. She has
no longer a public culture. No more grand national
fêtes, like those of antiquity, about which, for the whole
year, the family thought and talked. As to the religious
celebrations brought down from the middle ages, the
believers themselves deplore the lukewarmness with
which they are attended; they acknowledge their
feebleness. Can the culture of books supply the want?
Not at all. The diffuseness and parcelling out of the
serial publications which waste the intellect, have dis
gusted women, and many of them will read no more.

There remains, then, the living book, the personality
of the man, the speech of the beloved. Love is more
than ever called upon to merit its great title of The
World's Mediator.

The whole question is, to evoke by love all that there
is in this young being of love, of grace, of thought. In
her there sleeps an ocean which must be roused to
motion. The most unpretending will respond to the
attempt with an unexpected opulence of nature. He

who, without egotism, has thought only of saturating her
mind with all that he believes to be beautiful and great,
will joyfully find that she yields all to him alone, and
loves him with the growing strength of her augmented
love. She must be taken where she is, on her true
plane, which is to love ever more and more.

You must, in the narrow, concentrated love she has
for you, magnanimously inspire her with a sympathetic
enthusiasm for the great universal love of life and nature,
and in the end, by degrees, with the force of active love,
of religious charity, of social sympathy.

She is young, but from this day she must be made and
formed for the good things of God, prepared to become
what a woman truly is—a power of harmony, of solace,
of medication, and of salvation. She cannot yet, at
eighteen, acquire all these, but she may acquire the sentiments, the ideas of them. Many positive things, which
she can learn to-day, will be useful to her at a later period.

This must be carried on gently, without precipitation.
It is not so much a matter of science, and a course of
study, as to give, at apposite moments, living germs,
which, transplanted, removed from your heart to hers,
shall germinate, shall identify themselves with her, and
become her very self.

———

It is doubtless difficult to observe this gentle power of
germination, of incubation in the woman.

The power of man is in abstracting, in dividing; but
the power of the woman is in not knowing how to
abstract, in preserving everything, every idea, entire and
living, and so to be able to render it more living, and to
fructify it.

Nature forbids her dividing and separating. The woman is union itself. She must form a living be_ng, that is to say, one and entire. She cannot say, *two.* " I and my lover are one and the same," she says. An if he impregnates her, it will not make three. No divi sion in her; no plurality. The three are but one.

Your brain, an arsenal of the finest steel blades, con- tains scalpels which will cut through everything. Ana- tomy, war, criticism form the intellect of the man. But the organ of the woman is another thing. That sweet organ, which is a second brain to her, dreams only dreams of love. The peace of heaven, the peace of God, union, unity itself, these are the treasures of her heart.

By what means would you have her employ your methods, how seize that rough instrument of analysis? If one of your subtle thoughts should come to her, it is that she, by her maternal process of incubation, has brooded on it for your sake, has put it into herself, has *conceived* it, and of the idea makes a child.

That which gives an entirely peculiar character of fecundity to the reveries of the woman, is the manner in which time divides itself to her, not by the artificial division of the calendar, but by natural periods. Her month, of about twenty-eight days, reproduces itself with precisely the same incidents, the same developments, the same catastrophes and *entr'actes.* These conditions, but little varied, give to the following month a mental state analogous to that of its corresponding conditions, and often with the same thoughts. These thoughts, repro duced more than once, strengthened from month to

month, come at last to take form, to sway the enti.
individual, to fill her to all her capacity of love an-i
passion.

This is what may be observed in the solitary woman,
in her whom society does not continually draw out from
herself. These returns of the same thought make of
her a faithful being, in whom the culture of the heart is
aided by nature; and even, however little aided, a progressive being, who, once having received the germ,
gives it, at each new epoch, a renewed degree of life,
and of warmth.

All is poetry in the woman, but especially this rhyth-
mic life, harmonized in regular periods, as if scanned by
nature.

On the contrary, time is to man without any real division;
it does not return with new identity. His months are not
months; no rhythm in his life. It is projected always before him, stretched out like free prose, but infinitely mobile,
unceasingly creating germs, for the most part to be lost.

A few men (who unite the two sexes, and are yet the
most powerful of males) have the gift of incubation.

———

What we have just said about the rhythmical life of
the woman affects her whole education, and makes it
essentially different from that of the man.

Care must be taken to do nothing with her inoppor
unely, but to follow the suggestions of nature. If you
do this carefully, she will aid you. What an advantage,
for example, to commence every experiment of mental
initiation in the ascending phase of her sanguine life,
when the flood rises, and her sensibility is exalted with
a more abundant flow, and a more generous tone! On

the contrary, during her crisis, or the languor in which
it leaves her, she should not be fatigued with new ideas,
but should be left quietly to recover, to dream, to think
over those she has already received.

This should be attended to by the prudent mother, by
the wise instructress, who commences the education of
the young girl; and by the lover, the husband, who
continues that of the young wife. The impregnation of
the mind, as well as that of the body, demands that no
thing be done but in season, at the most favorable time.
For this there is needed a constant and unrelaxing watch
over, a tender respect for, the beloved. No violence,
no impatience; select her time, her day, her hour.

She will repay you for this care. The young wife
whom society will not claim from her wedding-day, but
who is left by solitude to the contemplation of this
solemn epoch, asks nothing but to believe and desire all
that her husband wishes her to desire and believe. She
is infinitely interesting. The new condition which from
the very first has given delight to the man, has almost
always aspects still painful for her. He is happy; she will
be so. But she is not the less very tender, with disinterested tenderness. You can from this earliest period
open your heart to her, talk to her about all the great objects of life, and seriously begin the mastery of her mind.

You will think what I am about to say very minute;
but nothing can be too much so on this subject.

Not only the period of the month should be observed,
and the condition of mental exaltation preferred to all
others, but the state of the weather is also an important
matter. I would not have you awkwardly choose for a

confession, or a communion of thought, of new ideas, the moment when she is suffering from the terrors of a tempest. The electricity of life with which she is charged, complicated with that of the air, of a storm, is enough for her to bear; do not annoy her with other matters.

The approach (if not too near) of the sanguineous crisis, when she is in a relaxed condition, is the holy hour I would have you choose to open your mind to her on those grand and weighty questions in which first impressions are of the highest importance : at first a very little, a word, a germ, the first glimmer of an idea, hinted in moments of freest familiarity, or while caressing her.

If your heart has touched her heart, if your idea has truly descended upon her, the approaching crisis of the month, even though it be painful, will efface nothing On the contrary, an idea is stamped on a woman by suffering. Every thorn, whether of love or of nature, makes it penetrate deeper. The necessary idleness which pain sometimes imposes will admirably nourish the germs which her mind has received.

Though still suffering, she will, in the week of agitation which follows the crisis, and the week of interval in which she is entirely calm, busy herself; her hands will work willingly ; and so will her mind. Women can do two things at once. Spinning, knitting, embroidery, needle-work, are excellent employments for ncreasing the activity of their minds. Oh, pleasant little labors, sweet toils, you shall continue despite all the interference of machinery ! No intrinsic advantages, no beauty of mechanical workmanship shall pre-

vail over the pretty trifles which charm away the long
hours of a chaste and industrious woman. In them she
sews up her gentleness, weaves her love, her dreams
and I always feel therein the warmth of the charming
heart which has been blended with them.

———

The French woman, who is called so frivolous, un-
steady, is even more capable than other women of this
double work. Her dream is not a languishing reverie,
vague and uncertain. It is much more a reflecting. At
times, for the sake of change, she accompanies a favorite
thought, which she pursues within, with little snatches of
song in a low tone, which have no connexion with it. But,
at moments, a louder strain bursts forth, and shows that
under the light carol or the monotonous refrain there is
quite another thing, earnest and passionate.

The French woman has not that servile dependence in
love which so many women of other countries betray so
willingly. Although she may be captivated at heart,
obedient, all devotion to the thought of her lover, she
still preserves an independence of form and of manner;
sometimes you are deceived by it. Something you
uttered yesterday from the bottom of your heart; and
because she seemed not to take notice of it, you believe
it was lost. Undeceive yourself; she has it safe. She
has been busy with it all day. And in the evening,
after supper, drawing up her chair beside yours by
the fire, she repeats it in her own way, in her feminine language, quite different and yet the same. Who
knows? those words may take root, and in the approaching period, fructified by the vital flow, may
thrive and blossom with thoughts, with new ideas, with

more warmth, more life, I may even say with more love, than in the month before.

———

To submit thus, without submitting, to acknowledge without embarrassment the profound ascendency of love, and her mental conquest, it is requisite that her gentle pride should be met with favorable occasions, with proper hours, when nature herself is disarmed and yields. Night, or twilight, is much better for this than day-time. Things that she could not have said at mid-day, she will utter in the evening, under a less brilliant light—words that she cannot say at a distance, but which she suffers less to whisper close by—in your ear.

M. de Senancour, who advises that there should be no bed in common, forgets (which is surprising in so thoughtful a mind) that it is the bed which is the conciliator of souls in all weighty and important communications. It is not alone for repose, not alone for pleasure; it is the discreet confidant, the propitious agent for thoughts and words not to be spoken elsewhere. It is the great *communicator*, or better still, a communion.

Religious subjects, for example, the most delicate of all, if discussed in the open day, breed ungentle thoughts—sometimes even dissensions, between the new couple. This is much less apt to be the case when they are spoken of at night and in the bed. There all is softened and harmonized. In the day, one encounters seeming differences, but in the night these disappear, or at least are much less prominent. In spite of these matters of mere form, the pair feel that they are for ever united in love, and the love of God.

The very large bed of former times, occupying half the chamber, very low, almost on a level with the floor, and surrounded on all sides by thick carpets, is infinitely comfortable. It imposes no constraint. It affords every facility for being together or apart. The conversations in the evening and in the morning become easy; so, too, the intercourse of sweet friendship, as well as of love; the most intimate words, often the least premeditated, escape one's lips, which, perhaps, would never have come from the heart if it had been necessary to throw them from one end of the room to the other.

These indescribable freedoms of repose and of awaking, the facility for words, and for unspoken language, are a natural temptation to the tender sensibility of a delicate young soul, which, long after you believe you possess it, preserves, even against its love, a hesitancy, a contracting or drawing back—I know not what to call it. Is it shame? Is it pride? How shall it be named? Whatever it may be, the man is rarely delicate enough to feel it much. And yet the ice is not entirely broken between you. She, married months ago, is at heart still a girl. Some moral cause is necessary, such is their natural nobility, to compel them to give themselves entirely up. This almost always comes when they have loved and adopted some good sentiment in the man, something sincere, glowing, grand, strong, of which they have caught a glimpse in him. And who has not had moments like these? The very worst have such gleams of light.

Thenceforth she is won by him. The gentle warmth of love which has risen to her heart gives her a little more courage; and in the evening, when he has been

7

asleep, he has the sweet surprise of finding her still awake. Alert and loving, this silent one suddenly speaks. It is night: she has not dared to speak during the day; but at this time she is often eloquent. She is happy; she believes him to be good, worthy, a man after God's own heart, and in God she loves him. Her heart melts, and she is his wife. From that hour marriage has commenced for her. Thenceforth she can bear his name. We hear no more of the girl of yesterday to-day the wife is born.

BOOK THIRD

———o———

OF THE INCARNATION OF LOVE.

I.

CONCEPTION.

Love in woman is an exalted and a noble thing. She stakes her life upon it.

Every time she consents, and yields to man's desire, she testifies her willingness to die for him.

What does he risk? Nothing, except to labor a little more, and to support a child. What does she risk? Everything. She submits not only to the crisis of a terrible agony, in which her life is suspended by a thread, but to the chances of a lingering death, and a thousand infirmities, so cruel. that their very author might be shocked by them.

Young man, you who regard love as so pleasant and so trifling a matter, I beg you to obtain and read but a single one of the numerous books afforded by the terrible literature of midwifery, and the diseases which follow child-bed. At the mere enumeration, your arms fall powerless; at the description, a cold perspiration stands upon your forehead; and if you persevere to the horribly-ingenious surgical details, to the operations (which torture but do not cure), the book falls from your hands. That which is endured by these poor weak creatures, alas! with their bodies, with their flesh, you, a man, can scarcely endure the thought of.

Love is the Brother of Death. This has been often said, and said again. But who has yet discovered to what extent he is the *Brother of Pain ?*

Let these solemn words be inscribed on the threshold of the charming world of Reproduction, into which you imagine you are about to enter as through triumphal arches of garlands and flowers. Read these words, not to recoil (for it is the law of nature), but to understand for once the supreme beauty of woman. She accepts every peril—death, the depths of suffering—to give to him she loves an infinity of joy, the life of centuries com pressed into an instant, the epitome of eternity.

"Be happy, though I should die! Be happy one second, though I should for ever suffer!" These are the words she has in her heart. And yet she has the genero-sity not to utter them to you; it would sadden you too much, it would cool your ardor, if that cruel name of death, which is in the depths of her heart, should come up to her lips among your kisses.—No, she will keep it all to herself.—To you the heaven, to you the joy! To her the dark foreshadowings, and the terrors of the future.

Unselfish devotion! It is a vain stupidity, too com-mon in man, to suppose that woman yields herself, over-come by physical love. This error may be pardoned in children and in novices, but it is very absurd in those who have had any experience. Whoever knows woman knows very well that, with almost all, there is in this act only kindness and compliance. In our refined age, the generating crisis distresses them very little. This cold

ness results from two causes: from their vast expenditure of nervous force in affability and conversation ; and,
on the other hand, too often from the unhealthy waste of
life going on in them, even during the intervals between
the regular crises of nature.

To state the matter frankly, even should the man's
pride suffer by it : they comply almost always wittingly,
in order to fulfil their destiny as woman, to insure the
love of the man, and to create a family ; they submit
from the exalted necessity implanted in them, of sacri-
ficing themselves.

———

The great physiologist, Burdach, our illustrious master, makes this beautiful and just remark : "In the animal races, the nobility of the female appears in this : that
she does not seek a mate except for the purpose of generation." And still another trait : "The male is fierce
before pleasure, in the blindness of his savage desire ; but
if the female is fierce it is only after pleasure, and during
her maternity, to protect her young."

The child is the recompense, the precious prize for the
sufferings and the perils which love has brought to the
woman. "It is to her the prize of pleasure," worthily
says Virgil. But, even without this hope, the wife can
devote herself. Fruitful or not, she accepts the sovereign duty of woman—that of renewing, of re-animating
the man. She is the *Fountain of life* (Genesis), but she
is so in two senses. If she does not give it to a child,
he gives it to her husband.

Ah, how little did the shameful and subtle science of
the scholastics, who spoke so senselessly of these things,
seeking in them only libertinism, suspect their holy gra-

vity! they saw nothing of the earnestness, the danger,
the devotion, which is the foundation of it all, nor the
profound bartering of life which is the true mystery of it.

. Our age, the age of labor, understands very well that
the laborer, the producer of all things, who gives his life
and his soul to it, has need of constantly recovering that
life from nature. The wife is in no wise ignorant that
she is nature herself: that is to say, reparation, consolation, happiness, and joy. She is the prize of the day,
the charm of the evening and of repose. In her alone
man finds oblivion: oblivion profound as death, which
daily regenerates him. He revives—through whom, if
not her? But how shall she renew his life? By hazard-
ing her own. She sees him blind in his joy, but she
makes him none the less the arbiter of her fate, gives
him full control over her. The generous security of a
pure heart which is doing its duty puts aside all care;
and she smiles in peace, risking only life. Nor does
she love him any the less for this—ah, what do I say?
even more, for her sacrifice and her danger; all that he
abstracts in passion, she gives him in redoubled love.

The wise and the foolish will tell you that all this is
instinctive, that in her self-devoting the woman follows
the blind enthusiasm of her nature, etc. Generally it is
exactly the contrary. She has very little ardor, much
serenity and tenderness. It is the man who loves in
gusts; she in perfect calm.

I blush to write this, but it is too *true*, and must be
acknowledged. Man's love is manifested much too often
at night from the base excitement caused by a luxurious
banquet, especially after winter and autumn feasts, when

the harvest is in, the granaries full, and the grapes gath
ered. Thence come those numerous conceptions of the
winter months, begotten infamously, without love, upon
the wife submissive, but not consulted.

With her, on the contrary, if at times she feels the
spark divine, it is at dreamy and poetic hours, in gentle
awakings, in the morning, above all in the spring time,
when God wills her to love; and when a breath of that
fruitfulness which is the duty of nature, reanimates both
the woman and the flower.

Woe unto the children of darkness, the sons of drunk-
enness, who were, nine months before their birth, an
outrage on their mothers !

He who is born of a nocturnal orgie, of the very for
getfulness of love, of a profanation of the beloved one,
will drag out a sad and troubled life.

On the contrary, it is a sublime, a mighty blessing to
be conceived in the light, when a man's love is directed,
not to the sex indiscriminately, not to any woman whatsoever, but to this single woman, to this heart which belongs to him, saying : " *She*, and no other ;" when it is
mirrored in her smile, in her beautiful quiet eyes, which
reflect the dawn on him—in her charming surprise, and
her artless impulse, which say : " Yes, yes, I was dreaming of you."

The profound and perfect harmony of the heart, the
exquisite sense that love, in its most obscured moments
nd its hidden light, preserves of the loved object, is
that which produces divine fruit—a son of liberty and of
light. Both are *desirous*. It is doubtless of the most
elevated voluntary love that heroes have been born

7*

But now the day is becoming brighter ;—he has gone business has called him away. The young wife rises, modestly, not without dignity, but a little strange to herself. . . . . " Am I truly myself?" she asks. " Yes, certainly—Great mystery! I have done my duty, and yet I am disturbed!

" Ah, wrong, wrong for thee to be so, pure diamond! which of us can boast of being as pure ?" So say the last stars, fading out in the morning-hour. They look down smilingly on her, the innocent one, as she walks, agitated, in her little garden.

The exquisitely transparent and limpid waters of the fountain from which she asks a little to refresh herself, those waters in which heaven is mirrored, say to her : " Chaste wife ! would to heaven that our waves, in which you think to purify yourself, were as pure as thy bosom !"

" But after all,"—she says to herself very low—so low that she is almost afraid of her own voice—" was I not too happy ? . . . And in that solemn moment, it may be of an infinite future, did I lift my soul above? God willed it, God ordained it. Did I preserve the thought of God in my mind ?"

" Ah, dear sister," murmur the flowers, as they bend to the ground to kiss her footsteps, " who would not be softened by thy tender heart ? . . Oh, that we might breathe the sweet perfume that emanates from thee ! . . . Do as we do, oh young flower ! open in peace thy inno-cent bosom ; grudge not that the dew of heaven swells thy chaste chalice. After, even as before love, we are, and, we remain, pure."

II.

PREGNANCY, AND THE STATE OF GRACE.

WE have said that woman is, indeed, Fruitful Life
Whatever she thinks of, is a living thing for her, and
her idea is a child.

We know now why to certain words she is so indif·
ferent, to others so alive. She is susceptible and sensible
only of an idea which can be incarnated. This she
takes, makes her own, sketches it out like a living dream,
endows it with her desires. Let the breath of love pass
over it, and the dream is embodied, and becomes a
child.

Of whatever you give her, which is abstract, general,
collective, she makes an individual. If you speak to
her of patriotism, of a free and heroic community,
already she has conceived its hero—the hero in action,
in art, or in science—the renovator, the creator, the
strong arm, the fruitful hand, which shall lavish unheard
of benefits on the human race. All this obscurely and
indefinitely. She hardly knows herself what she would
desire, but leaves it all to Providence. God will know
what is best to do. It is enough for the mother to know
—and she is almost sure of it—that the child is a mira·
cle, a saviour, a messiah.

She has never dared to speak of it, not even in her
bed, not even at the encouraging hour when kind Night
hides all, and allows so much to be said. She has not

dared. If he had laughed! what a cruel wound that would be to her! No; that sublime hope is the only thing that woman does not tell him whom she loves. She has a little bashfulness, a secret shame, of her divine romance.

I will tell you in confidence: it was this of which she was thinking the other day when her husband, returning before his usual time, found her serious, agitated, as if she had been surprised in something which she wished to conceal. He sought for it, he endeavored to discover what it was, but she embraced him in silence.

She, so discreet, and so unimpassioned, is herself astonished at the involuntary flight her imagination has taken. She does not know that her folly is the highest wisdom. It was the exaltation of our mothers, their effort to conceive an infant God, that has made you and me the little that we are; it is this dream that has given us the best that is in us. And if any is strong upon earth, it is because a woman conceived him in heaven.

This, if I may say so, was the solitary conception of the woman, between her and herself, while she was still mistress of her thoughts, still free and light, before the night when the Omnipotent God, the All-powerful Realizer, surprised her in her ethereal dream, and caught her in his storm. And now all is changed. She feels a dull heat, and sudden chills, shiverings, run through her body; her beautiful neck is swollen; her bosom is agitated and tumid; but this time the wave does not retire; the billow remains suspended, her breasts become enlarged, and lower down there is delineated—a shadow!—an undefined outline, like a new world.

A painful turgidness weighs her down. Even her head is a little weakened; that winged soul is for a moment borne down and oppressed by the body. She has no longer the free and sure direction of her motions. She vacillates, hesitates, wavers—what is there surprising in that? He himself, the blind author of the miracle, is almost as much disturbed as she. He is agitated, he is enraptured, but uneasy too, on seeing her launched on that great sea whereon he cannot follow her. She is beyond his power, beyond his protection. What terror for him who loves! He sees her fatally advancing, day by day, towards the fulfilment of this mystery. He can do nothing but make propitiation, pray, and clasp his hands, like a suppliant at the altar. A boundless devotion for this living temple has seized upon him. Before that divine globe, which contains the unknown world, he dreams, he is hushed; if he smiles, the smile is almost a tear.

Let no one accuse him of weakness. If ever a paroxysm of religion deserve respect, it is surely in this case. We are actually in the presence of the grandest miracle—an incontestable miracle, with nothing absurd in it, but which is not the less obscure. Every human being is a miracle, shut in by an insuperable barrier. Yet she has broken through it. It is a double prodigy —the formation of the child, the transformation of the mother. The impregnated wife becomes man. Invaded by the male force, when it has once seized upon her, she will gradually yield to it. The man will gain on her, will pervade her. She will be *himself*, more and more.

One or two years will suffice for a soft and delicate

silkiness, like the blossom of an ear of corn, to bloom on
her lip. Her voice, too, will be changed. She often
loses the high, and gains deeper, tones (but of such
wondrous sweetness !). And how many other changes !
The involuntary imitation of him she has at the bottom
of her being manifests itself unconsciously to her, in her
manner and her movements. You would not know her ;
but only to look at her walk, to hear her speak, to see
her smile (despite a certain softness, and a fragility of
form), you would say : " I recognise him in his wife, and
her in him."

Profound, marvellous union ! Especially in these
first months of pregnancy, when the new life, begun
within, does not yet reveal itself to her, except by the
confusing disturbance of a great fluctuation, she tells
everything to him who has injured her, by whom she
suffers, and whom she loves so much the more. Inter-
nally she feels that it is he who burns, who circulates in
her. Externally, she takes him as her only support,
leans on him, complains to him, and is as if suspended
to him. She wishes (and he even more than she), that
he shall pity her, spoil her, envelope her with the most
tender cares. In return, she abandons herself entirely
to him, she is thoroughly a good child. She becomes
his little daughter, and lets him attend her like a child.
If at first she forbids it, if it is a little in spite of her,
what can she do ? She has no power, no wish to
refuse ; she submits, since he demands it ; and not with
much trouble, for she finds it very pleasant.

While waiting for the child to come, she can surely
take his place. And, what is rather strange, she, but

now so serious, feels nothing disagreeable in this new
rôle. The liberties which the woman finds so sweet in
her little innocent, she knows well that he who loves
her thinks delightful in her. She knows that everything in her enraptures him, that he is so delighted with
the unrestrained felicity to which she abandons herself,
that to insure it to her he must shut his eyes. Among
other natural peculiarities a woman has at this time, she
loves now and then to hide herself, to withdraw apart,
in order to prove to herself that she is truly independent, and that the dear tyrant, who so follows her in
heart, does not enwrap her too much. She obeys this,
and retires, at most only smiling. She, on her part, is
not ignorant that in pretending to observe nothing, he
sees it all. No matter, she is pleased with him for
being so considerate and so good. Charming, innocent
game, in which no one is deceived, and no one deceives!
Ridiculous, do you say? Ah, no! Leave them this
child's play of the State of Grace.

To tell you the truth, madame, if this man spoils you,
there is no merit in it, for we are all like him. For
you, all of us (I am not speaking of friends, but of
strangers, men, everybody, all nature) are agreed to
love, to overwhelm you with votive offerings, to bless
you. Our houses are at your service. Take the flowers,
and the fruit; anything you may desire. We shall be
only too happy!

But you shall go no farther; come into my house, I
beg you. Deign to rob me, madame; rob me in preference to the others. I do not know what old custom
t is which allows the pregnant woman to take three

pears, or three apples; but it is too few. Oblige me
by taking the whole garden. That is, if you like.

But, clumsy fellow that I am, what have I said?—I
have spoiled all. She enters, and she is now full of
shame, will have nothing more, averts her eyes. ' Her
charming little mouth plainly says: "You should have
seen nothing."

I cannot forgive myself, I am disconsolate—for she
will listen no more to me; she passes out, and walks
away, blushing, and lowering her eyes.

It was the stealthiness of the thing which tempted
her. For she knows very well that all is for her; that
she can do anything she pleases, and it will always be
right. She brings infinitely more than she can carry
away, for she brings peace, love, a fragrance of felicity.
You cannot see her without smiling, but it is a smile of
beatitude; it is as if you had seen happiness itself; and
after it you are happy all day.

Wherever she deigns to set her foot, law ceases.
And the law entreats her to command. Her caprice is
the law; her whim, wisdom—her folly, reason.

If she, the innocent daughter of God, should sin
(a thing impossible!), her fault would come to our
hearts so slight, so softened, rather as another charm!
The only little sin which she perhaps must acknowledge,
is that agitated virtually by an atom, but one so
greedy, she is greedy herself; and if she consulted only
herself, if she dared to do it, she would follow this blind
impulse. You are happy to see her eat much, eat
always, often slily and in secret. Unwisely indulged,

this impulse may injure her. Her husband should beseech her to deny herself a little. He yields too much to the enjoyment of seeing her enlarged life, her dazzling beauty, so solemnly splendid. See! it is no her waist alone that is enlarging. Her beautiful arms her white shoulders, her bosom, all expand in voluptu· ous curves; and her whole person is in flower.

It was on St. John's day, I think, in 1825, that I was making a visit to an old friend at Saint-Cloud. The wife of the charming painter, Madame B——, who was a neighbor, and like one of the family, entered without being announced. The door opened quickly, and the room seemed to me to be suddenly filled with light and with flowers. I was dazzled. She threw off her straw hat, and cast down an immense bouquet she had just gathered in the fields. Although far advanced in pregnancy, she had done all this in a moment, with the vivacity of a young girl, and a spoiled child, sure of being approved by all.

She was in person very large, and in the positive plenitude of life. Her powerful electricity, which overflowed everything, prevented me from hearing what she said. What I understood best, was the light of life, of happiness and of goodness, which gushed forth from her eyes.

I lowered mine, and became sad. Again I raised them, and looked at her. Then, strengthened in heart, I took my leave, and sauntered back to Paris.

That oriental hymn, the true chaunt of the infinite, passed through my mind amidst its whirl of emotion.

"Oh sun! oh sea! oh rose! . . . .

"The circle of existence is fulfilled and finished in thee!"

III.

THE RESULT OF PREGNANCY.—THE RIVAL

FRIENDS should be true to each other. I ought to tell you frankly, without subterfuge—you have a rival "Great God!"—yes, a preferred rival. She loves you, and will always love you. But you must resign your-self to this fact: you are no longer her first thought.

Among the peculiarities which we remark in her, the strongest (not equal in all women) is that, at first, when she feels herself so invaded by you, so subjugated by you, she has weak little desires of contradiction, infan-tile refractorinesses, freaks of resistance. Her instinctive liberty timidly reclaims her from her full engulfment by love.

Love laughs at this, thinking to engross it with all the rest. He believes so, and he deceives himself. As everything in her is loving, the timid resistance was nothing but the new life which bubbled in her breast. The graceful little rebellion was no other than your child.

———

There is another man, another soul, another will, which doubles, and troubles too at moments, that dear heart, which believes it could never wish for another beside you. He is there, and he demands her. From the depths of the sea of milk, from the darkness in which he sleeps, he already influences, already works upon her. His world, that poor suffering, agitated world that contains him, he will soon govern ; and already at the fifth month, he has knocked at the door, and cried strongly: "I am here!"

"I have felt him!" she cries, placing her trembling hand on the spot where he has rapped, "He moves; he is indeed living! . . There he is again; he is restless Ah! my child, you have done me harm! But, O God what good too!"

From this hour he is her thought. She never escapes from him. To dream of him, to follow him, to watch for him, to note his movements, to wait for him, is all her life. Nor does he fail her at the rendezvous. He is her inseparable lover. Still, if she is unfaithful to you, she does not conceal it; she talks incessantly of him. How can it be otherwise? This progressive creation of one being within another is so absorbing, that the mother has nothing in herself to which she can withdraw, by which she can defend herself against him. And she shows no discretion in thinking of him. For, if his sudden movements do make her suffer every moment, she still enjoys the harmony of so profound a marriage. The tremblings of this sweet fruit are not always painful. She fancies easily that he already loves his mother. Sometimes her countenance lights up; she blushes—he has passed by.

She tells you all, or almost all. You are the happy confidant of their innocent amours. You take part in, and have a third share in them. But in her life, henceforward filled to this point with another being, what a little place have you! He is now the predominant, exclusive, only interest. What he desires you desire; and what he fears, you fear. Four months before he is born he is master of the house.

The husband always gives way to, must always give way to, the father. Every habit, every pleasure, is sacrificed in this crisis. Ah! who would contradict her, annoy her, give her trouble? Shall she not rather be surrounded with objects of joy, be cheered, be made happy, and smiling? Gain this at any price.

Still the man is always the man. He does not easily alter his life from its very foundation. And so there are little disturbances, I do not say of jealousy in such a heart as yours, but perhaps of a slight sadness; and you make some complaints. She does not wish to hear them. For the first time, she evades you; she would rather not listen to you; she goes apart. She does not go very far, she does not flee very swiftly, and has no fear of being rejoined. And, half-returning, with the tenderest smile, albeit a little malicious, she says: "Why, my dear, if *he* does not wish me to love you, what shall I do?" She wishes to try you. Perhaps the proof is a little harsh. She sees you aggrieved, and she hastens to console you. Divided between two duties, she submits to the one without neglecting the other. But if *he* does not suffer, does not recall her, the little tyrant will obey in everything; and, far from complaining, will say: "Ah, how happy I am! In loving him, it is you alone that I love. And through him I have the happiness of belonging the more to you."

In love all is worthy, all royal. Nothing elevates her more than her free servitudes, her voluntary humiliations. She was never more a queen than in this abnegation, when submitting to the exigencies of an inexorable love. Restless and uneasy, but unspotted, she leaves all to God. Her sufferings, the imminence of the approaching peril, bring to her the most solemn thoughts. In moments of happiness in which you, a little selfishly, embrace her (the dear slave of devotion and self-sacrifice), if you could see her face you would perhaps experience a pang of regret at finding it so calm and so exalted, so full of the light of heaven.

She is timorous, she is fearful certainly, in these latter days, but it is especially the fear of doing wrong. She confesses herself the sacred instrument of eternal creation, and that in transmitting to her child her blood and her life, she at the same time transmits her soul. And so we have a constant scruple, a touching heedfulness, to preserve that soul pure and holy.

Would to heaven we could give her a book which might sustain her, or some sufficing prayer—but not to ask of God that he will change anything in His laws; on the contrary, she desires only to harmonize herself with those laws, with the infinite order, and to do all as God wills.

Her true strength, in this path in which she is walking alone and trembling, should be you, if you are able to control passion by love, and not humble her continually to the dust. This is a solemn time. Her day draws near. You must think much of it, treat her tenderly, spare her. Ah! will Death spare her?

Have pity on us, O Death!

IV.

CONFINEMENT.

If you would see an image of fear, look at that man in this awful moment—frank fear, not concealed, too strong to be contained, which expresses itself by signs that would be absurd, if they were not so touching. I have seen men, and they too the most haughty, tearing their beards in desperation. Haggard, pale, exhausted, they could not but excite pity. Even the sick woman, in the midst of her agony, had to say : " Courage, dear, courage! Are you such a coward ?"

The woman lives in the child, but the man lives in the woman. In this truly formidable hour he presses close to her, he clasps her two hands in his, as if they would escape him. But her hands hold on by nothing—she is subject to another power which draws her away, drags her from his side. At intervals she looks around the world in which she still remains, at the anxiety of the assistants, at that distracted man ; but it seems to him, already, as if she were gazing from the other shore.

The crisis continues. The doctor shakes his head, walks up and down, is not self-assured ; and the husband follows him like a dog. Fear has humbled him. His cowardice—his flatteries, his quick and sudden friendship for one whom he scarcely knew before, but who holds her life in his hands, are the most curious things imaginable. The husband, once so jealous, is so no longer He unhesitatingly unveils to a stranger that dear and honored person. He does not even inquire if she suffers from this profanation. He assumes a severe expression, and scolds her for her modest hesitation. In short, he is absurd, imbecile, a complete idiot.

She has said the most reasonable things to him in regard to this matter; but fear will listen to nothing. She has told him that in the great work of woman, woman only is a useful auxiliary. That the presence of a man may on the contrary be the greatest obstacle—an obstacle absolutely insurmountable by some, even should they die for it.

Observe, that in the majority of cases all the skill consists in watching, with folded arms. If the child presents in a bad position, if dexterity be required, a woman's little hand, her adroitness, her habits of touching minute objects, all are most certainly better suited to it than a man's great paws. What hand can be soft enough, what manipulation delicate enough, to handle (great heaven!) the most tender object, terribly painful from such excess of tension, to touch the rents and wounds of that poor bleeding body!

Woman can nurse woman much the best. Why? Because she is at once patient and physician, because she can easily understand in another the pains she herself has felt, the trials she herself has undergone. Doctors are learned in science, but know very little of patients. There is scarcely one of them who has a clear understanding of a being so delicate, so full of mystery, in whom the nervous life is all in all.

Our physicians are a very enlightened class of men, and, in my opinion, incomparably the first in Europe.

No others know so much, nor with such certainty. None are so well trained in mind and character. But, after all, their rude masculine education in schools and hospitals, their severe surgical initiation, one of the glories of this country, are all qualities which involve a grave deficiency in this department. They result in the extinction, in them, of that refined sensibility which alone can perceive, foresee, divine the truths of the feminine mystery. The breast of the woman, that sweet miracle, on which nature has exhausted her tenderness, who but woman herself can touch it without impiety?

The fault is not in the physicians, who, I think, will appreciate this. It is owing to the weakness of the man rather than of the woman, at such times; it is the husband's fault, and nothing can reassure him but the presence of the doctor. I do not gainsay this. Although so many illustrious midwives, the Boivins, the Lachapelles, and others, might certainly suffice to tranquillize; although the testimony of Europe, through the whole extent of which they are preferred, might also calm our fears, there is nothing to prevent our consulting the doctor and profiting by his advice, provided that he does not officiate, and that he is not too near. His direct intervention is much less calculated to aid than to paralyse nature.

Women should be listened to. And they say frankly (when one ventures to press them on so delicate a matter) that all their strength, in this act of violent exertion, consists in the *liberty* of the exertion, and that this liberty is as nothing if a man is in the room. From this cause, at every moment, hesitation results, and contradictory movements. They desire and they do not desire.

They exert and they restrain themselves. You will say they are in the wrong, that they should be at ease, should, in such a crisis, forget their superstitions of shame and fear, the little annoyances which so humiliate them. But, however this may be, such they are; as such they must be treated. And he who, to save them, will put them in such peril, is certainly a fool.

My dissertation grows too long; it is done. An unnatural cry, which is not of this world, which is not of our race, it would seem—a sharp, shrill, savage cry, pierces our ears. A little bleeding mass has fallen among us. . . . .

And this then is man! . . . . . Welcome, poor shipwrecked soul!—She was exhausted, but she suddenly opens her eyes, " Oh my child, are you then here !"

And holding out her hand to her half-dead husband, " I was resigned to it," she says, " I accepted death for you."

Here is now a solemn compact between them, entered into on that day—a truly earnest marriage ; the contract of suffering !

She loves him, and holds him now by a bond that pleasure never formed ; she loves him, branded by him with an ineffaceable mark ; she loves him for the blood she pours out, and for her lacerated flesh ; for her awful sundering when the very frame of her being seemed about to dissolve.

And he, he loves her for the anguish, and the agony of terror, in which he was plunged, with no strength left him, more shattered than she, and more haggard

8

than at the grave. He has been mastered by terror and
by pity to-day. The weak has vanquished the strong.
She has branded him, in her own way, with an ineffaceable mark of fear and agony.

What a bond is this, of dying together—I should say
of having, together, seen and felt death so near.

————

And it is not yet over. The fear is not yet banished.
Behold her there in her laces, pale and beautiful, with a
touching grace. Ah, if you but knew, in truth, the
terrible reality which that beauty hides!

You must face all, oh man! These impressions are
salutary. It is well that you should know Love, the
great master of Pain.

"No; have pity," you say, "leave us our poetry; the
horrible is not poetical. What would become of her if
the shocking image of her torn entrails was depicted to
her?"

Let us spare her that sight; but you must endure it,
and it will do you good.

Nothing so strains the feelings as this. Whoever has
not been accustomed, inured to these sad spectacles, is
hardly master of himself when he sees a perfect representation of the matrix after delivery. A shivering
agony seizes him, and freezes the marrow in his bones.
The fearful irritation of the organ, the turbid torrent
which exudes so frightfully from the devastated abyss!
oh! what a horror!—he shrinks back. . . . .

This was my experience when this truly terrible
object was shown to me for the first time in the excellent plates of Bourgery's work. A matchless engraving
in the atlas of Coste and Gerbe also represents the same

organ under a less terrible form, but which still affects one to tears. It is shown at the time when, with its intricate plexus of red fibres, which appear like silk, or purple hair, the matrix weeps tears of blood.

These several plates of Gerbe (the majority not signed), this unique astonishing atlas, is a temple of the future, which, in a later and a better time, shall fill every heart with religion. You should throw yourself on your knees before daring to look upon it.

The great mystery of generation has never before appeared in art in all its charm, in its true sacredness. I do not know who is the wonderful artist. It makes no difference; I thank him. Every man who had a mother will thank him.

He has given us the form, the color, but better than all, the softness and delicacy of style, the tragic grace of these things, and their profound emotion. Is it but imitation! or has he, too, felt this? I do not know, but such is the effect.

Oh, sanctuary of grace, made to purify all our hearts, how much you reveal to us!

We learn first of all, that Nature, while lavishing so many beauties on the outside, has bestowed the grandest within. The most thrilling are concealed, as if swallowed up in the very depths of life itself. And we learn here too, that love is a visible thing. The tenderness our mothers lavished on us, their dear caresses, and the sweetness of their milk, all, all is recognised, is felt, is divined, and adored, in this unutterable sanctuary of love and of agony.

V

LYING-IN AND CONVALESCENCE.

BEFORE and during the lying-in, the usual company, the conversation of the sick nurses, of the neighbors and others, is generally injurious, even dangerous to the sick woman. They are garrulous, and inconsiderate in the use of their tongues, and often irritate a spirit so shattered as this, with disagreeable matters. Sometimes it is gossip, scandal, and a hundred little nonsensical details, which produce useless disturbances. Sometimes it is mischievous accounts of terrible accidents, of bad signs, of miracles, of absurd recipes, etc. At any other time she would not listen to them, would compel them to be silent. But now, enfeebled, passive as she is, she receives a gloomy impression only too readily, and keeps it to herself. All this, among the women, takes place, of course, in the absence of her husband; let him return, and they are hushed.

Yet the prime condition essential to her recovery is perfect tranquillity of mind. The presence of a stranger at this time will be no benefit to her; how much less that of a thoughtless babbler and fool who, in her capacity of nurse, deranges the order of the house, makes everything subservient to her ways, and gives more trouble than the invalid herself. The familiar servant, the good country girl, simple, kind, obeying the doctor's orders to the very letter without a question, would certainly have been preferable. Silence would then have been insured, and nothing would be altered. But the nurse, with whom I would be best satisfied, is undoubtedly the husband; he, with the assistance of this girl, can easily do everything.

I know very well that he is busy, that he has but little time. He must, he *must* make time—now, or never.

You should obtain leave of absence; you should post-pone all business not absolutely imperative. The danger is not yet over, and it may be much more imminent. She looks beautiful and smiling, as she lies dressed, in her bed. Death is nevertheless very near. A door or a window opened inopportunely, food given at the critical moment of the suppurating fever, a rude shock, may unsettle, may shatter her. A few hours, and all will be over.

Even this devoted servant may, from her ignorance, or perhaps in obedience to a whim of the invalid, strike the fatal blow in your absence. Truly, I can rely on no one but you.

First of all, understand that your presence alone is a sovereign remedy. When you are with her, she is tran-quil, perfectly calm; she falls asleep. In your absence, she is not well; if she sleeps, it is only an uneasy slum-ber; the strange nurse, who is put there for the express purpose of watching over her, the sick woman, on the contrary, feels the necessity of watching. Even the good servant, a little awkward, puts her out of patience. And though she were skilful, all that one could desire, she cannot supply your place. It is the loved hand, and none other, that she needs in a hundred little services. She must have by her side the dear one for whom she

suffers, and make him suffer a little   she must complain
to him, and be pitied by him; in short, even if she
wants for nothing, does not talk, is even sleeping, she
must know you are near her.

———

"But shall I be competent for this position of nurse?"
Yes, you will.   You do not know your talents and
accomplishments yet.   You do not know all you are
capable of.   If you are not restrained by the pride of
man's so-called dignity (ridiculous, aye, guilty, in so·
delicate a crisis), I assure you you will discover an unexpected skill, an unwonted tact, which will excite
shame and envy in the most experienced nurse.

There is little, very little to do (much more not to do,
to avoid).   The doctor has traced out the way for you,
and she, your wife, in case of need, will supply the
deficiency in a few words.   It will be a pleasure, a very
great pleasure, for her to direct you, and a source of
amusement to see you at work.   The clumsy ways of
another would irritate her, but yours put her in good
humor; your patience will please her, will fill her with
perfect serenity, even hilarity.   What matters it?   A
man of spirit who really loves is only too happy in such
a case to see impressions made, so favorable to her
health.

If your vanity suffers from it, so much the better.
You deserve that, and much more.   Who has sinned, if
not you?   Since she has suffered so much for you, it i
only just that you should endure in your turn, that you
should do a little penance.

And are you, besides, sick of waiting on a sweet woman,
who, if it were not for this occurrence, would perhaps

never have been willing to resign herself so completely to you? You should bless your fate! How many men would envy you for it! Everything that comes from her is a boon.

———

Exalt yourself, my friend, to the dignity of your situation. A good heart and a stout courage know how to make all circumstances honorable. The man naturally distinguished with a true nobility, dignifies every duty, and imparts a certain stateliness, a certain pleasing grace, to that which, in the hands of another, would not appear susceptible of it.

What happiness for her! and how will she be tranquillized and soothed, in finding you there so zealous, so nimble at everything! To tell the truth, the poor darling, if she does at times laugh at you, is a little ridiculous herself. Do you know what was her fear in her greatest danger (the common fear of women, all alike in this)? Death? No. Suffering? No. Even though that was awful; another thought possessed her. What was it? I shall tell you, for you would never guess it: The fear of displeasing, or in some way repelling, of being offensive.

To whom? To all; to the doctor, to the nurse, to her very maid, who is like her own child, and for whom she cherishes such hearty regard.

For the first time the young wife feels herself completely bound down in bed, incapable of helping herself. She is not at her ease with anyone. All embarrass her. What will become of her without you?

It is too true that the best mistress, the most refined, the most worthy to be beloved, is never assured that cer-.

tain things will be received by her servant. Even her perilous and affecting situation does not deter the latter from being sulky behind her back. The invalid under-stands this very well, and there is only one being to whom she is quite sure of being always delightful, always sweet, and charming in all respects.

It is one of the chief delights of the all-powerful master, Love, to transform everything; especially to change, to pervert, and to transpose the senses. There is no doubt that whatever is unpleasant to those who do not love, is agreeable to those who do. Which is wrong? I do not know. Are our usually cold, calm, mournful feelings, which declare this or that object disagreeable, certain to be in the right when opposed to the superior senses to which every manifestation of nature is a charm and a delight?

An original engraving, by a master of the seventeenth century, the facetious Abraham Boss, shows this very naturally. A pretty woman is in bed (recently confined no doubt), sick, but evidently cheerful. Her old grumbling servant is shuffling around the room, groaning over a nurse's little annoyances. But there is a pendant to this. It represents the husband, a young and elegant cavalier, in the full costume of the time, freshly starched, hatted and plumed, equipped with sword and spurs, having a Spanish countenance, dark, resolute, soldier-like. Armed not with the sword, however, but with the peaceful badge of his new calling, he stands in a triumphant attitude, making himself ready for his task; and for the rest, full of inspiration and of spirit, his hair flying, handsome as a man leading an assault. It is easy to see that he hesitates at nothing that he will carry the affair

successfully, that he has genius for the thing—love and
dexterity.

———

To be able to do nothing, to wait for everything, to
live entirely by the beloved hand, to receive food, and
every other necessary from it, is a more perfect identifi
cation of two beings than even that of the child at the
bosom of its mother. For the infant does nothing, but
receives without volition. *She* does not wish to do anything but to receive, and she does receive, enjoying
this state of infancy with all her heart and all her mind.

He is her complete world; she does not love, she
does not move, except in him. Her lovely, loving,
languishing eyes follow him as he moves about the
chamber, walking lightly on tiptoe. She will not drink
from any hand but his. Soon she will not eat but from
his hand. Even the involuntary organs of animal life—
as for example, the stomach—have become so strongly
habituated, that, without him, they will refuse to act.
"He is not here—I will wait till he comes."

One admirable result of this single life in two persons is this: that the well half exerts a powerful physical influence to the advantage of the sick half. She
loves him with her feebleness and her sickness; he loves
her with his health, his cheerfulness, his hope. It is the
healthy, the confident one, that sways the other; he
draws her on as by the influence of a superior magnetism, and leads her back to life.

———

What a joy it is when she can leave her bed, when
they show her her garden, and the changes they have
made in it for her, when the sun smiles on her, and her

8*

dumb pets leap with happiness at seeing her again; when, at length, for the first time, they draw up her large arm-chair to the table, and her place, so sadly vacant, is occupied again.

She recovers her spirits, and her harmony, always through you. Weak as she is, she keeps her eyes fixed long on yours, drawing from them happiness, health, strength, renewing that union which forms your lives; and then she tenderly says: "Through you I am my-self again."

———

What more can be done for her who has suffered so much? One thing, one only, will recompense her. We are still too uncivilized for it; but it will certainly be a sacrament in the future. A lady suggested the idea to me. "The highest happiness for the mother," said she, "is, after her recovery, forty days, or more, as the case may be, to take her husband's arm, and in company with the whole family, and all the kindred and friends, to carry her child herself to the altar (required, by a law of '91, to be erected in the commune), to announce its name to the magistrate, and by this means give it a place in the community, and introduce it to life."

"I am very sure that at the sight of such a train of friends, everyone would follow as a friend. There would not be a passer-by but would take his place in the proces-sion, but would wish to be of it, that he might do honor to the mother, that he might thank her for being a mother, and congratulate and bless her."

———

They return, and her tenderness for her husband ex presses itself by an outburst of love and of gratitude.

'Here I am then, still at home! I know well it is you who have given me life; it is you who have given me my child!"

Seated in the sun, with him at her feet, she—the white rose—bends over him, and says: "What can I give you? you have me, I have kept nothing back. Still, if I can do anything, here I am! Demand even impossibilities ; I will perform them." "You wish me to? Well, I demand "—"Oh, anything, everything!" "Give me, then, a yet deeper place in your heart!" " How can I do that? you are myself; we have ceased to be two."

But he insists: "You have told me of the past—what you did, suffered, desired, ... and I loved you the more for it. What I ask of you now is your thoughts of the future. Promise me that you will tell me your dreams, your cares, if you have any, your caprices (ah! who has them not?), your griefs, the causes of complaint you have against me. And if, at length, fate ordains that the light of love shall pass away from you, if you are troubled, ill for one moment—take me for your physician. You will find in me abundant stores of compassion and indulgence. We will put our strength together. Still united, we will seek, in that trial, the aid of God and of reason."

But she laughs: "Is that all, my darling? That is very easy for her who thinks only of you !"

Then, leaning on him, in a close embrace, she says.

You have been my lover, my husband; to you I have given my body and my life;—aye, even more!—my life before I saw you; for I have told you all my little secrets. You have been my physician, my tender nurse,

and my indulgent guardian.   And so you see me through
and through, as if a ray of the sun had lighted up my
body and my soul.   And what do you see there? Yourself.   I feel I am transformed into you.   How can you
help seeing whatever is in this heart, in this body,
since they are yours?   The faintest germ, the dimmest
dawn of a sentiment, when it is born you shall seize
with me, and even sooner."   And, joining hands with
him: "Dearest, be assured you shall know my soul,
even before it has thought."

BOOK FOURTH.

———o———

ON THE LANGUISHING OF LOVE.

1.

NURSING AND ESTRANGEMENT.

The house is changed; it has become more stirring, more lively. A new centre exists, the cradle, around which everything revolves. The *milky age*, the supreme innocence of the little one, throws its spell over all. Compassion and tenderness enslave the family to him. The father serves the mother, and the mother the child. It is seemingly a world, ordered not like the outer world, but according to the law of love, and of God: in it the strong wait on the weak; dominion belongs to the least.

The house is more open too, and less lonesome. The infant suffers pain, and cries; what is to be done? You call in new aid. The mother nurses him; but she, so feeble and delicate, cannot suffice for all there is to do. Another servant is needed, who, with the infant ever in her arms, is always in the midst of the family, seeing and hearing. After a while she will edge in her word, and, through the child, become an important character.

Farewell to solitude! The old servant lived apart from you, and was not considered. You were two; now you are five.

There is ever a complete change. The mother lives

entirely in that cradle; the world is as nothing to her.
This is as it should be, for it is the saving of the babe. So
frail is he, he would perish but for his absorption of the
mother.

The forgotten father may suffer, but he has to adore
her. She is so beautiful and touching, in her state of
exhilaration, of fond solicitude, that even he says to himself: "She is scarcely the same woman! I have never
known, never understood her, until now!"

When, bending over her son, throbbing with rapture,
she catches sight of a celestial smile in his wandering
eyes, the light shining from her transfigures all around;
no heart can withstand it; all must yield. [Correggio
at Dresden, and Solari at the Louvre.]

Love has surpassed love. He thought to incarnate
himself, to renew himself, to reduplicate himself; and he
has made something mightier than himself. He thought
not of making a God. All that is left for him to do is
to fall on his knees.

But does this mean that the miracle has set at naught
him who, after all, performed it? No; kind Nature
takes pity on the first love. At the very moment the
woman appears to have no thought for him who loves
her, she belongs to him more than ever. The perfect
impregnation received from him remains in her, is growing, and will grow. The active love with which she
endues her infant has no effect on the passive love—
involuntary, and by so much the more invincible—which
possesses her. She dreams less of her husband, and
loves him less in her thoughts; but more in her blood,
more in her transformed life. Even in the midst of this
apparent forgetfulness, which seems to separate them,

the metamorphosis which blends them more and more, is being confirmed.

Nor is this all; the flood of life ascends. The emotions, so diverse, of nursing—joy, sadness, at times a mysterious voluptuousness echoing through her lowest depths—cause her (by a sixth sense which cannot be named) to mingle her two loves. Troubled by her babe, she tremblingly turns to its father. When the beautiful fount flows freely and smoothly, when the child lets her go, and drops off, from sheer excess of fullness, she falls back as from a narcotic, in a half dream, in which between her life and theirs there is no distinction. Her personality flows from her; she is all three at once, but most of all in the two she loves.

If she should think, in the beatitude of that reverie, it is to compare you two—you whom she has in her heart, and you whom she has in the cradle. "Oh, how he resembles you!" This is her constant exclamation, and she utters it in good faith. It is a sweet sensuality of abnegation for her to say: "I have received him from thee, and he is all thee. I have scarcely anything in him. Thy features, thy soul, even thy movements, thou hast given him. Part of thyself passed from thee in that fiery flash." To which there are not wanting friends, neighbors, and servants to applaud, each after her own fashion observing some new feature. "This one especially!"—"No, no, that one!"

In this joyful carol, the little creature, by his unformed features and a thousand changing shadows, according to the light, or the direction from which they look at him, invites every extravagance. He recalls or reproduces whatever they desire.   Such and such a thought of that happy day, such and such an incident of that night, such and such a physical peculiarity, known to one alone—all are shown in him artlessly.   "Ah! I recognise that mark on his face very well—that delight-ful dimple in his cheek I have seen somewhere, else.   He frowns; I know why, and I know it isn't his fault." A little cloud was passing at that moment. . . . .

Thus the babe, a living history, charms them by tell-ing them their secrets, even the very things they had forgotten.   How can they help loving the delightful confidant who knows things they never told, who repre-sents with supreme purity the moment of glowing rap-ture.   A confirmed and a faithful image, he has caught and fixed that lightning flash of the moment which created his future.

So well does he preserve it, so completely is he him-self the light of life, the incarnation of joy, that by his side the intoxication begins anew.   The sight of him cannot so soften their hearts with impunity.   If they did not love, he would suffice to light the flame.   His father glows at the remembrance.   And she too has blushed. She is agitated—desires and does not desire.   But she is the first to recover her reason at length, and (was she ever more charming?) she begs for mercy: "Spare us —have pity on your son!"

He is touched.   Behold them hanging over the cradle, uniting there their souls, and mingling together their thoughts of the future.

What a glorious day it will be when the eyes of the babe are opened; when his hands are stretched forth, when he shall try his first step! What feelings, what words will be exchanged between them! What things then to be told! and how much to be listened to! The infant is the occasion, the necessity, of a thousand new relations between them; or, to express it better, he is the communion of two beings in a living form, exacting a sweet intercourse, on which the neces- sity of nursing still imposes a half divorce.

It is not necessary to remonstrate with the husband. Neither the doctor nor the mother has any need to reason with him. His love for his wife, his love for his child, speak forcibly enough to him. He withdraws himself, but the very least possible, and remains in the chamber.

At first he has his bed apart from them. This is not enough. Even his wife, out of very love for him, makes him go farther away. The child will cry; and if the father is awakened, how shall he arise in the morn- ing in time for business? She begs, and insists, and he struggles a little. "But, my dear, suppose you get sick? We have only you to depend upon!" That is an irresistible argument, for which he has no reply. The poor fellow resigns himself to his fate. Dispos- sessed of the dear society in which he had hitherto lived, every hour of the whole world of sweet familiarities which made that life enchanting, Adam is driven from Paradise.

But in the evening at least, when he returned from work, he once had the happiness of hearing a woman's song, the song of that worshipped heart. In this too the separation is complete. For now the infant is suffi- cient for her; he is her song, her melody. Bound up, day and night, in that thought, she needs no other, "My dear, I have no voice. My confinement has taken it from me."

The instrument remains there—a thankless though versatile instrument—the piano, over which she spent so many years. Oh, now how inadequately its dusty keys seem to her to respond to the sublime harmonies in her heart, as of a cathedral organ—profound maternal love!

If the husband should think of it, if he should beg her to recall a few notes, she would undoubtedly try; her amiability never fails her. But what can she do? After so many months, this piano has suffered very much; *the best string is broken.*

II.

THE BUTTERFLY.

The Book of Love cannot, should not, contain a second book on Maternal Love. Therefore I must, to my great regret, suppress here what flows from the point of my pen: which is, the charming educational development that the child bestows upon the woman, as well as the woman upon the child. That she may influence him, she goes back to his age. She begins again to lisp; and imitates him, that he may imitate her. What an admirable comedy, in which she evinces such

Indomitable patience, and sometimes almost genius!
Without this extraordinary effort, there would be no
initiation into human life; we all start from this point,
and we should, none of us, become men, but for this
patience of the woman, in making herself a child.

We insolently ask why the woman, checked at an
early age in her development, has learned no art. It is
because she has had to concentrate all the efforts of her
best years on a superior art—that of forming the man,
of laying the foundation for those mental superstruc-
tures, those powerful faculties, of which you are now so
proud, and so ungrateful.

This wonderful perseverance in breaking down the
barrier between herself and the thing of which she
wishes to make a human being, in conversing with a
mute, in drawing out signs from him, and at length
causing speech and intelligence and feeling to burst forth
from him—this is far beyond the powers of the man.
He may encourage the comedy, and even take part in
it for a moment, perhaps for an hour, but that is a great
deal for him. Let her repeat the same thing twenty or
thirty times in succession, and he thinks it very agreeable, very charming from her mouth; her pretty tricks
to amuse and enliven the little baby sometimes amuse
the big baby. But when the comedy is repeated a
thousand, a million times, repeated day and night, and
for ever, almost always the same—he pretends to listen,
to take part in it, but he cannot; he is thinking of something else.

These four years (eight years, if a second, a third
child succeed) will establish an increasing divergence,
and one that becomes wider and wider, between the

most closely united couple. The woman, absorbed in her office of nurse and educator, renovates herself but little, is even restricted to a narrow circle of ideas. The man, on the contrary, by the progress of the times and of his affairs, by the effect of the solitude in which he is left by his wife, whom the children engross—the man, I say, enlarges the varied circle of his activity, and his relations. He yields more and more to the mighty vortex of life in our age, to its terrible mutability, which takes possession of and destroys the individual, reduces him to dust, plays with him, and throws him to the winds.

In this you have the invariable error which the best households present. The woman (the best woman) is crowded into a very small circle, and the man (the best man) is infinitely dispersed.

The man must needs have a great, a very strong and fixed passion, to prevent such a separation, such an immense divergence, from annihilating the union.

How can this woman, engrossed by her duties, this admirable mother, contend with her competitor, the World, and its variety ?—the giddy, glittering World of to-day ?

No personality can hold its own against an adversary which opposes to it a thousand different powers at once.

She is beautiful, engaging; she lends a charm to the fireside. But the prodigious mobility of modern life, which carries us in one moment, as it were, from one continent to the other, on wings of fire, gives to man the whole world for a home, and dazzles his eyes with the thousand beauties of humanity and nature by the ray, which at least prevent him from thinking.

Even though she be still *spirituelle*, entertaining skilfui in freshening herself, that giant with a thousand arms, the Press, brings every hour to her husband the world's novelties—the novelty of events, of accidents of facts, which render the novelty of ideas in the most fruitful mind less piquant than they. This brutal training of the mind by material facts blunts and deadens the perceptions.

Let her follow, if she can, that ingenious being, that varying, entertaining kaleidoscope—Fashion; she is still in the most uncertain competition with Change itself—with all the risks of the Unforeseen.

And what resistance can possibly be offered by a delicate personality to violent stimulants, ardent spirits, that barbarism of civilization, which cares only for bold strokes, for factitious paroxysms and outbreaks—those true demons of the mind?

We have said that two brutal and cruel powers, which are contending for the world, wage bloody war on love: 1st. The desire, the mania for variety (*La Papillonne*—a very good word of Fourier's), which, long restrained by the monotony of the Middle Ages, has since burst out, to avenge itself to-day, and is the rage, in every form working with all the violence of a reaction. 2d. [We have desired this, welcomed it with enthusiasm, and now it crushes us.] Already wearied, bewildered, palled and disgusted with this hurly-burly, this *Papillonne*, which robs him of all his strength, the man takes cowardly refuge in a different and more fatal enervation, in a dull *Narcotism*, in vague and barren dreams—the fumes of tobacco, the stupefaction of alcohol.

How much right has the woman to reclaim him here!
The man who is, I do not say blinded by passion, but
who on the contrary forbears, and lives according to
reason, will easily understand that the two alternated
intoxications, the two opposed deliriums, which bestow
balance of wisdom, are found, healthful and vivifying, in
the breast of woman, rather than in all this false life.
She constitutes the best narcotic, and the best stimulant.

The cerebral paralysis and torpor which wither the
morrow for you in advance, are dismal means of forgetfulness, compared to those she would afford you—the
paradise of the evening, the sweet repose by her side,
with that gift of renovation which would have endowed
the dawn with a charm for you.

And as to this infinite diffusion of objects which per-
plexes you, these many new books which are but old ones,
these many railroads stretching to no point, all this—
(shall I tell you ?)—produces on me the effect of a grand
conspiracy to destroy your mind, to overwhelm it with
a world of indigestible matter, buried under which it
cannot stir. Thus Herculaneum in one day was overwhelmed with five hundred feet of ashes. Thus a mea-
dow of the Loire that I have seen, having in the famous
inundation received two hundred cart-loads of stones,
was abandoned, and ever since is good for nothing.
Save your soul from such a fate; preserve it from this
inundation. Guard it with love and wisdom. Reply
to the muddy ocean which comes to you and offers you so
many things, that all these are as nothing to the treasures
which the husband and wife keep watch over for each
other : that of the man, a nothing, an infinitesimal, an
atom of fire which incites him to love, work, and create—I

will name it in a word: it is The Spark; and that of the
woman, the sweetness of a pure heart in which you rest,
the fruitful sea of milk, the eternal youthing. All this
under a modest and virginal charm: holy simplicity,
divine infancy!

When in the evening you return to the fireside, and
she comes to meet you, the little one in her arms, dispel,
my friend, dispel the cloud left upon your heart and
your eyes by the things which have harassed you during
the day. Recover your sense of the reality after that
phantasmagoria, that mischievous magic-lantern which
has shown you so many shadows. Let this woman with
her child, let her charming smile, her joy at seeing you
again, her loving kiss, and her mute embrace, purify
you, and restore to you the wholesome light of nature.
Renew, I beg you, your amiable intercourse, which has
been a little disturbed by your business, by mater
nity, by the nursing which has estranged you. . . . . Ah,
bear no ill-will towards her! Is it her fault? What
has she not suffered to give her blood and her milk to
this greedy, inexorable child, who has torn her very
heart-strings? You love her, I know; you behold her
bewitching in her blooming beauty, bearing her divine
fruit. Oh, the spark for her! You have found each
other the same as ever.

Is it, in truth, the poor little fellow who spoils your
tête-à-tête? He is, at least, an accommodating rival.
Tolerate, then, both of them; or rather, love yourself in
all three. By-and-by he will grow, he will no longer
engross his mother. A few years more, and he will
escape from her; then, abandoned by him, she will come
to weep in your arms.

9

III.

THE YOUNG MOTHER SEPARATED FROM HER SON.

I HAVE tears in my heart, and for more than one thing. I have not passed (in history) the Styx, the river of the dead, so many times with impunity.

I am not insensible to my times, and I feel their mortal wounds.

Well, all this, which should deaden me to private sorrows, leaves a place in my heart plainly bleeding for what I have beheld so often, the mother separated suddenly from her child, the mother from whom they take away her boy.

Ah, how can the man do this barbarous thing? Because he foresees, you say. If the child is not put to school, how will he succeed in the trials and examinations required by the State?

Why have examinations? asks the mother. What do you, Madame, you so intelligent, not understand that it is the only barrier which remains? Without examinations, all goes by favor; it is an absolute reign of the king of kings—I mean the commissary

———

Eight, ten years have passed away. They have had children, and lost them; all the dearer, then, the one that is left. And this only child must be exiled. They have differences at times on his account. But at length, he growing older, the father insists on it, and he is *torn*

away! Oh, how different the case appears to them!
How unequal the sacrifice! He, busy, occupied with
his affairs, hardly suffers at all. But with her, it is her
life they take. The child had supplied the place of
everything for her—art, reading, all that formerly suf
ficed for her. He goes—an utter blank. She is alone
in the deserted house. When the father is absent, and
she is free, she weeps in every room. Here he was born,
here he played, here he learned to read. At meals, it is
much worse. She tries to put a pleasant face on the
matter, not to distress her husband, and to pretend she
is resigned. She does not look at that vacant place.
But—I don't know how it happened—her eyes have
fallen on it—she runs out sobbing.

What is left to her? You. You embrace, and console her? But that is not enough for a heart so sad.
That heart is out there; it is in that horrid school; it
participates in the sudden, the cruel change of situation.
The confinement, of a being hitherto so free, the thankless, fretting study, the cold and harsh repression! On
whom will all this rebound, if not on the mother, to
whom he writes, to whom he relates all? I cut short the
story of her sorrows; I have seen her sink into despair.

But this is not enough. The worst is to follow. We
become accustomed to everything. After a year she is
less unhappy; he has found friends; he plays furiously
in the brief moments of recreation. And, when his
mother, after a week's impatient waiting, in which she
has counted every day, runs, agitated, to embrace him,
she finds him cold and heedless, evidently thinking of
other things. She has interrupted his play, and made
him lose an hour; she speaks, and he hears only the cries

of his companions, who are enjoying themselves without him. Cruel, cruel wound! She feels how little already she is necessary to him; she has only been in his way, he sees her leave with pleasure. She goes forth without weeping, bearing up against her grief. But when she reaches home she is overcome. "My God, what is the matter!" She cannot speak, she can scarcely breathe.

What a blow! She has lost her son, her love of ten years . . . . . . and her last love here below! Its like will never return.

She is pure, she is good; she again leans on her husband. No other aid, no consolation but this, occurs to her. Happy moment for him, if he knows how to seize it!

This scarcely ever happens. There are too many changes, changes in him. The man has made terrible strides ahead during those years of half divorce, while she was thinking only of her children. He has passed through a thousand trials. He has arrived at an unpoetical age which they call *positive* (forty years), as a general thing already cold and barren. Is he even himself? I wish I could believe it. But even though he be a man apart, exceptional and peculiar, whose life has not eaten into his very heart, it has at least attacked the flower of the heart, that exquisite and -refined sensibility, which would enable him to feel the happiness of so sweet a return.

And she too is changed. How much for the better! I appeal to Vandyck. Pleasing at twenty, she is admirable at twenty-eight. And a curious thing it is: she has changed her class, so to speak. The first beauty of youth scarcely ever attains aristocratic distinction. The rose was a little *bourgeoise ;* but this lily is royal.

The refinement, the immaculate smoothness, the irreproachable purity of her complexion, proves that no base passion has defiled the sanctuary. Her visible innocence renders her still more touching in her melancholy. She suffers, and has done no wrong. "And what is the matter with her?" is asked. "Is it her husband who makes her unhappy?" "No; but her son is at college. That is the cause of her illness." They smile; and this grief, so little understood, which seems childish to them, is still doubted. That some other grief is concealed there, everybody is ready to believe; and all desire to console her.

This is not easy. For she has a horror of the world, a distaste for society, and idle amusements. When her husband drags her into company, she returns sadder than ever. "Ah, my dear, why alter our habits? Sad or cheerful, I am better at home."

How right and sensible she is! . . . . And are you wise yourself? What is it that her heart needs? Love; and nothing else. Is love extinguished in yourself? No, but cooled, dissipated. She desires just the opposite of dissipation in love: she desires concentration.

The hearth has been disturbed, and the embers, that formerly burned, are now scattered. But they must be brought together. Let them but touch each other, and the spark will revive.

Would you love, love much—that is, be happy? Then take by the hand the charming woman who comes and reclines upon you. Take her, press her to you, live much with her, and do not leave her. So, many living fibres will mingle together, will recover their force, will restore your unity.

I ought to premise to you, that she is at this moment richer in beauty and love than ever. Pain and sorrow have made her a new woman, have created in her exquisite graces of sensibility, profound joys inconceivable to you, and pleasures yet unknown.

Divine treasure! Fool indeed is he who will invoke the world to share his affections, when he himself seeks but a single heart upon which to bestow himself.

———

The world! the vast world!—As she utters these words the young wife is subdued, and I too become gloomy. The infinite, the unknown, is before us. What shall we find in it? A thousand presentiments take possession of us.

This book has been flowing smoothly on, and I could not check its course. It has made too convenient use of the blissful hypothesis of a solitary life, of a little world of harmony. But how can one be isolated from society?

That world will not permit it. If you do not go to it, it will come to you; it will growl at your door, like the waves of Ocean. And no bars can keep it out.

Who art thou, that knockest so loudly? Art thou my Country? my People? Art thou the Great Love to whom all should yield, to whom heroes offer even more than their lives, their very hearts? Ah! if thou art, then let the door be widely opened! If not, let it be shut, let the walls fall! For we are thine, we belong to thee, body and property, life and soul. And she too, woman as she is (or rather because she is a woman), will not disgrace us; on the contrary, tender towards individuals, she has no less than us the love of country.

But, O World, thou art not that world of grandeur and of light. Thou art confusion and chaos.

"It is no matter! I will enter, and you can do nothing; I am your fate. You shut the door against me. But you breathe me; I am in the air. You cannot escape me. Without within, everywhere, do you find me.

"Yes, I am, undoubtedly, confusion and peril. And therein am I a wholesome trial; there is in me a duty to confront and to perform. My true name is: *The Battle of Life*."

———►◄———

IV.

OF THE WORLD—HAS THE HUSBAND DEGENERATED?

THIS house is no longer the little house we had the happiness to describe. It has become larger in the very nature of things. Children, relations, business interests, have in every respect amplified it. Our couple, linked to-gether, and alone with their hearts, have been compelled to admit this dangerous third party, whom they hoped to exclude—the stranger, the unknown, the World. It has also, undoubtedly, become necessary for them to live in some great centre of business, where the activity of the husband may find full play. And last, and worst of

all, our husband and wife have, perhaps, become rich by
that activity, or by the mere progress of time, gifts of
the dead, inheritances, etc.

Observe, that in France one thing is wanting which is
the true foundation of English life, and which in every
sense keeps the family together. What is this? The
lock and key. Neither of them exists in this country
In England solitude is the rule (a voluntary, cherished
solitude). Here it is the exception, a peculiarity, and a
very rare one. Unintroduced and unrecommended, any
man may introduce himself, by his rights as a man.

The inscription over every English door—an unneces-
sary inscription—is " I do not know you." Over a
French door you read: " Have the kindness to enter."

From this handsome confidence, which does honor to
the nation, there results one inconvenience: namely, that
those who are not admitted, imagining that they are the
only exceptions, become your enemies. Those who are
admitted with reserve, with a natural caution, are still
more dangerous, in that they have a better opportunity
of injuring you, by getting into the place. They bring
in the Trojan horse.

The most dangerous and determined enemies are generally relations, who often, without the least congeniality
of ideas and sentiments, aspire, nevertheless, to your intimacy. The woman who is closely bound to her hus
band, and reserves her confidence for him, is sure to have
all the women of the family against her. Mother, sisters,
cousins, all become her foes, and wage a petty warfare
against her. The friends of her childhood, who have
retained a foothold in the house, entertain much ill-will
towards her, for they cannot pardon her steadfastness in

the right path. If they do not quarrel with her, it is
because they wish to watch this singular house, this ex
ceptional character ; they still hope that, sooner or later
she will flag, and thenceforward will become so much
the more dependent on them, in proportion to her pre·
vious propriety; and having an overwhelming fear of
rumor and of scandal, she will become a slave to the
friends who have detected her secret.

But even though they find her still innocent, young
in heart (her child having engrossed her), quite inex·
perienced in spite of her twenty-eight years, still they
do not despair of seeing her reach that moment of weak·
ness. For this they must have tact; but above all, the
patience, the wily patience of the Indian hunter. The
envious are not wanting in this. Years are as nothing
to them, provided they win a little in the end.

It begins in harmless matters. The one whom she
trusts, and consults about dress, may also, at times,
touch on other subjects. On some occasion such a one
may, as if jesting, and in sheer thoughtlessness, throw
out a trifling remark about the husband, and playfully
alluding to some slight fault, shake the woman's faith,
that had hitherto, blind at least by habit, believed him
to be almost perfect.

———

He seems to confirm this. It cannot be denied that in
middle life (thirty-eight years, we will suppose) the man,
engaged in business, excited in his profession, bound
down to his particular career, cannot but have notably
declined.

He has husbanded his resources, concentrated his
mind ; he is stronger, but no longer genial. The beauty

9*

he possessed at twenty, at twenty-five, when his mind and his heart took an interest in everything, and enjoyed everything—that young budding greatness, which was the chief attraction to his wife—has he preserved this? I doubt it. Why was he loved? Because in him she saw the infinite. But it is precisely a special strength which alone has given him success in his profession—his art, or his science; it is exactly this which has narrowed him, and robbed him of the infinite, that imposing illusion of love.

This is the admission we owe to woman: It is too true; the husband has declined.

It is too true. He was a man when she first loved him; ten, twelve years later, he is an eminent lawyer, an excellent physician, a great architect—that is fine. But to the woman he was finer in being a man; that is to say, in being everything, in having the range of thought in all things, hoping all things, and soaring above all things.

Now, let the woman (who is happiness here below), let her, I say, judge us fairly. What would have become of that man if he had soared for ever, if he had never descended to seize on the realities of life?

Let her judge. But a great mind has taken exception to this privilege; he says, "Woman is the destroyer of justice." She is all love, it is true; and love, it seems, is favor and proffered grace. Still, who will maintain that there is not also in love appreciative generosity, tenderness, profound pity, for the effort of the will, for the nobility of labor, from which comes well-earned success? And what woman is insensible to glory? Even to relative glory, which is the same in trade as in art. It is as plainly visible in the humblest circle as in the im, ising sphere of nationality and humanity. Woman is keenly alive to it. She takes a strong interest in it. She is impressed by it. She will admit no doubt of the glory of her husband. And if he is a blacksmith, never dare to say in her presence that he is not the best black-smith in the world.

Then, Madame, you wish for glory, for success; you desire that this man shall make his mark in works, which alone prove strength. Only you do not always take into consideration the very difficult conditions, the de-termined efforts, often violent, extreme, and I may say desperate, by which success is purchased.

Of these conditions, the hardest for the man is that of being branded by the effort in that member which he must employ the most, and so of being no longer sym-metrical. He who hammers iron, were he the very genius of his art, were he even a god, must infallibly have his right shoulder too high. What can you do for this? Deprive him of his art at an early period. And whoever forges in any other line shall also bear the mark of his trade—some mental or physical defor-mity. The gravest deformity results from the unem-ployed faculties becoming atrophied. If the artist does not take heed, by ever strengthening one faculty, which shall become colossal, and leaving the others unde-veloped, he will become a monster—a sublime monster, it is true.

———

The antique man remained strong and beautiful, and the progress of years was to him but a progress in beauty. Ulysses, at fifty, returns from Troy, returns after a long and terrible voyage, in which he has undergone every hardship; and he is the same Ulysses—so entirely the same, that he alone can bend the bow which the young braggarts can hardly lift. His Penelope recognises him by his strength, by the majesty of his beauty, which suffering has but increased. How is this? He has preserved himself by his energetic use of all the gifts that belong to him. He remains the symmetrical man who went to the siege of Troy.

Now take what modern man you will, of the best blood, and the best endowed, grand in genius and in will; at twenty he finds before him a great and terrible test, the gauntlet of the arts and sciences, which he must run before he can arrive at distinction. The object of life is changed. Ulysses was born to act; he acts, and remains beautiful. The other is born to create; his speciality (the machine by which he creates) marks him; the work is beautiful, but the man is in danger of becoming deformed.

Woman, have pity on him then!

Give us credit for this great effort; and if we lose,—since the human race gains by it,—look at the work, not so much at the workman.

You give your beauty liberally to your children; we give ours to our work, our intellectual child; but almost always too liberally, alas! and without any reservation.

———

Now, what would come of it if we should remain as we were, beautiful in our aptitude for all things, of a brilliant facility—if we should stand at the luminous threshold of science without penetrating its shadows? We should be, not the antique man, in the complete

symmetry of Ulysses, but the agreeable society-man,
who knows everything; one of those held in such admi
ration and request in the time of Louis XIV., and who
was known as "*l'honnête homme.*" He was a gentle
man, who turned his hand to nothing, but who plumed
himself on a fine, delicate appreciation of everything.
We would in our day call him "the connoisseur." Such
are the heroes of Molière, Philinthe, and, if you please,
Clitandre.

He is a monarch in the saloon, a nice judge of many
things, the admiration of the ladies, accepted and appealed to by them. He knows everything *in general.*
He pleases them because he resembles them. They
always know and do (when they do anything) *in general.* They remain mere *amateurs*, having no power to
understand works of conscience, and the master-pieces
of herculean talent, like a Ruysdaël, for example,—
l'Estacade aux eaux rousses — that prodigy of the
Louvre.

We do right in not requiring from woman such terri
ble works as these, which involve a martyrdom to art.
Her glory lies in living works, far above all art. In her
is the spark by which they are inspired.

As to man, it is a different matter. The age will not
hold him guiltless if he remain Philinthe or Clitandre.
The modern man, that all-powerful male, must incessantly generate.

But if child-birth is at the cost of agony to the woman;
if she must suffer nine months, and then scream for
twenty or thirty hours—the grander generations of the
man often require nine, aye twenty years. And what
stifled cries, what suppressed groans! The *hah!* of the

carpenter, his heave as he lifts his axe to drive it well home, we have uttered all our days.

———

Women love energy and grand results, the principle and its goal; but they are ignorant of the long road which leads to that goal, appreciating neither the time nor the continuity of effort necessary to success. Believing that everything is gained by strokes of genius, by happy hits, they are sensible of no achievement but that of improvisation. The fortunate lawyer who carries home to them a triumph every evening, the sparkling journalist who dazzles them with his display of fireworks—these are the beloved men. But even improvisation, in great matters, requires time, and a great deal of it. That of Michael Angelo, so rapid, took six or seven years of solitary application to paint one church.

Observe that a too frequent effect of great performances, of grand efforts, is the loss of language. He who acts or creates, talks little. "Deeds, not words," is his motto. The brilliant gifts he may have had when he was yet on the surface of things, are lost to him when he enters into the thinking, exacting intercourse of art, where only results are called for. The smallest of small-talkers may take precedence of, and keep silent, the greatest of inventors. I have sometimes beheld the strange spectacle of an insignificant character, in a circle of laughing ladies, lording it over a poor man of genius, one of the three or four who will give their names to this century, who shall reform its very art, who shall compel it to study.

———

It is still worse in business, properly so called. For. a woman there must be no business. She herself wishes to be the only, the essential business of the man, and every other is odious to her. She scarcely ever gives full credit to the mind, the talent, the superior faculties so often displayed in the management of varied interests. She desires to know nothing of all this. At the slightest word uttered about his plans, his efforts, what he does and what he hopes for his family, she yawns or turns away her head. In short, she desires to be rich, but to hear nothing about the way of becoming so.

What shall the husband do? He often works solely on her account. Some, moderate, and not extravagant in their desires, can live, like so many others, in that free and simple style so much liked in France. It is his marriage, his enlarged household, his continually-arriving. children, which have attached him to labor—a thankless labor, of which he cannot even speak to her. She goes and comes, idle and disdainful, while he wears himself away, in reality alone, and keeping to himself the thorns of life.

————

How is it, if you please, that the novels which, it is pretended, represent our manners, never touch upon all this? Why are the men we meet with in them— husbands, lovers, whatever they may be—always idlers with incomes? Why do messieurs and mesdames, the authors, usually choose their heroes from the vagabond class (help me to the popular expression, strong and graphic), drones, and *people for fatting ?* Why is this? Because the weakness they retain, for all their democratic speeches, is for the dainty world, for the gentry

I regret to see so much genius wasted in this cen
tury on this dreary style of novel, made to probe our
wounds, to aggravate them. The novel has taught us to
weep for ourselves; it has extinguished fortitude. It
has made universal evils of the wretchedness, of the
moral deformity, which exists only in certain classes.
Out of thirty-six millions of Frenchmen, thirty-five are
utterly ignorant of all that is depicted by these grand
artists.

Nevertheless, this morbid literature takes no hold on
healthy minds. It brings disease only to those already
diseased. It is not very dangerous to the little household for which we are concerned. The young wife who
has not been forced into premature ripeness in her early
youth, pierced and poisoned by the mystic worm;
tainted and spoiled by religious equivoque, is not ripe for
the novel. First, a healthy love, loyal and strong, and
then maternal love—two powerful purifiers—have
guarded her against contagion. She would not understand Balzac; or if she did, would reject him with disgust.
His book on *Marriage*, which he himself calls a skeleton,
would seem to her a corpse.

She will not be won over by vileness. The friends
who sound her, and would shake her virtue, will not fail
to lend her secretly something from Madame Sand.
What does she find there? That the lover is no better
than the husband. The husband is often infamous in
those books, but the lover always contemptible What
do I say?—he is base, loathsome! Raymond shutting
his door against poor Indiana, who has no refuge but in
death, is certainly as powerful a warning as could be
written against adultery.

No single book, however, should be taken separately from the painful mission of this great writer. You must peruse all. The husband illustrates it to his wife, and gives her the leading idea of it. It is, after all, a historical monument of the weakness of the times, a passionate impeachment of the want of character in our middle classes. A woman, born for all that is great, and therefore justly exacting, has sought everywhere for the strong, and has not found them. She has uttered aloud what every one thinks. That is, that *man has declined* (husbands, lovers, it matters not which), that such men will not do for the women.

If you have no intention of responding to this appeal, of renewing your energy, you certainly have reason to fear these books. They are your positive condemnation. But the men who daily prove their prowess, who create new life, or risk their own, have no fear of novels. They know very well that, even if their wives should spend the day in perusing the portraits of husbands which Madame Sand draws so well, they could not recognise *them* in the pictures, which are those of strangers. I write this in the town of the most beautiful women in France, whom their husbands leave every night to go fishing. And, what is more, six months in every year they go in a body to Newfoundland, where numbers of them perish. Well, in this place there are no bastards, no adulteries, no amours. If there is ever any scandal about a woman (and this in a population of eighteen thousand), it is in the upper classes, or sometimes among the *bourgeoisie.*

Admirably abstemious, they are yet rich in liberal development of beauty—with large hands, fit for the employments of men. Many of them are in business. In the night they wash their linen; in the day they run among the rocks in a fearless nudity which would be a blessing to a painter. They appear, however, to be ignorant that a *gentleman* is a man. They will bathe him, in case of necessity, as if he were a nurseling. They could fight wonderfully if an enemy should come, as did their mothers once, when they took English prisoners with their own hands.

There is not a novel in this place. The poetry of the ocean is enough and to spare; it furnishes only too many tragedies. But I declare to you, all the novels in the world might come here. Husbands might allow their wives to have them with impunity. For two considerations protect them: One is the idea of death, the idea of the danger which their husbands are braving, far away, brought ever freshly to their minds by the sight of so many widows in the streets; that keeps their hearts lofty. The other is the vigor, the superiority of the men, daily facing more dangers than a soldier ever meets. From this comes profound security. The men know that their brave partners will not be deceived, that they know well who the true men are.

This original place, with full, fresh healthy breezes, and heroic inspirations, is that where the English and the Vendeans fought—Granville—rightly called, since '93, *Victory.*

V.

THE SPIDER AND THE FLY.

WHEN I see the singular ardor with which women wage war on each other, the exquisite enjoyment that intimate friends feel in losing a friend, I may well fear for the household I am following in this book. One thing reassures me. It is this: that in despite of the accidents of position which may have relaxed the bond, they communicate everything, trust everything to one another— every act and every thought. The table and bed in common afford natural opportunities, favorable hours, even to the busiest man. He tells her of his business, his ideas, he tells her everything; and she appreciates the trouble he takes to make her understand even those matters which seem out of her sphere.

This effort to have her always participate in his life, is of infinite influence on her. In it she feels his enduring love, steadfast through so many pre-occupations. In it she feels his loving consideration for the wife and the mother. She is elevated by it, honored in her own eyes. So strong and so earnest a tenderness renders her own no less profound, and independent of the changes (all external) of humor and caprice. It renders her scrupulous, mindful to tell everything too. She takes in true earnest the promise she made (end of Book iii.) to confide to him all her sentiments, and all the emotions of her heart. Sometimes it costs her very much to keep her word Still young, morally a virgin, it gives her a little pain to acknowledge this fugitive thought, that dream, that illu

sion of nature, which sometimes comes to the wisest
But then she has promised! A just and right instinct
tells her that her best security is to live in open light,
under her husband's eyes. She has a confused idea of
the snares which surround her. She does not affect to
know everything. Hitherto separated from the world
(by her child), the surest plan for her is not to take a
step without relying on the experience of him who lives
amid the warring of affairs and interests. Women (almost all) ruin themselves by pride. They refuse to acknowledge that the husband, compelled to mingle in so
many intricate matters, living in open battle, is much
more positive than they. He needs must be so in his
affairs, when there is a daily chance of his being ruined,
and bringing starvation upon his dear ones, if he errs from
the right course one line, or even so much as a hair.

Women are very subtile, you say. This is true. But
that penetration which they possess in matters of sentiment, those who have not mingled with the world do not
have at all in matters of real life. They really live from
hand to mouth. In the moments of the greatest danger
they leave much to chance. And if they consult any
one, it is generally the very person of whom they should
most beware.

You often see the best wives ensnared, even through
their husbands. They are vain for *him*, ambitious for
him, and through this they can be worked upon. If he is
powerful and influential, his wife, willing or not, must
have a court. She takes pleasure in this glitter, for it is
a reflection from her husband. She becomes an object for
intriguers. She has ladies come to her house (not once

or.ly, but ten times), ladies of good position, esteemed, often pious, active in good works, whom she has seen in charitable meetings, who bring with them, and introduce, a young man; he may be interesting, already capable of assisting her husband, devoted to his ideas, exactly in his line. He has lived among solitary studies. He is wanting in the polish of the world. But then, he is so gentle and so docile! If he is only received, and advised and directed a little, he will soon become accomplished.

When the affair is once begun and ·in good trim, an astonishing concert is established. No one speaks of anything but the young man. It seems as if every part had been assigned. Some cousin, admitted in the morning, mentions him accidentally; she has seen him, and thinks he is delightful. And in the evening, another female friend will say jestingly: "I am in love with him." The *femme-de-chambre*, even bolder yet, soon breaks the ice, and ventures, while she is dressing her mistress's hair, to say he is dying for love. Yesterday you had to bribe Lisette; she made you pay for her tongue. But to-day there is no need of it. She knows very well that if her lady is once embarked in an adventure, has once given her a handle, and allowed herself to be surprised with a secret, she will become mistress of her mistress, can have full sway in the house, and reign and ransack without control.

How much faster they will all go to work, if her husband, instead of patronizing, has himself need of a patron; if he is, for instance, some little functionary waiting for promotion, some manufacturer in poor circumstances, who can make no progress without being backed by a capitalist. In this case, the mode of corruption is insolent and daring.   They hesitate at nothing, push bravely on, at the risk of rousing the indignation of the young wife.   The good friend, the female confidant, already a woman of experience, to whom she has art lessly told some heart-sorrow, will tell her that after all she is not surprised that she should grow weary, being so poorly married; that her husband is a pitiable object, a person of dispiriting incapacity; that he will keep her vegetating for ever.   She says so much of this, that the self-respect of the little wife, her good heart, the affec tion she still preserves in the bottom of it, are sensibly wounded.   She cries out, she flies into a passion.   And the awkward woman must change her tactics: at any rate, we must aid this poor man who, after all, works very hard.   He should have some one to depend on, who would take him to his heart, who would be sure to succeed, who has power and credit; he need only raise him from the earth; he could then trust to his own wings; a little help at first will do so much.

There is nothing older than the way of making two people love each other, who would never have thought of it.   But it always succeeds.   It is only necessary to tell each that the other is in love.   The patron and the lady, thus prepared, and brought together by a favor- able opportunity, which is never wanting, will both act as is desired; and the young wife rarely fails to justify what had been said of her, by some trifling piece of coquetry, which she thinks harmless, or at least allow- able, since it is for her husband's interest.

But they know that she loves her husband; they know she will not go much farther, that it would not be safe to make any overtures to her.   It would be at the risk of spoiling all, of having her escape them. Doing is a surer. way than talking. Boldness, a half-violence, will carry the thing successfully, and force her into it.

You will say this cannot be.   You believe that these odious acts are seldom seen but in the lowest classes. You are completely deceived. They are very common affairs. But the matrons are a great deal more discreet about it than the young girls. They keep the affair to themselves; they swallow their grief and their tears.

Sometimes the thing is revealed, in one way or an-other, long after it happened. A number of facts of this nature have come to my knowledge, and from true sources. I have no desire to give the shameful details of them. The spider has always circumvented the fly, and dragged her into his web.

There is one essential point to be noticed. It is this that in these affairs the weak creature had not the least intention of being false, that in the act her will counted for nothing, or almost nothing; but that, on the con trary, the very act itself (a compulsory one, almost en tirely) corrupted her will.

Another grave point is, that the female friend, who betrayed the wife, herself knew the circumstances of life, of temperament, of health, of menstrual epochs, etc., which enabled her fully to understand what she might dare, and to take the situations, the moments in which the woman is always most feeble, and most easily agitated by any emotions whatever—by surprise, or certainly by fear.

And the third point is, that the more unexpected and improbable the thing is, the more hatefully absurd, the

easier it becomes. Indignation is very powerful, you
say. Yes, but surprise is more powerful: it is blasting
paralysing. The will, not warned, not expecting anything to happen, does not act at all, and fatality effects
everything, not allowing the dismayed personality to
assert itself until afterwards, and then perhaps only to
draw from it a moment of physical consent, which is, after
all, not a consent.

———

She weeps—she wishes to tell all, and yet does nothing
towards it. Her friend shows her the danger of such a
terrible exposure—and that, too, for something which
cannot be helped. What would be her husband's rage,
his transports of fury! Would he believe she had
been forced, or consented? He would demand satisfaction
from this man, who, much more skilful, more accustomed
to arms than he, would kill him for satisfaction. "My
dear, I beg you, for your husband's sake, not to say anything about it. Who knows? It may result in his
death; at least he will certainly die from grief. Your
children will be ruined, your life blasted. . . . . . This
man has such power to harm you! He is very wicked
when he hates or is enraged. But it cannot be denied
that he is also very zealous in the cause of those whom
he loves. He wishes to atone for his offence, to propi
tiate you. . . . . He will do everything for your family,
for the future of your children."

And, in fact, some one will come and tell the young
creature the next day that he is driven to despair because
he has been too happy; that he will kill himself if she
does not forgive him. For it is her heart that he wishes
to win. He has already been at work for her husband

He burns to be of service to her; and never was there
seen so much good will. " My dear child, what is done
can't be helped. Alas! we women are all obliged to
suffer, and to hide many things. I have had my
share too! . . . . But then, in this vale of tears we
must always be resigned—must always humble ourselves, my child, and forgive. We must always have
the right feelings about these things, and not be impla-
cable towards our enemies. And, really, he is in a most
terrible state! He seems wild—you will have pity on
him ?"

This eloquence leads to a meeting, this time a voluntary one. The interests of the family have begun the
work of corruption. Then comes a violent scene, an
admirably performed play of sorrow and despair. Large
promises, eternal devotion to the husband. And all so
pathetic that even the female friend weeps! Sensibility
wins the day. The young wife is not inexorable. How
far will her forgiveness go ?

Still matters drag. Nothing comes of these grand
promises. She is dying with regret and remorse. They
make her I know not what excuses. At length, every
pretext exhausted, the friend profits by her impatience.
" Why, my dear, I would write; yes, if I were in your
place, I would call upon him to perform his promises; I
would make him blush; I would say that after all he
has done, and all you have pardoned—after so many
new favors, it is horrible for him to forget." This
speech, or something like it, written by the imprudent
woman from the other's dictation, betrays her for ever.
Both *friends*—the man and the woman—hold her henceforth for their own, and are sure of her. They speak to

10

her in another tone. They begged before, now they command. She has a master. At any day, at any hour, here or there, he bids her come, and she obeys. The fear she has of scandal, and a sort of magnetism, which I cannot understand, like that which allures the bird towards the serpent, draw her on weeping. They find her more beautiful thus than ever. They laugh at her. As for the promises, they scarcely remember them.

When he has had enough of her, she is at least free? Not at all. Her friend has the papers, and she lures her on with new hopes, which are improbable and absurd. No matter, she *must* go on; she must sell herself again and again; must submit to another patron, who, she is told, will do better, but who still does nothing. What a frightful servitude, which lasts as long as she is young and beautiful, which sinks her lower and lower, casts her down, and thoroughly depraves her! Ah! would that she had had courage rather to risk everything, to go to her husband, and throw herself into his arms, and to tell him all! Whatever might have been the rage of the first few moments, she would surely have found more compassion in him!

But this life of shame has shattered the little nerve and resolution she had. She bows down to it, and is less capable every day of freeing herself. If at times her female tyrant, who hardly treats her with decency, should goad her by some bitter, ironical speech, and again arouse her, so that she resists for a moment and says, "I will reveal the whole!" she will answer, "Why, my dear, everybody will laugh at you; not one will believe you. And even should they believe you, they would laugh none the less." "There is the law, ma-

dame." " Oh, that's a mistake, my child, juries in
these cases require proofs clearer than sunlight. More
than one would envy the guilty man. Such is the sentiment in France. People always start with the idea
that she who resists the most consents in her heart, at
least for a moment. What can you do? They have
always thought in this way, and therefore they have
always laughed."

This is only too true. The very men who will read
this, they who see the manners of our time, and the
readiness of so many women to seek renewed dishonor,
will, I think, say : " There's no need of such an outcry
about the matter." They do not, or will not, understand what is still true, though it is more concealed.
It is this : that numbers of women take the first step out
of the path of duty in spite of themselves, led on
unknown to themselves, skilfully drawn farther than
they are aware of, and at last surprised and compelled.
I mean that there is a half-violence, strong enough to
master the weakness which has gone too far, and which
finding itself captured, loses its self-possession, and yields.
Thenceforth she believes she has gone too far to recede,
and will submit every day.

" She has consented," you will say. It can be proved
that she has made advances by some slight levity,
coquetry, an imprudent glance. It would be very harsh
to judge her by these facts. Were they a serious encouragement, a pledge to dishonor? You know very well,
they always want to please. But they are wrong in
believing that man is generous, that he of whom they
expect some worthy favor, something for the family,
will feel repaid by a glance. Is it then nothing to have

the happiness of obliging a woman, of having her feel
for you that affectionate sentiment which the most innocent grant to gratitude?

If it be her misfortune to become *enceinte*, so much
the more harshly will they say that she consented.
This is an old error, the fallacy of which is now known.
Nature has nothing to do with consent. It is the occasion more than anything else which decides it. The
complete opposition of the will, a passionate sorrow or
despair—none of these are of any consequence.

———

I am angry at Cervantes, who has, in other respects,
such admirable good sense. He has flattered a brutal
prejudice, and courted a vulgar laugh, in the trial
imposed by his King Sancho on the girl who complained
to him. The strength she employed to defend a purse
of gold before the court, and in open day, and that too
with no fear of anything, does not by any means prove
that she would have been able, when surprised and
terrified in the night, to defend her honor as well.

An old German law (of Swabia), which went to the
other extreme, nevertheless understood well that in this
case surprise is everything, that the crime consists
entirely in the boldness of the attack, in the strong hand
fastened on a timid being, mastered in advance by excess
of emotion. It ordains the death of him who has laid
his hand upon a virgin, and rumpled her hair (*disca-
pillata*).

———

Those who think that they effectually establish the
fact that woman can defend herself, speak of her as a
cold, lifeless thing, with no emotion, like a piece of marble

oi a block of wood. But every physiologist, every physician, and every one who understands this poor nervous being, who vibrates and quivers at a breath, whom nature desires to be feeble, and whom she monthly disarms by suffering—such a one will tell you that nature also desires that she should be always protected, that she should walk holy and respected, that every man should take up her cause as his own, giving serious ear to her complaints. It is for us to defend her, since she is unable to do it herself.

We should leave to the scholastics that absurd opinion which draws a precise line, puts a well-defined severance, an abyss, between *consenting* and *not consenting*. In a matter so blended of the influences of the body and the soul, so blended of liberty and compulsion, there are infinite shades, and I know not how many intermediate and mixed states, in which, not consenting, she yet yields.

I have passed my whole life in upholding the rights of the mind against the nauseating materialism of my age. I must, however, make use here of some plain words, words of good sense (not materialistic). The body, remember, acts also ; it is concerned in the motive, and the two actions cross each other, each prevailing in its turn, each succeeding to the other with a terrible rapidity and confusion.

Our voluntary powers must not be spoken of as you would speak of a bar of iron, or a bolt, which you draw, and simply open or shut. This will by no means do. They are very much more complex. It would be juster to compare these powers to a thing infinitely susceptible of rise and fall, like a thermo-

meter divisible into I know not how many degrees. In
order to measure her true morality and the degree of pain
caused her by the act, we must discover what was her degree of will, what also was the degree of constraint which
is almost always blended with it. Without this careful
appreciation, the best judge may err, and be too mild
or too severe. One whom he would spare, has desired
and ventured; another whom he would crush, has not
consented; not even with a thirtieth part of her will.

"And the twenty-nine remaining parts which have
decided the act, how do you reckon them?" Put
down twenty of them for the surprise, the terror at
feeling herself under a strong hand (and cruel too, if
need be). Then, if her resistance continue, add, say
eight or nine degrees, for what his fierce impatience
hardly spares her, the rude shock, the sharp pain which
paralyses her. And last, her emotion (for the poor
woman is not made of stone). If to this sudden suspended agony, there succeed a sensation not painful, it is
to her like a reprieve to the criminal on the scaffold.
This is the wretched thirtieth part of will which is not
will, of pretended consent. And is the culprit less
guilty? No, he is more so; this very fact, far from
extenuating his guilt, adds horror to it. He has defiled
the soul.

A wise magistrate has said that in all causes in which
women are concerned, and even in many others, the
tribunals have need of the permanent assistance of a
medical jury for the elucidation of the real degree of
will and of necessity concerned. It is not enough to call
in some chance expert for the proof of material circum-

stance. They should always be present to clear up the capital and obscure question—that is, the degree of will.

All the aids of physiological science are needed for this. And when the doctor shall have told all the physical, material, fatal facts, let the judge conscientiously commence his work—the blame, the correction and redressing of the soul, the medication of patience and of amelioration.

In the Middle Ages, when all science was theological, the magistrate took care to have by his side the *clergyman judge*, that is the *savant*, whose duty it was to enlighten his conscience. In our day, I have no doubt, our tribunals have a continual increasing desire to keep the light of science before them, which at least will explain half of every case. I allude to the physician, the physiologist, who, without pretending to too great an influence, will nevertheless afford great aid, and often give the clue to the judge, by means of which he can himself penetrate into the shadows of the will.

VI.

TEMPTATION.

If I have spoken of these tragic matters, to which the little household, which is the only object of this book, is a stranger, it is solely to warn imprudent flies of the manœuvres of the spider. It is to remind those who

neglect their wives, and almost forget them, and are
then astonished when they hear of their sad fall, that
they themselves are the cause of it, and are very justly
punished by it.

Those, on the contrary, who are but little removed from
each other, who remain together, and daily mingle their
thoughts, have no cause to fear these plots. They see
them beforehand, they talk of them, and laugh at them
in scorn or in pity.

All honor to the woman, for preserving herself free
and pure amid this universal withering, when her relations, her friends in girlhood, almost every one of them,
undergo a bondage to shame. They affect at first to
consider her strange and ridiculous. All this makes but
little impression on her. And then, seeing her remain
unshaken, unassailable, they are compelled to be resigned. The public voice, the suffrage of unconcerned
and disinterested persons, assigns to her her true moral
rank. In her simple dignity, still young, without knowing or desiring it, she assumes authority. She is consulted, and those whom she receives are esteemed. She
is trusty and discreet, while she nevertheless plainly
warns all that she will have no secret which she cannot
tell her husband.

———

Can she ignore the advantage of such a position, and
not be proud on account of it? This is a difficult thing,
but it is but little perceived by any one. She presents
only the modest gravity of a young matron, honored
by her husband, queen of his heart as well as of his
house, who rules in her own sphere, and is often con
sulted in her husband's sphere, being conversant with

his affairs, and able sometimes to advise usefully. Even
.n general ideas and conversation, the woman of thirty,
with a clear and unsullied mind, which has nct been
drawn down to low thoughts, often shines with a light
unpossessed by the man of forty, given to his speciality,
and a little enfeebled.

She has reached the summit of her strength. You
feel it in a certain grand and serene expression which
her beauty has taken on. She blooms and thrives with
a charming plenitude. Never was her skin whiter than
now, and it has again become delicately rose-tinted.
Always abstemious, she is yet not indifferent to the table.
She should walk more; but she has so much to do in
the house, that she finds it difficult to leave it; and her
sedentary life gives her a little too much blood. She
blushes easily, often without cause. The flood rises
suddenly to her head, and then her beautiful eyes glitter
more than they should.

She lives and enjoys life, but with a moderation
which would weary others. Her only sensuality consists in going alone at times into her garden to gather
herself some fruit—one, then two, then several. Why
should she do it stealthily, when she is mistress of all,
and can rob only herself?

She gives herself holidays ; she becomes a sluggard.
Her sleep, sometimes heavy, is not, however, always
peaceful; she has sudden heats, when she blushes
deeply, and tosses about. Her husband, awakened in
he morning, and watching her, is not without a certain
uneasiness. What is it? She is but dreaming; or
rather her young blood, so abundant and generous,
dreams for her The malicious fairy of dreams makes

10*

sport of even the wisest; she causes precise'y those to submit to her follies in the night who have the least to do with such things in the day. But our wife is so scrupulous, that almost before she is awakened she makes an effort to tell everything to him; and confessed, absolved, embraced, she is happy and blooming, unmindful now of herself.

The physical life of woman is often awakened very late, at a period which it would seem should bring more calm, when her health is strengthened, and when she is free from the maladies of youth, and the first trials of maternity. All in regular harmony, all going on with perfect order, her position improved and easier, her child grown up, and established at school, her motherly heart calm, the good wife having accepted all that is in her husband, knowing his strength and his weakness, and ruling· him a little, her whole existence glides on with the imperceptible motion of a railway train, at moderate speed. . . . . But what a trifle would suffice to throw it off the track !

———

Our tradeswomen, the most intelligent in France, who live in public as in a glass house, and are consequently very easily observed, give rise to this remark : that there are many among them, otherwise discreet in conduct, who have a weakness for their head clerk. You say at first that this weakness is at the husband's expense, but this is not always true. If you penetrated deeper, if you knew the interior of this house perfectly, you would often find that he is none the less loved, that the predilections of the lady are for the one whom he himself loves and esteems, whom he believes, not with·

out reason, to be the most devoted to him. I have
sometimes seen this idyl in a shop. An innocent idyl it
seems to be, but notwithstanding dangerous; for the
ground is slippery. The young man, delighted at thus
being adopted and so well liked by both, may be truly
loyal at first; he loves them both, and scarcely discrimi-
nates in his affection. But still things work on their
way, and the handsome eyes of his mistress trouble him
more and more, and make his life very unhappy. All
three presently reach the end of the affair—the idyl is
turned into a tragedy, and makes its denouement: separation, downfall, perhaps suicide.

I wish you to notice only one thing in this, which is
remarkable, but which is also very true: that a good wife,
with a true and tender heart, who has the misfortune to
give way a little, does so only on the side towards which
her husband also leans; I mean towards the one whom
her husband prefers, whom he appropriates to himself,
and holds subordinate; of whom in short he makes another self. On the contrary, far from loving the men
who are superior to her husband, the wife is ill-disposed
towards them; she is envious of the greater renown
they have, hates and fights against it, and is not at all
ensnared by it. I have seen this, not ten, but a hundred times, in our *bourgeoise* classes.

The worst women, on the contrary, those who are unfaithful, who sin not through weakness, but by express
desire, do not fail to search after and to attract a man
whose real or apparent superiority will humiliate the husband, will render him ridiculous, will overwhelm him
with shame and irony. Which one do they love in
heart? Neither of them. Their fall is not an affair of

love, but of pure vanity; and it is from pride that they dishonor themselves. The absence of the heart explains everything; so, too, they seldom reform. Where the heart is wanting, nothing will supply its place.

To return to the young wife, so perfectly balanced in moral harmony with, and bound to her husband: if any misfortune should happen to her, it can only be a surprise of the heart, of which he himself will be a little guilty. Their position, their virtues, the magnanimity of that excellent man, may lead in the most honorable way to an accident, not dangerous, but afflicting to her, which shall remind her that she is a wife, and make her poor heart bleed.

A nephew of the husband, suddenly orphaned, has fallen to them at the age of ten; they are eager for him to come. He arrives (from Pau or Bayonne) a graceful child, with no timidity, full of pretty and roguish ways. Madame, then very young, not over twenty, receives him like a mother, weeps with him for his own, even more than he does, and covers him with caresses. He is sent to school, to return every year in the vacation, more and more lively, agreeable, charming, and bold, with plenty of confidence in himself. He becomes twelve, fifteen, and is still received very lovingly, like an elder brother of her own child. They do not grudge her her innocent caresses any more than they do those she bestows on the little one. Only the effect is different. One day she is romping with him in her husband's presence, and, as you may imagine, caught by surprise, and captured; he must be paid with a kiss, and she lets him take it. But it is not the only one: at the second, she loses her self-possession; returns it, with more than he gives; she lies a moment in his arms without strength, breathless. He turns very red, then very pale. He laughingly leads back the trembling dove. Her husband laughs too; but she not at all; she has a fever all day.

From this year, it may be believed, she begins to be a little afraid, and becomes more prudent. He, on his part, is developed with all the vivacity of Southern grace, is a good talker, a charming and witty story-teller, perhaps a braggart; but he is always believed. The damage done the Northern woman is great, and the contrast strong which he presents to the earnest, busy man, whose manners are undemonstrative, but who concentrates his fire for action and great results.

The agreeable arrival of the young man is a holiday in the house, and works a sudden change in everything. There is more sunlight, it seems, and more noise and laughter (not much heard where true happiness is). As for her, she laughs and she is sad. This contrast strikes even herself, and makes her uneasy. She is not very well, and the gentlemen go out together, while she remains; she wishes to collect her thoughts, and commune with herself.

There she is in that little garden—in that same garden where ten years before, on the holy day she became *enceinte*, she walked in the dawn, not less agitated, though so pure. There she is in the presence of the same flowers which were moved to pity for her, and swore to her that she was innocent. "But what would they say to me to-day? I have done no wrong, and I have wished none. It I had, I should have told my

husband.   Still I am troubled ; I do not feel well.   Yet
I have nothing to tell him."   " Very much, madame."
" Why, who was it that spoke ?   There is no one here
but this rose and I.   How brilliant it is, and so red
(at least so it looks to me)—red with fire.   Does it speak
by its color, and what does it mean ?"

VII.

A ROSE FOR A COUNSELLOR.

Do not pluck the rose, Madame, or it will become for
ever mute.   Removed from Nature's bosom, it would
but wither on yours, after having intoxicated and agitated you with its perfume.   Bend over it and listen ;
this is what it tells you:

"You go and come at will; you are endowed with
the power of motion.   I remain always on my stalk.
You admire me in my calmness, in my rosy royalty.   I
am such because I always remain faithful to my nature.

"I am not a plaything, fit only to be stuck in a
woman's hair.   I am an earnest creature, a powerful
and living energy, a work and a worker at the same
time, set here to solve a mystery.   My time is short; I
must hasten to accomplish a great end, the perpetuation
of a divine race, the immortality of the rose.   And
hence it is, Madame, that I am one of God's Roses.

"I have my stalk, and I cling fast to it.   Spare me

the honor of dying upon your bosom. Let me remain pure and fruitful; and be so, likewise, yourself."

"Ah! you have spoken well," replies the woman "how I should like to resemble you, to be also one of God's roses.

"But, dear Rose, do you really think I ought to make a confession? And what shall I confess? It is all a cloud, a mist with me, in which I can scarce distinguish anything. And if I accuse myself, it will break his heart."

"But you have promised to tell him everything."

"Oh, Rose, you understand the love of flowers, but not that of women! The very moment that I confess this thing, this love for another, it will assume a sudden strength in my heart, become more ardent than before. To reveal it, is but to increase it."

"Then you are indeed unfortunate. You guard your secret, brood over and caress it as you would your child. You tremble lest it may be discovered, and be dragged into the full light of day. And you are right, Madame, for nothing in nature is more delicate. From the time that a secret love is acknowledged, it is compromised. It may still burn on, but it burns towards total extinguishment. Such profanation brings it to shame. If you had but to tell it to a female friend, to a kind and indulgent father, you would not hesitate a moment. You would delight to talk of this love, and nourish it, and your tears would be an additional sin. But you must tell it to the victim, to him who is to suffer from it, and share with him this painful secret. How his heart will bleed! but yours will bleed also, and will put an end to this love for another. Your

dream will be stript of its wings, and you will come
down again to the real, to the infinite sorrow in which
his bleeding heart is plunged. You are kind and affectionate—love will return to you through pity."

* * * * * *

She heeds this counsel. She summons all her strength
and courage. At the breakfast-table, from which the
young man is absent, she will tell all. She takes her
seat, weak and haggard, feeling like one condemned to
death. But her heart beats too loudly, her tongue is
tied. At last, with a superhuman effort, she asks her
husband if this life of idleness is good for his nephew.
His studies are finished. Is it not time to put him at
something, to place him in a position which will prepare
and open for him a career ?—The husband regards her
with surprise :

"Why, my dear, he has but just come. We cannot
send him away yet.. I noticed, indeed, that you were
very cool to him. Have you taken a dislike to him ?"

"Oh, no !"

"Do you love him, then ?"

"Ah ! If it should have come to that . . . ."

To have lifted a mountain would have cost her less
effort. She falls back powerless ; she is almost fainting.
Both are extremely pale. But he, though heart-
broken, is strong even in death, is grateful to her for
her heroic loyalty. With her, one danger alone is to
be feared, that she will die of her anguish and of her virtue.

He convulsively clasps her hand, and they separate
in silence. But, like a fire from which the ashes have

been suddenly removed, her passion breaks forth, her agitation, her internal distraction cannot be concealed.

Love is so powerful a thing that, though you catch but a flash of it, by its reflection alone, it sets every-thing on fire. The coldest heart is warmed thereby; the boundless pride, the sudden joy, the violent delight of its discovery, creates in the least susceptible young men an immediate blazing forth of passion! How this passion may have been expressed, favored as it was, under the guise of a natural and, so to speak, filial affection, is not known. But the poor wife, almost beside herself, and too weak to resist these struggles, as evening and bed-time draw near, throws herself into her husband's arms, choking with sobs.

He kisses her, tries in vain to quiet and encourage her. It is only after a long time, after a deluge of tears, that, keeping him still close to her, and not letting him go, she succeeds in saying:

"Defend me, have mercy on me, sustain me. I feel that I am sinking. My will is so feeble that it slips away from me hour by hour, and soon it will desert me entirely. No; for it drags me with it; I have only strength left to drown myself. I did wrong to be so confident of myself until now; I am punished for it. I am weaker than our little one was in his cradle. I en-treat you to look upon me as a child, to treat me as one, for I am nothing more. You have been too kind to me heretofore—be more severe, be my master. Pun-ish me. If my body is humbled and mortified, my soul will be cured. I must hold you in dread, be a little afraid of you. Let my will perish from this moment! I will have nothing more to do with it; I deliver it up to you. You are my veritable will, my better self. But do not leave me, that I may ask you about every thing—whether I may desire it, and whether it be right for me to desire it."

This profound humiliation of a person who was innocent and irreproachable, fills him who loved her with pain. Alas! to see this queen of purity fallen so low! He conceals his true impressions, and makes an effort to smile: "My dear," he says, "it is not enough for you to ask me to act thus; I must also find the will to do it. Do you not feel that there is nothing about your beloved person that I do not hold as sacred as my mother's grave? Where shall I find the resolution to treat you with such harshness?"

"But if it does me good," she answers, "if it cures me? Fear, said Solomon, is the beginning of wisdom. I feel a need of fear, of humiliation. I should love you the more for it. Madam —— , whom you know as a very proud and self-confident woman, said to me the other day: 'she who has once felt the weight of her husband's hand, is so much the more attached to him for the severity of his affection, recollecting and fearing a repetition of it.'"

"No," he answers, "we shall not yet go back to the barbarity of past ages. Great Heaven! have I married a soul and a body, to make of them a thing, a nonentity? I slander them to think of it. But, my love, whatever your self-abasement may be, remember that my love's dearest wish, my heart's greatest desire, was to reach your soul, to enter wholly into its inner temple. What will become of me if I listen to you, if I break your will, if I deface you by fear? I shall have

lost for ever my most cherished hope. What truth or
fidelity can I expect from a servile person, who has
once trembled before me, and who, brought thus low, can
never regain her former position—would not, perhaps,
if she could? The soul is but too ready to abandon
itself, to take delight in its shame, to seek and to feel in
it a sensuality of love.

"And if I exterminate your will, what will you have
left to love me with? No, I wish you to become more
and more an independent being, a free intelligence, opposed to me if need be.

"I have always wished you to be thus, but not
strongly enough. I have not cultivated and nourished
your heart with sufficient constancy. Hence comes this
fatal accident.. Whose fault is it? It is the fault of
the labor, the business, the outside interests and the
cares with which I have been occupied, for the accumu-
lation of your fortune, and that of our children. Im-
provident man that I was: for the family's sake I forgot
the family! And for an uncertain good I have jeopard-
ized that which heaven placed in my hands—this, my
incomparable treasure! Thanks for this cruel blow; I
am warned against myself. Without it, I had been a
man no longer. Now I return to my former self, I feel
and recognise myself through affliction. You will find
me again what I once was. We shall be inseparable for
the future. And you must needs love me, for I shall be
great and noble again.

"As for this boy, even were he not already related to
me, he should become so. He, upon whom your eye has
once dwelt, who has occupied for a moment your cherished thoughts, is a chosen being who should ever after

experience the benefits of this great good fortune. I will adopt him. I will put him forward to the utmost in his career. Though far distant, he shall be ever present to me, and he shall always find in me a helping friend I shall be pleased if, in writing to me, he speaks often of you. May so noble a souvenir keep his heart worthy and pure, and always in the straight path."

———

Our invalid was not one of those who do not wish to get well. She did not let her husband lull himself into security with this imprudent and magnanimous confidence; she allowed no delays, but prayed and insisted upon the sending away of the young man. An occasion presenting itself, the nephew departed the next day. She felt that in these matters no procrastination, no middle course, is possible. A partial separation, permitting him to return frequently, would have been more dangerous than a permanent stay. More timid than Rousseau's Julie, she would have feared even the boat of Saint Preux and the rocks of Meillerie. So she desired and exacted of him a complete separation, which should cut off everything, even at the risk of breaking her own heart.

But she was surprised that he who she thought must suffer the most, resigned himself to the separation with great composure. The attractions of the unknown, of travelling, of a new life, of a rapid and brilliant career, with a friendly providence to help him along, all combined to form a powerful distraction to the sorrows of parting. The lively imagination of the South is often found joined to another gift with which it would seem at first irreconcilable—a lively appreciation of the actual, and of self-interest.

However virtuous and courageous she may have been, she was vexed to see herself so calmly obeyed. Her husband saw that she suffered intensely. Any other person would have felt exultant. But he, who loved her so, shared her grief. Nothing could be gained by the separation, if this sorrowing love was to last, and perhaps increase. Of what use was it to outwardly preserve her, if the fatal shaft was still to rankle in her bosom?

She would have perished in her mute sorrow, not daring to confess the affliction of her love that remained to her, nor the undefined regret, which a weak nature associates with its grand sacrifices. If her husband had yielded to the ordinary temptation of jealous men, and removed her from society, shut her up in solitude, he would have fulfilled her dearest wish. If he had put her in a tower, built on the summit of a rock, or in the malarious castle of the Maremma, where Dante's Pia passes out of life, she would have thanked him for it. That was what she needed, to keep her ideal ever before her eyes. Solitary, and a prisoner, she could uninterruptedly have enjoyed the happiness of tears.

He did just the opposite. He wisely judged that if the illusion remained, it was because the loved object, so promptly sent away, having become a permanent vision, still retained all his former charms. Far from granting her the indulgence of solitary dreams, he took his patient out into the living, moving world, subject to the teachings of reality, and convinced that her false and fantastic creation could not survive such contact.

———

One of the most frequent causes of a lover's illusions

and exaggerations, is the belief that the beloved object is
a marvel, is *unique* by some quality, which is found to
be commonplace when one learns a little more of the
world.

A young man sees in Paris a beautiful girl, with deli
cate and regular features. He is enamored. He marries
her, and afterwards is anxious to see the birth-place of
his wife, the city of Arles. There, he finds at every
turn this woman whom he thought unique. The marvel
is to be seen any day, in the streets. He sees a hundred,
a thousand girls as pretty as she. It is the beauty of
an entire people, the Arlesian beauty that he has fallen
in love with. And his ardor is at once cooled.

In like manner, an uninformed Spanish woman, who
has never been out of her own country, and for the first
time beholds, with his tutor, a young Englishman, with
that blooming complexion which is found only at the
North, is completely bewildered. Shut her up in a
convent, and she would die. The opposite course is the
one to pursue. You must take her to Germany, to
our Normandy, or to England, the entire zone, in fact,
of blonde beauty, of millions of women and children, and
young men even, just as white and red as the one whom
she thought unique. When she has seen this ruddiness
on numberless faces, destitute of all charm, stupid even,
she will conclude that the quality, common to a whole
race, does not suffice to make an angel.

The attraction of Southerners, for us of the North,
is more common still. Such a man at Lille, at Rouen,
at Strasbourg seems irresistible. Is it through his own
merit? Not at all; it is only because he has, in his look
or his speech, the sun of Provence, the grace of the

Bernese, the piquancy of the Gascon. The most ordinary men from these favored districts, if transplanted to
the North, produce an astonishing illusion. At an official dinner, where many of the guests found themselves
together for the first time, I was seated opposite a gentleman from the South of France, whose charming eyes
seemed fairly to sparkle; however much you tried, you
could hardly support a glance from them. In those
eyes were countless romances, in the style of Ariosto—
everything that was brilliant and sparkling; at times
they seemed to contain the divine fire of genius.
I at length asked his name of my neighbor. It was perfectly unknown; he was a deputy from the central depart-
ments, who never said a word in the Chamber, but was
extremely loquacious elsewhere. So that, in this human
firework, the race was everything, the man nothing.

It is then to the South that our prudent husband takes
his ailing young wife. He does not allow resignation
and sorrow to close in upon her. He insists upon a
change of air, and of habits. The beautiful horizons
and landscapes of southern France elevate and fortify
the heart. Rousseau has admirably told how, at a time
when he was sinking, the mere sight, the austere and
grandiose sight, of the Pont du Gard lifted him up.
How much greater the influence of the sublime spectacle of the Pyrenees! Their untrodden glaciers, their
immaculate snows, purify the eyes and the soul.

But while seeing nature, your delicate and intelligent
patient also sees and understands man. She finds everywhere, in this part of the country, the young man who has
parted from her. At first she is pained by this. They

all have the same vivacity as he, the same grace, **the**
same fluent and brilliant speech. In fact, she sees here
every quality which she imagined he alone possessed ·
the same quickness, that charming clearness of glance,
at times sparkling, again more profound, retreating into
a semi-tragical sombreness, which has its effect, but
about which, however, there is naught of seriousness.

That young man talked excellently, and was very amusing. So is every one here, and several have an astonishing fecundity in conversation. A mere clerk, to induce you to buy his wine, will exercise more diplomacy
than the Talleyrands. If you hesitate, his eloquence increases till it resembles a whirlwind, a maëlstrom. It is
like a Pyrenean torrent, sweeping its banks along with
it. It even reaches the pathetic, the sublime, carries
everything before it. But how he will laugh when you
leave!

A loquacious, and yet a charming race! They lie
without lying; it is their nature. Do not blame their
fictions. They have a poet's license. It is planted so
deeply in their nature, in their blood, that on every occasion it comes up to them unconsciously, in spite of themselves. I have seen some who for days together would
pour forth a torrent of assertions which could not deceive any one, false as facts, but true as ideas, which, if
they did not exist in the real world, had a brilliant existence in the domain of creative fancy.

When we see this mirage for the first time, we are
dazzled and amazed. This it was that the Northern
woman felt in seeing it in but one person; but when she
finds it in a crowd, in a whole people, she grows calm,
becomes herself again, and smiles.

The god falls from his pedestal and becomes man, like
other men.   He is subordinated, classified, returned to
his genus and species.   If the celestial being has disappeared, there remains an agreeable young fellow in
stead, a little frivolous and not much to be depended
upon, but not without his merits.

---- ▸◂ ----

VIII.

THE MEDICATION OF THE HEART.

ARE the adultery of the woman and the adultery of
the man equally guilty ?   Yes, as an infidelity, a violation
of vows.   No, in a thousand other respects.

The treachery of the woman carries with it fearful
consequences—that of the man does not.   The woman
does not simply betray her husband ; she yields up his
honor and his life ;   She makes him gossiped about,
ridiculed, pointed at, hissed ; she puts him in peril of
death, of either killing a man or remaining a butt ; it is
almost as if she let an assassin into the house by night.

He will suffer a moral assassination all the rest of his
life, never knowing whether her child is his child, obliged
to rear and provide for a doubtful progeny, or to amuse
the public by a trial, which, whether he gains·or loses,
makes his name a byword and a jest.

It is folly to say that the woman has no more responsibility than the man.   He, by his activity and strength,
supports the family ; but she is its heart.   She alone

11

knows its mysteries. She alone holds the secret of domestic happiness, the sole assurance for the future. She alone can attest a legitimate inheritance. A wife's falsehood may falsify history for a thousand years.

What is the bosom of woman, if not our living temple, our sanctuary, our shrine where burns the light of God for ever, where we each day are recreated ? If she deliver this up to the enemy, if she permit this fire, which is her husband's life, to be stolen, it is more dreadful than to plunge a knife into his heart.

No punishment could be severe enough, if she knew what she had done.

But she is nearly always very far from even dreaming of it. Premeditated infidelity, prompted by hate and malice, is a thing of infinitely rare occurrence. The first false step, at least, is nearly always accidental, the result of a negative weakness, less an act than an inability to act, to resist.

Warm, *full-blooded* woman are dazzled and bewildered, and at certain periods have an actual vertigo. Those of a lymphatic temperament have an extreme placidity of will; they are wont to yield; they know that it becomes them, and hence they never resist. It costs them too much of an effort to refuse.

Those who are not forgiven often suffer the bitterness of remorse. I myself have seen two striking examples.

A very beautiful woman, rich and happy, arrived at her fortieth year without a shadow of reproach, having a dear husband and grown up children, one morning, as if tired of a monotonous happiness, yielded to a man whom she did not love. Her inexperience in evil-doing caused her to be discovered. Her chagrin that she had fallen at that age, her shame in the presence of her children, weighed her down, and she died four months afterwards.

A young woman of twenty-five, elegant, high-spirited, and full of life, with a face of noble gravity, expressive of a pure mind, had, to her misfortune, a beautiful and impassioned voice, which was continually in requisition at *soirées* and in the *salons* of Paris. A duet turned her head; she succumbed to the transports of her art, not to passion. Her heart still belonged to her husband, who was young and pleasing, and certainly adored her. Overwhelmed with her misfortune, she went to him without delay, told him all, and threatened to kill herself at once if he did not find means by which to make her expiate her crime. But he, crushed by the blow, never found strength to punish her. In this contest with herself she began to sing. She had lost her wits.

I was young at the time, but the memory of that occurrence is ever present to me. I saw her in a lunatic asylum—a pit of madness and misery, to which her physicians had consigned her. Her husband came to see her every day, and swore to her, with the tears pouring down his cheeks, that she was forgiven, that she was thenceforth pure and innocent. But she understood nothing of all that. Her madness was only cured by exterminating it: the treatment she received annihilated it. It may be said that she came out of the asylum a living corpse, and it was not long before she died in reality.

It is a pity that this same terrible word, adultery, is

applied to two very different things, to the perverse infidelity of her who mocks her husband, who really wishes to disgrace him, and the heedless self-ruin of an imprudent woman who does not even know that she falls until after she is fallen.

A wife awaits her husband's return from a journey with lively emotion, a strong physical impatience. His supper is ready to receive him, but he is not able to come. He sends a zealous friend to tell the cause of his detention, and to reassure his wife. Through a violent storm the friend arrives, wet to the skin. She is touched with sympathy, has his clothes dried, gives him supper, and orders a bed to be made ready for him She prepares for him a heating wine, which only her husband drank, and of whose dangerous powers she is ignorant. In short, they both lose their reason for the time being.—The friend, truly in despair, seeks out the husband at the earliest opportunity, confesses all, and offers to submit to any punishment. What is he to do? "The real culprit," says the husband, "is the wine. And I also am guilty. There are times when no woman should be kept waiting."

A storm like this, which brings together two persons with strong passions—evening amusements, romping country games with relations, with boys who are considered children, are but too frequent occasions. A thoughtless girl, by her wild hoydenness, provokes a bold act. She had not dreamed of it, nor desired it, but she comes home weeping.

But the case that most frequently induces infidelity is ennui, the excessive ennui of woman's solitude The man's life is busier and more animating.

What a sad thing it is to see in our country towns women, married but two years, yet already forsaken; to see them go, at vespers, to yawn with five or six old crones.

How often, too, in travelling, as I entered a German village, have I seen at a balcony, or in a little glass con servatory, surrounded by flowers and birds, a sweet womanly face looking through the window at the passers-by! How languishing she seemed! "She is not loved enough," I thought. "Where is her husband? Spending his days between smoke and beer, while his house contains for him the most charming of God's gifts.'

The most faithless are often those who had the great est need of love, who loved powerfully, strongly, and would have been the most faithful. French women, for the most part, are not at all contented with the cold conjugal observances which suffice for the women of the North. The latter, being gentle and resigned, exact but little; and if marriage is for them only an exterior relation, a simple living together, they sigh, but make no complaint. To our women you must give everything or nothing. The French woman is either the worst or the best of her sex. Union with her must be either null or complete.

It is very wrongly believed, and often she herself yields to the belief, that she has constant need of amusements and distractions. In reality, it is quite the opposite. They do not know themselves. Those who fly from pleasure to pleasure, shake off their thoughts in the pursuit; but they own that they soon weary of it. What they really need is to be *very much loved* and *very much occupied.*

Even the woman of business, but partially occupied, though always kept behind the counter, has not that excitement of outside affairs which continually draws her husband away from the shop. I see now, in imagination, a young and pretty saleswoman, in the back part of a dark, damp booth, in a dingy little street of the city of Lyons. Her husband loves her, but he devotes his days to business and his evenings to his café. She languishes in this living tomb. How can you expect her not to listen to the friend, or the customer, who comes and goes every hour, amuses and interests her? If the husband really loves her, he should take pity on her, liberate her from her loneliness.

Even without leaving the city, it will often be found sufficient to raise her from the bottom to the top of the house, from darkness into light. The little woman, exposed to the dangers of the counter, and fickle by the necessity of her situation, rather than from any willingness of her own, can work very well in a room on the fourth floor, whence she may see the verdure on the hill sides of Fouviéres, or better still, a glimpse of the Alps, which shall elevate and purify her heart.

"Is that all?" No, that is but a small part yet. The great point is to love her, to interest yourself in her, not to turn your back when you see her weary, to sympathize with all her sufferings. Not only go to her frequently, but do not leave her. She will feel grateful for this, and disclose her thoughts to you, at last; she will go so far as to say, "I am dying with sadness." That means, "I want a love."

But do not be offended at that; it is only a love, not a lover that she wants. Love applies to so many things

It is perhaps the love of a child, or the love of an idea, of a great work, of an entirely new, busy, exacting life in a strange country.

No half-way manœuvre will remedy this; do not imagine that a slight and transient diversion, a trip to the theatre, or an excursion into the country, will suffice for her state of mind. No, she must have some outlet for affection, or a great change in life.

Whatever may happen, even if she should fall, do not abandon the wife of your youth. If she has fallen, she has so much the more need of you. If she is humble and repenting, you must treat her as an invalid, wait upon her, and hide her from the world. If bad influences have perverted her, you must, without losing a moment, take her away from them, and place her amid better surroundings; act with energy and moderation, correct her gently.

She is still yours, whatever she may have done. The share that she has in your name, the profound and complete blending of your physical existences, renders all separation illusory. She who has once been fruitful, once impregnated, will bear her husband with her everywhere. This has been amply proven. How long does the first impregnation last? Ten years? Twenty? a life-time? It is not known; but one thing is certain, and that is, that the widow often has by her second husband children resembling her first.

She has surrendered herself *entirely* to marriage; what would she have beside it?

Man has such an advantage over woman, both by nature and the laws, that it goes against his magnanimity ever to ask for divorce. If she demands it, she who loses everything by it, it is to be regarded as an astounding, senseless act, except in cases of cruelty and maltreatment, from which she must be delivered at all costs.

You cannot abandon her. For how dangerous will it be for her, when the lover who receives her, experiences the disgust of finding your reflection everywhere in her person, transformed through you ? In discovering in her, your voice, your words, your gestures, and traces even still more profound !

She belongs to you to that degree that even should the lover impregnate her, it will probably be your child, one marked with your features, that she will give him. He will have the punishment of seeing that he can have nothing real or profound from her, and that in the capital point, the generating union, he is unable to render her faithless.

What would become of the unfortunate woman if forsaken, and driven from her home, by you? she would not even have the friendly shelter of his roof who desired of her but the pleasure of a moment! Do not abandon a woman whom you have loved, who was and who is yours, to the chances of such an experiment. Rarely does she risk it herself; if she be not too badly treated, it is seldom that she leaves her home, the home of her habitual associations, and where perhaps she still has a bond of love. This is singular, but not the less true ; more than one capricious woman cares more for her husband than for the object of her passing fancy ; and, if she had to elect between them, would prefer him who knew her as a maiden, whom she has in her blood, and whose life is her life.

"Do not strike a woman, not even with a fl)wer though she has committed a hundred faults."

Our hearts would have prompted this sentiment, if India had not said it before us. Strike a woman! Heavens! a woman, our queen of love, and a queen so submissive that she gives the man illimitable power every night, the power to render her *enceinte!* It is almost the power of life and death.

To humiliate and break down a weak, gentle creature, by a servile punishment. Oh, base cowardice!

The women of the Middle Ages (and even now those of certain races) underwent, and endured patiently, conjugal discipline. With the nervous women of our day, this would be a dangerous attempt. Some would die at the least blow. Even when taken in her guilt, the woman should be spared. In but one case, where the despair of a great remorse threatens her life or her reason, if she offers herself up to punishment, begs and implores it, a slight bodily suffering may be granted her to lessen that of the soul.

The best remedy is in travel. Leave your business; cut the bonds that confine you to it, and take her away with you for a season. Do not utter those vile words, too often used in these days: "No noise about it . . . I will keep her here in spite of herself. I will inflict upon her and her lover the daily torture of my partnership n their joys. She shall be for me, henceforth, like a hattel, the passive instrument of my pleasure. And vhat matters the rest, after all?"

No, you must go to the root of the matter; suffer yourself, that she may be purified. Once taken from her

11*

associations, and brought into a new society, where a dJ
ferent language is spoken, intimate only with you, she
will be quite a different person.   With him who works
for her support, who never reminds her of her misfor
tune, never makes her life bitter to her, treats her as
. kindly and gently as on the day after their marriage,
she literally renews herself, and retains no more of her
past than a vague souvenir, as of an unpleasant dream.
In different circumstances, surrounded by a thousand
new necessities, you will both be renewed.   In Europe
you have had two children, here you will have a dozen.
At home, your pretty wife, with her self-willed and ardent
spirit, would have ruined you.   Here, on the contrary
she is the making of you.   Be exemplary, courageous,
and industrious;   she will assist in making your fortune.   She will love you with the old love made new,
for having regenerated her; and in your old age you can
both return to your native country.

IX.

MEDICATION OF THE BODY.

A CELEBRATED surgeon, who had much experience of
women, makes this remark: that, though often a little
cold in their first youth, they have, on the contrary, at
the middle of life and at the beginning of its wane, a
real need of being loved.   Often about their thirty-fifth

year, ten years before the normal cessation, the blood circulates with less regularity, stops at times, and becomes obstructed. From this come maladies of all sorts, impassioned dreams, languors, devouring flames, the desire of love, regrets.

Her husband deserts her, deceives her in his habits, and runs after thoughtless girls, who make fun of him, and are in reality so little worthy of him. His true province—the profound heart, the intelligent mind, the poetic soul of his suffering wife—he utterly forgets. What a prize he might have possessed! How powerful and delightful! The fruit of all fruits, the peach, is improved by the bite of the wasp, and woman, in like manner, by the sting of pain.

The man who, having eyes, sees with them, appreciates this period, when the face wears its most touching beauty, when the creature of Love, under the hand of Nature preparing for herself an age of suffering, already more humble in that, cares least for show and most for happiness She especially, who has lived a life of duty and virtue, who has walked side by side with love and with discretion, is very touching at that hour when, imagining it taking to flight, she sighing, says: "What, gone already!"

If you except the malady of northern countries, consumption, an effect of climate, there are but two great maladies in Europe, both having their origin in our passions, in our thoughts, our wills.

The man wishes to be strong, and he takes the wrong course, carrying invigoration to excess. He eats and drinks a great deal too much. All his maladies proceed from the digestive organs.

The woman wishes to be loved. She suffers in the organ of love and maternity. All her ailments, directly or indirectly, arise from the matrix.

This Proteus takes a thousand shapes. Its actions are remote. If you retrace, observantly and patiently, the life of the invalid, you will find at last that the affection of the chest, or the stomach, or what not, that you thought entirely foreign to any such cause, was prepared ten, fifteen years before, by some deep sorrow of the heart.

There is nothing low or vulgar in woman. Everything is poetic. Generally she is sick from love, man from indigestion.

Nothing is more serious than a reply she often makes, and at which men laugh. " What causes your head-ache ? your tooth-ache ? your colic ?" " Not being loved enough."

———

Having given the key to this mystery, and being now extricated from the mire of my 8th chapter (on Adultery and Divorce), I can follow the inclinations of my heart and return to our ideal, to the woman who has not fallen, to her who, reclining upon a loving husband, and concealing nothing from him, has skimmed over the wave without foundering in its depths. We have seen how she could arouse herself from her dream, and see the idol of her illusions vanish. · But does no trace of it remain ? Yes, for the most virtuous of them does not lose this illusion without a pang, does not confess to herself without pain that she has loved without being loved in return. The love of her husband is not doubted. She has felt the strength and the tenderness of his heart; yet even here she suffers also, feeling her former position gone, in having acknowledged to him that she was not the heavenly being, the angel of God, that he had believed her to be—finally obliged to confess to herself that without him she would have fallen, that she needed his protection. She is divided between these two questions: "Have I not sinned at least in thought? Or (O shame!) do I not regret having been preserved from sin?"

Thus, between two loves, between doubts and scruples, in the ebb and flow of a heart but partially cured, she gives way, loses her strength, languishes and grows pale. After the plethora and the storm comes a great exhaustion. The disease may be already prognosed.

———

In addition to our own diseases, we of these times have all to cope with an ancient and mysterious curse which we get from our ancestors. This latter, which never appears to us in our strength, lies waiting within us for the day of our weakness, and on that day pounces upon us, conquers us—breaking forth often in the most astounding forms, to our great terror and mortification.

My book is not an idyl. If the frivolous young man, the fastidious or disdainful young lady, chance to read it, they must have courage. For it will be ever sincere, and will not recoil from Nature. Besides, this is not an accessory. It is the heart of the subject, the strong proof of love.

The love which boys bear for a white and rosy Iris of fifteen can hardly be called love; it is a surface desire, a slight arousing of the senses. But he of whom it can be said, "His love is as powerful as death," loves in

quite a different manner. You need have no scruple in
setting him, not before Death, but, what is harder to
bear, in the presence of Disease.

What disease? That which is often hereditary and
fatal, of which this your poor mortified wife is innocent.
The purest, the most virtuous, has none the less a germ
in her blood which sooner or later will betray her.
This soft flower of love, this dazzling blonde (beautiful
as the *Néréide* of Rubens a the Louvre, if you will),
may soon detect the reappearance of the scrofula that
she had in her childhood. That other beauty, with the
large, lustrous eyes, the dark complexion, whose love
seems to burn its way into your heart—alas ! the very
shaft of love that she directs at you in her heart-rending
smile, is the twinge of the fierce cancer which is devouring her bosom.

The story goes that the brilliant Spaniard, Raymond
Lulli, once pursued with his suit a lady who loved him
but yielded him nothing. In the audacity of his desire,
he followed her into a church. There, indignant, and
emboldened by the darkness (Spanish churches are very
ill-lighted), she turned round and displayed to him a
bosom which was the prey of disease. What think you
the lover did ? He ran away from the place ; and the
knight turned doctor, preacher, schoolman.

He did not love her. Had he really loved her, how
such a discovery would have bound him to her ! What
a strong tie, what an opportunity for devotion, I had
almost said what a tender attraction, this would have
proved ! To the honor of our age be it said, that an
eminent thinker, in a similar case, doubled his former
love. He surrounded the innocent victim with atten-

tions proportioned to her misfortune. Delicate precautions were taken to veil her from the gaze of others, and
almost from her own. How he must have loved! This
single instance, among many, where the two combined
against fate and nature, will be envied by all those whose
hearts are worthy to contain such a sentiment as theirs.
And may not this indeed be the true temple that Love
the conqueror of death, has wished to consecrate to him
self here below ?

Suffering is the very life of woman. She can suffer
better than man; she is much more resigned to it.
But the intolerable part of it to her is, that disease, that
cruel revelation of our nature, displays her in numberless
low, sad, ungracious aspects. Every woman has had a
period, a moment of divinity, when she was thought to
be, when she almost thought herself, freed from this
earth. The remembrance of that time follows her, and
ennobles her in her own eyes. Even the drama of child-
birth, which keeps her in bed for a short time, leaves
her very poetic. Disease, alas! has none of these effects. It drags on, heavy and dull, displaying wantonly
what nature most strives to conceal. A triple disgust—of the disease itself, of its phases, and of its remedies!

When the truth can be concealed, the invalid suffers
in silence. But it would seem that disease has the per
versity to show itself by unpleasant appearances, treach
erous efflorescences which bring it into relief. There are
certain pimples that come and go upon the face, or an
eruption on the scalp, enough to drive one to despair. I
have seen this last affliction attack a young woman,

of resplendent beauty and freshness, so that she would gladly have died of it.

From that moment all witnesses are in the way. The femme-de-chambre is sent off, dismissed. Questioned by her husband, the patient weeps: "I am ashamed, my love. That girl will go and blab it about."—"Do not cry," he answers; "I alone will take care of you, and no one shall know of it." "But if I should displease you? For it is on your account that I suffer most."

A serious and terrible cause of the maladies of a woman who has passed her days of youthfulness, is in doubting her own influence. This doubt will cease on the day when, contrary to her expectations, her husband, in the height of ambition and success, holding perhaps an important station, forgets and sacrifices all, waits upon and attends to her with pleasure, proving to her that she is always his cherished and only thought.

"My love, it is really a pity to see you turned aside from your career to this extent—leaving great matters to occupy your mind with my misery. I am ashamed of myself; I pray you, leave me." She says this, but she smiles, and is truly happy. Her mind is very tranquil now.

———

Disease is discord, and health is harmony. Your first care should be to establish around the invalid an exterior harmony. You will never succeed in this if every-day neighbors, friends and relations, bring their advice to bear against yours, or call in their own physicians, thwart you at the very turning point of the disease, and even inspire the vacillating mind of the invalid herself with doubts. These doubts are in themselves a grave malady which will lengthen and aggravate the other. There are no means of curing them. Solitude and quiet are what are required.

The organization is about to relax, and in the majority of maladies this is the true commencement of a cure Nearly always it is an exaggerated idea, or a passion, which has overstrained the nervous system, upset the general equilibrium. Removed from the causes which have produced this evil, weaker and more depressed than before, she enters of her own free will, with body and soul, into a sort of retrospective meditation. She takes a clearer view of things, gets rid of her exaggeration. She blames herself, wishes to make herself better, and to live in perfect accord with the general harmony and the will of God. She comprehends that she is not innocent of her illness. She accepts it with resignation; she no longer accuses Nature, who never lets us off otherwise. One who does not complain of sickness, and is not impatient to be well, is in reality very nearly cured.

But nothing so inspires the invalid with patience as to be tended by the hand of him she loves, to feel herself enveloped by the being who is all the world to her. In this long tête-à-tête, which brings back to her the sweet solitude of the honeymoon, she is resigned to being ill; she expands her nature, and morally unbosoms herself.

In the deepening twilight, putting her little hands, now thin, into yours, she unburdens her whole heart to you. She speaks to you as she would to her own secret thought. You kiss her hands. She goes on without perceiving it, saying things that cannot be expressed here, but which, however, a feeble woman has need of saying. Her dreams, her invalid fancies, her little wo-

manly fears : " What if I should die, my dear ? I can
not leave you. But God will have mercy on us.' From
this she goes further, confesses this thing and that, a
certain great sin that she has concealed from you. In
fact, she has soon told you everything—had a complete
confession.

" What, so little ! is that all ?" you ask ; " And it is a
great deal," she answers ; " If I have done anything else,
I do not remember it. But, my dear, what is the matter,
that you are bathing my hands in your tears ?"

Now night has closed in. The moon is not up ; but
the twinkling stars are bright enough for you. She is a
little fatigued. She falls asleep without letting go your
hand ; and from that day forth she sleeps much more tran·
quilly, feeling a great harmony within her.

Marriage is confession. The union, the peace of two
hearts, begins in this, that they tell everything to each
other. And it is through this that they enter into peace
and the good order of the mind, which in turn will
bring back that of the body.

To confide in a third person, a stranger, who after all is
but a man, is not the way to become pure ; it is tempting
both, passing from a storm into a tempest. That the
unsettled soul, the sickly body, the whole suffering crea·
ture, may find perfect rest again, her other half, the
sharer of her pain, must open to her the infinite of love,
the infinite of confidence, and without exacting any·
thing, lead her on to tell him everything—she being
sure the while that she will be loved none the less for
the confession.

Once relieved by this, you must strengthen the poor

timid soul. Remember, that she is afraid of death.
Let us state the facts fearlessly, without any unreason
able heroics. It is very easy for us, educated in the
religion of the indulgent God of nature, to look our
common destiny in the face. But she, impressed with
the dogma of eternal punishment, though she may have
received other ideas from you, still, in her suffering and
debility, has painful foreshadowings of the future state.
She does not conceal these, and like a helpless child
seeks refuge in your arms. Then deal with her strongly,
though gently. Betray no lack of decision with her;
control, or put off your tears, and let her find in you a
firm resting-place. Expand her feminine soul, narrowed by pain, confined by fear, to a conception of the
great harmony—having which, we should be as willing
to die as to live, in the just and unalterable law of all
things. Here I know what a great effort it will cost you
to accept, as an agent of God, him of whom the name
even seems now so horrible to you—Death. Yet, believe me, he often spares those who look upon him without
fear. If this your beloved, who rests entirely upon you
and who lives upon your heart, resigns herself to the
idea of dying there, when God requires it, she has so
much the greater chance to live. The hope of immortality does not a little towards prolonging our stay upon
earth.

May we ever retain the strength and authority necessary for these great and solemn moments! May we
ever keep in the right path, and remain, to the one
whom we love, the capable confessor, the natural priest.
Let her who was an altar to the man, who so often
afforded glimpses of the divine, recognise in him, this

day, her mediator through whom is transmitted to her t↓ ‹
pardon of God.

But, even though you were less worthy, even though
you had, in passing through a life of trade, carried off
some of its stains upon you, love would renew you still.
Its flame would consume all that. And you would find
in an unexplored corner of your heart, the grandeur of
divine desire to sustain her who depends solely on you
She is yours, and she has but you with whom to live or
die. Upon you alone does it depend, whether she shall
live, or ascend to her Maker in your arms.

———

I have never understood in what respect the priest
and the physician were distinct from each other. All
branches of medicine are null, blind, and unintelligent,
if they do not begin at complete confession, at resignation to and reconciliation with the general government
of the universe.

Who can do this in the case of a woman ? He who
knows her thoroughly beforehand, and who is herself.
He is the one who was born to be her physician, a physician of the body and of the soul.

These two things, so completely harmonized in them
selves, are inseparable. Let the young man think of
and prepare himself for this. What an immense encou
ragement it will be to him, in his studies of the mind and
of the body, to anticipate the profound happiness he
will feel in being all in all to the object of his love!

———

In the coming age, education (relieved of its useless
features) will always comprise a course of medical
study. The present state of things is absurd. Who·

ever would live must first know what life is, what are its distempers, and what its cures.   These studies, more-over, are such a marvellous discipline to the mind, that he can hardly be called a *man* who has not pursued them.

Even to explain to the physician exactly how we are ill, to make him clearly and unmistakably understand that, we must be three-fourths a physician ourselves.

Most people will tell you that you cannot doctor your-self, nor your family—which amounts to saying, that we are most incapable of treating those whom we know best.   I am, then, guided in this case, rather by what a physician of the South of France said to me : " Never shall my son or wife be treated by any one but myself. Not that some of my compeers may not be more learned than I, but that here I have an immense advantage over all of them—that of knowing completely, from top to bot-tom, the subject to be treated : the child springing from my loins is myself, and the woman finally transformed into me, is also myself."

Individualization is ever progressive.   The ignorant physicking of former times often effected cures; but why? because all things went by large classes, both the sick and the diseases.   In those days, if I may so speak, the people were doctored *by wholesale*.   The class and the trade, indicating the temperament, afforded all the infor-mation that was necessary, and suggested the evil and its remedy.   But now classes are done away with, and so too is doctoring by classes.   Its last glory is he whom I have already mentioned, the illustrious physician of the remains of *la Grande Armée*.

Everything has changed, no one man resembles another everything is special, original, *individual*, very compli cated, and not to be determined beforehand.   Much study is necessary in order to seize this individuality, a long series of observations, an extreme assiduity.   This, and especially the time required, is denied to physicians in large cities.

This enigma, this *individual*, is incurable by whoever does not know him completely, from head to foot, and through and through, in his present and in his past, to him who is not as it were inside of his other self, him who is not another himself.

The more you are one with him, the more able you will be to cure him.

And so, if you have lived long with this woman, if your existence, identical with hers by habit and love, pro- duces each moment in you phenomena similar to those which are passing in her, so that your functions are the revelations of her, you are far advanced in her being, and may decide almost exactly what is fit and what is unfit for her, the real malady, and the possibility of erring.

You are her health, and she is your disease.   When she is cured, she re-enters into her harmony with you.

" What is woman ? Disease."

HIPPOCRATES.

What is woman ? the physician.

The greatest outside doctor you can call, is more than satisfied after a few questions.   He knows nothing of the disease but its crisis.   But that is nothing at all; the life of the patient must be known.   What a stock of time, patience, and let me add genius, would be required to completely confess her ! But could she answer him ? would she dare ? . . . He is often obliged to content himself with very little.

The husband, on the contrary, knows everything.

You smile incredulously ; I assert that even the subtlest dissembler, who manages to conceal certain circumstances from him, cannot, on the whole, prevent him, from the sole fact of their cohabitation, from knowing her entirely. He has noted her, by his finer senses, in all her exterior manifestations.   He knows her in all her internal operations, her months, her days, her hours of steadiness and caprice. He foresees her humors, her thoughts, and even her smallest desires. Who could know the terrible details ? he who loves or has loved, and who, eager and insatiable, has felt all, noted all, that she herself had forgotten. Still more, he has wondrously acted upon her. By their life in common, by fecundation, impregnation, and the profound metamorphosis which accompanies it, *he has made this woman !* The husband is as much of the wife, in this sense, as he is of the child.

He has made her, he can re-make her.

At least if any one can, it is he.

The creator of all things, Love, is also the all-powerful restorer. If once it languished and grew lukewarm, now, in these circumstances, it resumes its old ardor and intensity. Who could help loving the sick woman, who would not give all his heart up to her ? Even if the poor suffering creature has been a little thoughtless, how can you remember it now ? Humiliated under the hands of Nature, so fearful of displeasing, she is in reality more charming than she ever was. She excuses herself, and asks pardon for everything, even for the most innocent things. ,The force of her gratitude inspires her with delightful and touching remarks. Her heart has become quite a different one; great thoughts take possession of it. And this because illness, that severe natural discipline, draws from the soul a refinement that no human culture could have effected. Love is even deepened by · its own humility. At this time, the woman has the timidity of a child, is all love and trembling shame. And how can we help adoring her?

A touching contest this, between love and shame. The latter must yield, however, when they come to the remedies which so frighten women—if it is decided, for instance, that a blister must be applied. She would rather die than suffer that, if she were left to her own will; but she fears worse than death to displease or disobey. "And yet," she adds, "must I let him see me every day in this state? put him to such a trial? Ah! this will be the extinction of all love!"

The poor creature is so humiliated, that, bowed down each day under the loving hand that tends her, she does not even suppose that in her he still sees his wife, and she asks only for compassion. She thinks that desire is done with for ever. And great is her surprise, extreme her emotion, when she sees the flame still burning on, and the glorious ignorance in which Love remains of all that it knows, and all that it sees.

She then begins to understand that great and sovereign power of the heart which changes and transfigures everything, the independence of Love which is thought to be the slave of Nature, but which is also its king.

"What!" she exclaims, "have I still the power of pleasing! What! are my caresses still a happiness to him! My kiss his recompense!"

And behold! she is up again and reanimated. Her womanly royalty returns to her. Health will soon follow.

Everything that appertains to the woman we love is of precious importance. Everything about her charms us, and makes us adore her. Love comes from her by all the senses. Her physical life, taken in its ensemble and without omitting anything, is a universal enchantment. Hence results for her a state of infinite serenity of profound beatitude, the same state of grace that she catches a glimpse of in pregnancy, but now under what more difficult circumstances! To see that all that rendered her afraid and ashamed, all that she would have wished to conceal, is to him a joy and delight—that she is waited on by him, not as an effort of patience, but with desire and transport—is the miracle that saves her. She will live on, in spite of nature.

BOOK FIFTH.

———o———

THE REJUVENESCENCE OF LOVE.

I.

WOMAN'S SECOND YOUTH.

How severe is Nature upon woman! Man, even though ten years older, is in his prime, strengthened in active and productive life, when she is failing. And even now, though beloved, she is no longer the same. Suffering has matured her, and made her look pale. Melancholy hours of reverie come to her in her convalescence. She sighs. For what?—she so beautiful, so touching, so accomplished! For Time, the great artist, the great master in beauty, has given to hers that supreme touch that disarms and melts all hearts. Yes, but even this charm owes its origin to her advancing age. The circulation of life, already less regular, announces to her (from a distance, it is true) that she will be cured of love, which constitutes woman, of that divine rhythm which month by month measured out her time.

Man, on the contrary, who has not suffered from the vital flux and reflux, man who, of love, has had but the happiness, who has not loved as she has (to creation and the point of death), man, relatively speaking, has lived a prosy life. He has worked much and hard, but slept and repaired his forces. The perfect equilibrium of physical receipt and outlay has been maintained in him. He is equal, or superior to, his former self. If he nas had no excesses up to his fortieth year, beyond that he will be found much stronger than before. He has escaped those alternations of health which so try one's youth ; he has hardened himself for life, has taken root in it. And, as life then most certainly goes on by itself, as he lives without knowing that he lives (which is the physical perfection), he often works much more and much better, with a certainty, an infallibility of execution that a young hand never shows. Even among the most prolific of men, those who let out their lives in great floods for the nourishment of the human race, we see that their great works, those which have left their mark upon the world, have appeared at this age. Molière thus gave us the *Tartuffe*; Rousseau, *Emile* and the *Contrat Social*. It was even later in life that Voltaire published the first great product of his genius, that which has created Modern History. So in political life, Sully, Richelieu, Colbert, did nothing great until they were forty.

To sum up, we may say, that at the age when woman has finished her principal work, and is about to lose, or already has lost, her creative faculty, man exercises his with powerful effect. And this in every sense, in love, in business, and in the sphere of thought.

Is it all over with the woman then? Far from it. The charmfulness of heart and beauty, the grace, the brilliant mind, the elevation of her views, of her character, which often come at this age, all announce that she is called to a mysterious duty, more invisible, more inexplicable, more connected, perhaps, with a touching and a holy object. What this will be we cannot tell ; but I warrant you beforehand that it will be a work of love. Seized in the cradle by love, living on and by

t, she will go on till death, always loving more and
more.

Would you know the real cause of her sadness? It is
not her bad health, nor her fleeting youth; neither her
prospectively dreary life, nor even Death, to whom she
has been very near, and who obscures the horizon with
his sombre clouds. What saddens her is the semi-
divorce which, in spite of him and in spite of her, is
made between them by the mere force of circumstances.
He who formerly sacrificed everything, abandoned everything for her, still loves her. She does not doubt it.
But, after all, now that she is better, he rushes off again
to business, labor, and the struggles of life. He is getting old, and has no time to lose. The more pure and
faithful a man is, the more active he is; ever impatient
to move, to do, and to create. He looks forward to
glory, it matters little for what. The proved ability
in matters of grave import, the fidelity with which
fortune favors only those of strong will, are the honor
and glory of the man, the pride of the woman. But we
must confess that it is also a cause of uneasiness to
woman in her middle age. He said, "You will love
me, I am sure; for I shall be great." And he has kept
his word. His successes have made him great. He
knows that she has indirectly contributed much towards
this. Never, without the happiness, the peace of heart,
the mutual comforting that he has found in her, could
he have been each day equal to such efforts. She has
prepared his triumphs for him. And the invincible
strength with which, at the decisive time, he carried off
the prize, he took from her in the morning, when

serene through love, she commanded him to return that night a conqueror.

By the mercy of God all his undertakings have prevailed. He is now powerful and influential in matters of greatest moment. His ship now rides upon the waves, with both wind and tide in its favor. She, seated on the shore, admires him, but follows him no longer. Sometimes her eyes are dazzled, and she can scarcely keep the reckoning of this great and fortunate voyage. Fortunate, did I say? It is far from being so to her loving and faithful heart, which says, " He is off yonder. Oh, that I were with him!" .

Mockery of Fate! When she was younger and less intelligent, in reality even less loving—when she only suffered herself to be loved, when she was nothing but one of God's beautiful creatures, a pleasant thing—she had the unspeakable happiness of being united to him in an apparent oneness; but now that she is an intellectual being, an individual, now when her expanded heart contains an ocean of love, fortune and success hold him apart from her. So far, though so near! One day of glory for him perhaps, and to-morrow her life will have passed away.

In regarding his manly countenance, his powerful frame, all the royal beauty and the vigorous joy that Nature bestows upon the lusty man from whom she still expects great things, his wife admires him, dreams of him, is happy . . . . and sad. Youth is intact in him ; his powers of loving are unimpaired. When the torrent of life is stirred into action will he not return to the illusions of his youth? All think so. Every one believes that the treasure he has at home, that gentle and toucning beauty, that too complete perfection, will not hold him back for ever. On all sides the world of depraved men and equivocal women, by all the means in their power, by intrigue, cunning, audacity, ridicule, irony, everything, work together to disturb the serenity, to break in upon the privacy of the successful man of the day. Is the poor little dove in the cote ignorant of this? No; from a distance she sees enough of it to crush her heart down. What can she do about it? She takes good care not to approach this monster of a world, which frightens her so. The world, which, on its side, has come to her and learned that she is too pure for anything to be hoped from her, turns its back upon her, and goes after a more easy virtue.

Humbled by solitude, she dares not compare herself with the reigning beauties of the day. Those haughty Amazons, whom from afar she sees passing by, she admires sincerely, and not without a little fear. They must be queens, princesses, or at least great ladies, to be caracoling on such splendid coursers. She considers herself defeated beforehand. "Alas! what virtue, what discretion, what heroism of love can resist these Alcinas, these triumphant Clorindas? woe to poor Herminia! . . ."

She is completely ignorant of what her husband, nearer to them, sees: their misery and moral repulsiveness. All the efforts recently made to deck up that pitiful idol of the day, the *kept woman*—a base term of distinction etween *la dame galante* and the woman of the town— nave failed to invest her with beauty. Still ideal, though painfully inconsistent, in *Isidora*, she has sustained a terrible fall to the real in *la Dame aux Camellias*. The

12*

skill and talent of the author have not sufficed to conceal
the shocking inharmoniousness of this creation, a refined
consumptive, who, nevertheless, he tells us, "drinks and
swears like a street-porter."

If our husband, going by chance into his friend's
house, sees his shocking mistress, so gross under all her
elegance, he will remain faithful for ever.

Rousseau was right in making a distinction between
a woman and a lady. Is this a matter of rank and fortune? Not at all. It is a distinction of the heart. I
have seen an old washerwoman who was a lady, and
more than a lady; she would have graced the throne
of the world.

Some day, when the husband returns from visiting the
friend in question, when he has been bored and worn out
with his "little girl," who can talk only after drinking, he
finds his wife surrounded by earnest men who have come
on business. She astonishes them with the extent of
her knowledge and her practical mind. "How is this?"
he asks. "Who has taught her this? .. She knows
everything without having learned it."

How interesting is she at this moment! I have often
had the pleasure of observing the excellence of the wife
when she wished to become the auxiliary of her husband,
when she entered into his ideas and his business, took an
absorbing delight in them, and upheld his opinions with
even more vivacity than he could have brought to bear
on them himself. Far from taking sides against her, I
have joined her, nearly always adding a word to her hus
band's honor, to strengthen their union. I have alway
present to me, in this world, the Religion of Love, and
the desire of propagating it.

Picture then to yourself the happy husband at the mo
ment of his unexpected return, when he sees her fighting
for him. How surprised, how delighted he is! She is
Shakespeare's Desdemona, with a helmet on. He smiles
as he embraces her, saying like Othello: "O, my fair
warrior!"

But these word-combats are nothing to her. How
happy would she be to really aid him. Is she not as a
younger brother to him? She has his movements, his
gestures, his handwriting even. If he has gone to bed
late and sleeps a little longer than usual, he does not
find her beside him in the morning. At his desk sits
some one who has quietly got up at four o'clock, and is
writing his urgent letters. And this is apparently some
one who fully understands his thoughts, knows or divines
everything. A scholar of his perhaps, or a charming
little secretary? Style her what you will.

She has taken both sexes upon herself, and in her timid
audacity are combined the charms of the young man
and the child. Her thirty-six years are but as fifteen.
But the docile scholar, if he but deserve it, will be
transformed into the loving and obedient woman. In
the morning he wakes up, and not seeing her beside
him, is alarmed and calls to her. The pen is thrown
aside, and M. le Secretaire hastens to his bedside, an humble page.

How he is affected by this! He gently draws her towards him. But in her chasteness she seats herself on
the side of the bed. In a sacred transport, he would
pour out his heart to her, place it in her hand, disclose
to her, at last, the mysteries of his art, or the secrets of
his business. "Why can I not suppress time for you!"

he exclaims, " do away with the long succession of efforts and thoughts, with which we buy so dearly the results of life ! give you, without fatigue, the world and its science ! infuse it all in a kiss !" But, almost at the first word, he sees the miracle performed. God accords to purity a singular gift of intelligence. Her sense of right, which no lie, no corrupting sophism, has ever warped, enables her to seize at once the very essence of the abstruse enigma. How surprised is he ! how happy is she ! In her childish vivacity she exclaims: " I have understood you then !"

But nothing that she touches can fail to be embellished thereby. She timidly essays to take up what he has just said ; into what seems dry and tame, she infuses her womanly grace and the freshness of nature. It is as if the barren sea-shore, gladdened by a brook, should suddenly bloom with flowers.

A delicious discovery it is, to see her for the first time unfold to a loving eye her infinite mystery of grace, which, with a certain maiden modesty, she had always kept back. This virginity, reserved for the present moment, and which could not reveal itself before she now gives up, and offers it to love—the unlooked for flower of the soul.

II.

SHE PRESCRIBES AND REGULATES HIS DIET AND HIS RECREATIONS.

SEEING her so obedient, so docile, and so attentive a pupil, following out her husband's ideas and treasuring up his words, you imagine that he is master in everything. It is exactly the contrary.

Now that she is himself, imbued and impregnated with him, now that she is his soul (and his soul reserved pure), it is greatly to his interest that she should administer, rule, and reign in the house.

To speak frankly, he is no longer capable of this. The hurly-burly of life, the increased action, has so hustled him along from day to day, that his little interior world becomes almost foreign to him. This is an effect of the progress of the age, of absorption in a special business; it is even the effect of success: the man, as if in a vertigo, gets farther and farther away from himself. What would become of him if he should give himself up entirely to this centrifugal movement? if the centre should fail him, if the fixed point to which nature obliges him to return each day for a new supply of strength, should become vacillating, and no longer afford him support or rest? Yet may all this be observed in the house where the wife, the sure guardian of the man, does not keep watch over his fireside.

Strange is the inconsistency of the times. If the object be to outshine our fellows, to amass a fortune,

every one is what is called *positive*, that is grossly material. If it be a question of supplying or renewing the
strength and activity by which we shine or make money,
we have all the indifference of a spiritualist, who believes that he owes nothing to the body but everything
to the mind. We are generally fed by our servants,
that is to say, our enemies; or what is still worse, by
those great cooking laboratories which daily supply the
same food to thousands of men, all differing in health,
temperament, and social position, having each different
necessities. What is wholesome food for one is poison
to another.

If you despise the body thus (though it is the indis-
pensable agent of your faculties), respect your mind,
your judgment, which, you must know, are day by day
influenced by your diet. We must drop pride, and
speak of things as they are. Your cook governs you.
The unhealthy and irritating food that she has given
you for dinner will to-night disturb your stomach, and
thence your mind. To-morrow, or later, by its inward
irritation, it will impel you to hasty and violent resolu-
tions, perhaps to some act of libertinism or egregious
folly.

I maintain, Gentlemen " on 'Change," that it is the
influence of food, more than any forethought of your
own, which, holding dominion over your moods, decides
the rise and fall of stocks.

I who have always defended the rights of the mind,
must here be permitted to speak of these matters of
plain common sense, which every one else talks about
but idly, as everything is talked about nowadays, without even a thought of remedy.

To the evil Circe who transforms men into beasts, we
must oppose the good Circe, who will transform beasts
into men. . This good Circe is the loving and foreseeing
wife, who day by day expends her solicitude upon your
physical life, who knows no duty so noble, so imperative,
so sacred, as the preservation of the one whom she loves.
She would leave an important letter, an urgent and
serious work in which she had been engaged, to help
you, if a superior task required her presence—the pre-
paration of the dishes which are to refresh you at dinner.

She does not readily trust to that stupid and careless
girl, who will irritate your stomach, or feed you on
mere nothings, tickling your palate instead of renewing
your strength. She will put her own hands to the work,
those hands so royally beautiful, that nature seems to
have made them solely for the homage and the kisses
of kings. Your life is her life; who then has more interest than she in renewing your strength? She will
slight nothing to this end. For whom then is the first
smile of re-blooming nature, if not for her? It is for
you to repay her in love.

She has constantly before her eyes, in her memory, and
in her heart, the complete balance and poise of your
life; she sees clearly your material equilibrium, and the
equilibrium of your forces—all your expenditures in labor,
in words, or in exercise, to which she makes your appe-
tites subordinate. We have ample reason, while scolding
a little, to call her *economical*. Of what is she most
economical?—money? No, but of that of which she
speaks the least, of that which concerns herself. She
is your never-resting physician, but one who administers a preventive medicine, who is ever cautious and

moderate, and who especially takes care that by spend ing little, and gaining a great deal, repairing always largely, you shall remain equal, more than equal, to the exigencies of your profession. It is love that, at her expense, makes you admired in society, for the intense brilliancy of your glances, your vigorous life, your energetic activity.

In nothing that relates to love is she ignorant. She knows, as well as any one, not only the nutritive value of varieties of food, but the time required for their digestion—some rapid in their action, others, on the contrary, slow, but which will exert a powerful influence in time. She also knows perfectly well that strong and exciting food will not act with its full power on the day that it is required, if it is not preceded, a few days before, by a simpler diet which shall restore the organs to their youthful susceptibility, and augment their powers of assimilation.

———

So anxious is she in this matter, that she often watches her husband eating, instead of eating herself. With all her respect for him she does not trust him entirely. The man who comes home, having spent much vital force during the day, is naturally too anxious to restore it to take any heed to the means. Devoted to works of strength, every man has animal inclinations; he wants tonics—often too much of them. She, who is not fatigued, having much more temperance and judgment, does her best to check him in this error, to deceive him a little, if necessary. People admire women without art; for my part, I like them to have a great deal of it, all sorts of pious ruses with which love inspires them for our happiness.   This woman, so pure and chaste, who takes such good care of. him, would not, however, hesi · tate to sacrifice herself, if need be, in order to turn his mind to other matters ; she is his nurse after all.   And if the child is not reasonable, it is better for her, without making any disturbance, to play the child a little herself.   This tender hindering, which surprises and charms him (especially through his vanity), makes him think that the most sensible woman has sometimes her weak moments, while in reality it is at this very time that her loving intelligence performs its well-considered office, as a mentor and a physician.

Women do not know their power, or else they do not care to employ it in the interests of the family.   For it is certain, that with a husband of uniform habits, who is in good health, and neither has, nor wishes for, any outside attachment, she can at certain times do anything she pleases.   Man's love is impatient and incapable of waiting ; hence it is easily brought to terms.   The generating crisis, which in woman occurs every twenty days, solemn and painful, and much less exacting, returns to man every four days (if we assume the average given by Haller).   And this is not, as is believed, a mere requirement of pleasure, but an actual necessity of a mental and physical renewing.   If this be not fulfilled, it leaves the whole organism in a state of heavy dejection and discomposure ; the vital fluid deprived of issue, is like a pestilent stagnation.   True life is in action.   Woman, who is often sickly, exhausted by confinement and habitual loss of vitality, seldom understands the very different constitution of man, whose strength, subject

to no exhaustion, remains uncontracted, hence the per
sistence of desire, which he experiences often at a very
late period of life. He soon fatigues and wearies her.
He is frequently put off without pity or consideration,
and sometimes with ridicule.

In short, they so manage things that, not to annoy
an already faded wife, he takes a young mistress.

What has created, and set up against wives, the *Dame
aux Camellias?* Their own haughty prudishness.

When the husband hazards a word of love in the
evening, you say to him, "How silly you are! You are
jesting!" No, Madame, he is often very much in
earnest; he suffers, and requires forgetfulness. He
has need of that sweet and maternal consolation
which woman owes to the labors of man. It is
he who braves for you the great battles of this life,
whose repose and pleasures you enjoy. He needs to
forget his business cares, the injustice and tyranny of his
employer, the intrigue and calumny of his rivals. A
kiss from you, a smile from you, a sweet return of affection, a sympathy for his efforts, in short the happiness of
that mental and material union which renews the worn-
out soul, is what he needs.

"But, my dear, at our age" (they are perhaps forty
years old), "now that we have grown-up children! It
is ridiculous."

He has seen her all the evening appear youthful and
agreeable for a pretentious fool, on whom she has lavished her sweetest smiles; but now she calls herself old.
He takes her at her word, and goes off elsewhere.

He goes away, not only denied, but mortified. In

mar.y cases the divorce may be dated from that evening. He avoids her, he hates her. The change is often a rapid one. To-morrow he has a mistress, and launches forth into another life. Woe to his wife and children!

She will say, perhaps, "Why accuse me? I know perfectly well to what I am bound by the commandments of God and of the Church, by the marriage vow I was to give him children, and I have given them. I have refused to do no duty that I owed him. I undergo everything that must be undergone. But I will do nothing for empty pleasure, for amusement, for caprice."

Do you think that dreary passiveness, which, even in the embrace, communicates a death-like coldness, is acceptable; that the cool irony which observes, criticizes, and even sneers, in this sacred moment, is regarded as reciprocation? . . . . No: rather is it the solitude of solitudes, a divorce in complete union, despair! . . . . . What celibacy is not better than this? Rather settle the matter like Origène, and let the sword end it.

We know that she is chaste with her husband; but now how is she with others? Are we sure that what is denied to him is not granted to a friend?

You, Madam, who know how to measure out happiness in such nice proportions, listen to this:

The mother asks the child, in helping him to sweetmeats, how much he wants? He answers: "I want *too much*." Every time that preserves had been given to him, he had been told that more than *that* would be *too much*. And it is just this "too much" that he wants.

It is just so with love; *enough* does not satisfy it at all

"But," you ask, " does this *too much* mean those ex traordinary and humiliating things that the ancient casuist grants so liberally to conjugal exigencies—which so lower the woman, by giving her over completely to the senseless caprice of her husband ?"

Have no such fear.   To the clever, amiable, innocently gay and loving woman, this *too much*, which frightens you so, is often very little.   Often it is such a trifle that she would scarcely dare to speak of it; it would appear so silly, the merest child's play.

The more intense, care-laden, planning and combat ing, that a man's life is out of doors, the more kind comforting he requires at home.   A sensible woman knows what he needs at these times.   She knows that he does not consider her less thoughtful, less worthy in reality, for any playfulness she may treat him to; on the contrary, the more he finds her even so, the more pleased he is at the contrast.   He feels her affection in this, and he is soothed by it.   That this dear partner, whom he knows to be so zealous for his sake, should suddenly forget all other affairs, and be alive but to one alone, that of consoling, entertaining, and amusing him, affects him powerfully.   He laughs, but he is touched by it.   A loving word, an unlooked-for caress, the familiarity of some little action in which the young girl again appears, will have wonderful effect.   No seriousness nor sorrow can withstand them.   Never did the changing sea, in the dark hour when you could see only clouds overhanging it, present, in the shifting of the wind, so lovely a clearing-up.

Woman is not formed, as we are, in the uniformity of an educational mould.   It is this which leaves her, at every period of life, beautiful in instincts, in surprises, in unlooked-for graces. She has wonderful originality. The simplest has in her often, endless responses to nature, hidden and secret beauties, a smartness and charming-ness of reply, a youthful and pretty movement, that her husband in ten, twenty years, has never shown. Such a one, though long married, does not the less retain a certain relative innocence, forgetting (through frivolity, if you choose) all that would have faded her and made her old. She remains new, in one sense, and being pressed by love, replies with singular artlessness, and a charming ignorance of what she has learned every day of her life.

This cannot be imitated. The innocence of the wife is a mystery of the holy of holies, which no one out of it can imagine. All other women are premeditated, or are unconstrained only in the ugliness of intoxication. But she who is yours for life, without any thought for the future, with no reserve of coquetry, gives herself up to nature in complete sincerity, and is thereby so much the more beautiful, more touching and delicious. Hers is not the cat's play, nor the calculated obscenity, nor the false and discordant graces of your cold mistresses, whose hearts are like a violin, without a soul, squeaking under the bow. The sweet sportiveness of a woman who laughs, frolics, and says, " I am silly; but what of that, if it is for you ?" is the Divine Comedy, the secret Christmas carol of marriage, of which you will find elsewhere but a dismal counterfeit. This laughing grace, which we so adore in little children, is in a different way charming (because unexpected) in the young wife—so discreet in the absence of him she loves, and so grave to all chance-comers. Everyone says: "She is not cheerful; perhaps he renders her unhappy." But when he returns, she feels herself at ease, and gaily locks the door.

------- >< -------

III.

SHE REFINES HIS MIND, OR INSPIRES IT.

Savages are afraid of pleasure. "It hamstrings a man," they say. Of course, if a warrior were about to start off fasting on a hunt of two hundred leagues over the snow, as often happens, or to be chased to the death by a hostile tribe—in such trying circumstances he would do wisely to husband his strength.

In the civilized state it is different. If love weakens the animal force, and that material imagination which, under the influence of the blood, inspires the mind with its grosser fancies, in return it refines the nicer faculties of a man. The contact of a pure and beloved woman, whose heart throbs responsive to your own, communicates something of the moral excellence of her sweet serenity. The mind is harmonized thereby; the days are gloriously clear. The sanguine flood, and its companion, that carnal and animal poetry which belongs to the temperament, are for the moment suppressed; and the fantastic clouds, with which they obscured the mind, rolling away, disclose to you the Real in an intensity of light. Logic, and the faculties of observation and of analysis, that trinity of Invention, have their complete freedom and fertility.

For whatever requires continuousness, and is to be attained by pursuing a long train of thought, successive problems of the known and the unknown, a harmonious condition is needed; this is procured only by subduing that plethora of life which would retard all progress. The feverish mirages which this occasions, make us absurdly poetic or pitifully fanciful, turn us to the right or to the left, and cause us constantly to wander from the right road to the truth. Nothing obscures the mind more than this rutting, or the sickly and negative condition of complete abstinence—a condition really impotent, for virility then paralyses or devours itself.

There is no doubt that the great drags on life are desire and virility. But, that these may bear fruit, their ruggedness must be grafted on the softness of the feminine organization. What a miracle does nature here perform! Genius, arrested yesterday on the road to invention by one of those problems to which there seems no solution, having turned it over on every side, at last gives it up in despair, and sadly sits down by the fire. *She* soon observes his sadness: "Why, what is the matter with you?" she asks. "I cannot bear to see you looking so sad. Let your ideas alone; forget all about it, I pray you, and be happy now." It is precisely this moment of forgetfulness and happiness which has changed everything. His insight is renewed, his powers refreshed, he is newly electrified for performance. He has become another man. How is this? Magnetized by the woman, by that natural grace and amiable facility which she has, and communicates to all, he laughs at the slight obstacle which had impeded him the day before.

Being at Montpellier, I was inspired with religious feeling on seeing an old and stained sheet of paper, a fly-leaf from a book of Puget's, where, among some indistinct sketches, he had written at the top of the page these lines of the old poet:

> "Casta placent superis. Castâ cum mente venito,
> Et manibus puris, sumito fontis aquam."

I experienced such emotion as one feels in entering a great church or a Roman tomb, or the amphitheatre at Arles. It is evident that this man, whose mission it was to express the suffering soul of a century, in beginning his work makes to God and to his art his voluntary sacrifice. He feels that he is responsible, and he longs to be strong and worthy.

Every work of his is a sigh. Was it Milo caught in the oak? was it the broken down and suffering Atlases of Toulon, or the poor little Andromeda, swooning with pain even in her preservation, that he dreamed over then? I know not. But I see that then he gathered himself up, and concentrated his energies, asking strength of pure love, to create those everlasting works which will for ever fill all hearts with tenderness and pity.

Human art has no processes of its own, no power but to imitate divine art. What has the latter done, and what is it doing? From the great torrent of life Love creates generations of men, the whole ascending progress of races. And with a concentrated drop from this torrent it has created, and still creates, the world of invention and all the procession of ideas.

At what price is this concentration of vital force, through abstinence from pleasure, fruitful in works of thought? On the supreme condition of its being free. A sacrifice is only a sacrifice in being truly voluntary. Liberty alone deserves; liberty alone is fruitful.

Captive love, entrenched in walls, chaste in spite of itself, is barren. It turns against itself. Its flame but adds to its torture, and never grows. The boasted age of celibacy (the Middle Ages) was only productive of really great results in married men. Abailard was married; so was Dante. The Free-Masons, who have found and realized their proper art, lived around the churches in families, and continued those great works from century to century by hereditary labor.

Marriage is the only thing which at once supplies Genius with its two essential powers: harmony by pure happiness, and at times brilliancy by voluntary abstinence, and a free postponement of pleasure.

The beauty and efficacy of this sacrifice lie in its freedom, and in that it results from the mutual understanding and perfect unanimity of two persons who love each other.

Woman is very noble in this instance. She desires man to be strong, useful, and productive. Individual love is sacrificed to a greater love, and so shares its grandeur.

Here the two souls are the same. The gratitude of posterity must not separate them.

Puget was married, and in his palpitating works one perceives sensibly how much it must have cost him.

13

You may trace there the heart, the magnetizing purity, of a wife who desired him to love in art, to bestow upon marble the love he would have given to her, the excess of life's essence. She was not jealous of the charming Andromeda, but immolated herself to her rival. When the great artist, burning with the sacred fire, rose to write the lines you have just read, I imagine I hear the voice of that sainted wife, saying: "My love, remember Andromeda, and let us reserve all our energies for her. Love her, for she is my child!"

He did well to write: "Purity pleases God." It helps us to imitate God, and to create like Him.

But purity is not a savage isolation. It is increased, at times, by contact with what is pure. Who has not passed one of those troubled nights when an inward storm rages; when the mind, pitifully oppressed by shameful desires, flounders in the mire? Fortunately, dawn comes at last; beside you you see innocence and serenity. She opens her eyes, smiles—and all evil spirits take flight. Your dreams you dare not tell; you wish to forget them. In love's holy chalice you find all your former self, your soul, your virtue, your intelligence, with a ray of the dawn, with a pearl of the dew.

The pure woman, in whom her husband has set up his altar, who is united to him in heart, who thinks and desires as he does, has in her a strange mystery of spiritual fruitfulness which no one has yet described. What the fable tells of the Son of the Earth, who, to regain his strength, had but to touch the maternal bosom, she realizes to the letter. She is really Nature, loving, kind, and holy, who, by mere physical contact, by the virtue

of love, starts a flood of mental life. If you have a
great thought, tell it to her in the evening, or at night.
Happy in your confidence, happy in the hope of seeing
you attain still greater eminence, she is thrilled, her
heart is full of joy, and she embraces you. This is a
sacred moment; respect it. Your heart is rich in its
fulness; keep it exalted. Arise in the kingliness that
he feels who is loved ; arise with the proud sentiment of
preserving your love entire. Only to have touched your
divinity is happiness enough for that day.

The austere joy of sacrifice, the charm of paradise,
both these powers are with you. Now you may
say : "To-day I am in force, I can do whatsoever I
will."

So the Reuss or the Rhone, those swift Alpine
streams, in traversing the beautiful lakes which detain
them momentarily, do not so end their courses. They
gather there immense scope and power. Re-issuing,
nothing is impossible to them. Changed to a brilliant
blue, they roll on, mirroring in their bosoms the
sublime scenery, and the beautiful skies which overhang
them.

IV.

THERE ARE NO OLD WOMEN.

VASARI made a singular remark about the old master
Giotto, the creator of Italian art. " He was the first to
put goodness into the expression of heads."

The lustre of goodness is the soul of modern art. Its works affect our hearts precisely in the proportion that they are expressive of goodness.

The noble Madonnas of Raphael are admired as pictures; but who was ever in love with them? On the other hand, the Magdalen of Titian (a simple head, of Venice), a fisherman's girl, good, pretty, and strong, though not very young, is so touching in her tears, that you at once exclaim, "Who could have the heart to afflict such a good creature? Speak, say what you will! I should so like to console you!"

Titian preferred to paint beautiful women at thirty. Rubens goes without difficulty as far as forty, and beyond. Van Dyck does not recognise age at all; with him, art is free. He entertained a sovereign contempt for time. That powerful magician, Rembrandt, does more: by a gesture, a look, a smile, he banishes all age. The life, the goodness, and the intelligence, suffice to charm us: "What was the model?" Adorable! " And beautiful?" I do not remember; I have forgotten entirely.

The ignorant art of the Middle Ages held that youth and beauty were synonymous. For the mother of Christ, it gives us stiff and insipid little girls. The great painters of modern times, being very intelligent observers, soon saw that beauty, like everything else, needs time to become perfect and complete. They were the first to discover the mystery, unknown to antiquity, that face and form do not reach the fulness of their beauty at the same time. The first is faded, when the second is in full bloom.

The habit we have of judging woman by that which fades the soonest (the face), is a serious cruelty. But

with us, in France especially, where the mobile physiog
nomy, the quick eye, the graceful, smiling and eloquent
mouth, are in constant agitation, the muscles, quickly
trained to every movement, have a flexibility and sup-
pleness opposed to the fixed and tense firmness of
Northern beauty. A French woman has a thousand
tricks and changes of feature to every ten of the German woman. Then the face soon grows *weary*. Is that
as much as to say that our flesh is less firm? On
the contrary, a wound for which the German woman
would require surgical aid, in the French woman cures
itself.

It is not a rare thing for the body of the latter to be
twenty-five and her face forty—wrinkles form around
her eyes, and in her cheeks; while on the other hand
her knees and elbows, which were formerly angular,
have now pretty little dimples. The same contrast is
visible in the skin: in the face, where it has been
stretched by the constant play of the muscles, it has
already grown rougher; while everywhere else, delicately filled out, it is still young, and combines the lovely
hues of the lily and the rose.

This fullness of form does not produce a sensual effect,
as much as might be believed. It has also its moral influences. It is singularly favorable to the augmentation
and display of that expression of goodness which the
woman often wears when, untroubled by rivalries and
feminine crosses, she follows the kindly instincts of a
sympathetic heart. Her beautiful white arms, her exquisitely rounded and delicate chin, an inexpressible tenderness everywhere visible in her, present the most
charming idea of maternity. Not the exclusive mater

nity cf a young wife, wholly concentrated on her child, and often indifferent to everything else ; but an extreme kindliness towards everybody. This is manifested in her looks and caresses; and, if there be any work of charity to do, any unfortunate to help, in the moist eye, and the agitation of a bosom rich with pity and love.

It is a very bad sign of the times when the men do not appreciate this beauty of goodness—a hateful time, indeed, in which, having no longer the need of recipro- city, and really seeking only solitary pleasure, they demand it of the youngest of the young; and, by an accursed climax, of childhood itself.

These barbarians are punished in more ways than one. They become more and more barbarous, gross in man- ners and in language. A generation which does not spring from women of standing, is a generation of boors.

Selfish, cruel, and brutal love eats out everything, like aqua-fortis. Where it has once passed, nothing is left ; that place is barren for ever after.

And after all, to come to what their depraved tastes, their vile and impotent fancies, look for and require even at the price of crime, the poor young victim has nothing in reality to satisfy these fierce exactions. Badly nou- rished and of meagre form, what, alas! can she give but pain ?

As for the gay and splendid daughters of luxury and notoriety, of the theatre and the promenade, who pick your very bones, are you sure that those beauties, with their bacchanalian revels, their infernal lives, their sleep- less nights, could bear comparison in another Judgment of Paris, with the lady who, discreet and pure, has

always led a sober life?   If such insolent *lionnes* were
even twenty years younger, they would still be humiliated.

Besides, a lady is always a lady.   Her natural elegance,
the harmony which is in her, suffices to enchain the heart
more powerfully than the "*half* lady" can ever hope to
do, whose harmony is easily disturbed by any trifling
vexation.

In the Middle Ages, the grand lady, whom the little
page always waited upon on his knees, or whose train he
bore, was infallibly both young and beautiful.   For her
were his imagination, his emotions first aroused.   It is
the same in all times.   The fine lady of to-day, who, at
her morning toilet, among laces and perfumes, thinks it
of little consequence to give an order or a note to her
young attendant, even though she be quite mature and
almost old, often sets his heart throbbing ; she is young
for him in that elegance and perfume, from which he de-
parts like one intoxicated.

Who is deceived then—the child or his mistress?
Perhaps it is not he.   His instinct tells him that in his
lady, who has lost somewhat of her external splendor
and visible charm, there yet resides a great power which
she can still exercise.   *There are no old women ;* every
one of them, at no matter what age, if she is good and
loving, treats man to a glimpse of the infinite.   And not
alone the infinite of the moment—often that of the future.   She breathes upon him, and it is a gift.   All who
see him afterwards say, without being able to explain it,
' What! is he possessed ?   He is a born genius."

There were numberless Rousseaus before Rousseau, all

cunning and eloquent reasoners; and yet not one of them
attracted the world's attention.   A woman breathes
upon *this one*, with love, maternal love, and Jean Jacques
is the result.

V.

AUTUMNAL ASPIRATIONS.

AT the close of September (while I am writing this),
the year is ripe.   It reaches its completion not only in
the harvest, but in all its other harmonies, in the perfect
temperature, and the perfect balance of night and day.
The sky and the earth correspond; veiled by the morning mist, the sun rises late, as if it had not much to do ;
and every one seems also to have finished his work.   It
is as though it were Sunday, or the repose of evening.   And what is autumn, after all, but the evening of
the year?

Beautiful season!—at once pleasant and pensive.   A
few flowers yet remain, but they drop off one by one.
The aster resists the season's advance.   The cold, splendid dahlia still struggles on, through all October, despite
the morning frost.   The swallows sail around and around
in the air, calling to each other.   In the north, the Stork,
having on one foot gravely planned his journey, prepares
to desert his favorite haunts.

All this is much more impressive in places by the sea,

which is near them, without being seen from them, so
that you cannot behold its sublime scenes, but can
hear its sublime voice. The earth, already in repose and
silence, hearkens to the lamentations and the wrath of
old Ocean, who strikes upon the beach, recoils and strikes
again, in solemn iteration—that deep bass which one
hears, less with the ear than with the breast, which
strikes the shore more lightly than it does the heart of
man. Melancholy warning, with the measured appeal
of the pendulum of Time!

I see yonder a lady (the one whom this book found
in her youth, and has accompanied to her declining
age), walking pensively in a small garden; it is already
stripped of its blossoms, but sheltered, like those we see
behind our cliffs in France, or in the lowlands of Holland.
The exotics have already been placed in the green-house.
The fallen leaves have unveiled the statues near them,
which afford increased pleasure now that the flowers are
gone. These are luxuries of art, which somewhat
contrast with the very simple yet modest and dignified
toilet of the lady—a blond or grey silk, relieved only by
a lilac ribbon.

Though without ornament, she is none the less elegant:
elegant for her husband, and simple to the profit of
the poor.

She reaches the end of the walk and turns round.
We have now an opportunity to observe her. But have
I not seen her already in the museums of Amsterdam
or the Hague? She recalls to me one of Philip de
Champagne's ladies—one who took possession of my
heart at first sight, so frank yet so chaste, intelligent but
simple-minded, having no subtilty with which to keep

clear of the snares of the world. This woman has clung to me for thirty years, persistently returning, making me concerned for her, and forcing me to ask myself what was her name? What became of her? Was she happy here in this world? And how did she get through life?

She reminds me of another portrait, a Van Dyck, a poor pale and sickly lady. The white-satinness of her incomparably delicate skin adorns a body which is wasting away. In her beautiful eyes is a deep melancholy—that of age, of the heart's sorrows, or perhaps of the climate. Hers is the vague and far-reaching look of a person who has always had before her eyes the vast Northern Ocean, the great grayish sea, utterly deserted save by the sea-gull in his flight.

———

But let us return to the one here. If I did not fear to disturb her quiet meditations, I would say: Are you also melancholy, Madame? What can be wrong with you, who are so discreet, so sensible and so resigned?

"What is it, sir?" she answers—"That which everything feels at this time, a desire for the great passage, a need of taking flight. But I have no beautiful wings—neither the white sails of the swan, nor the false wings of the swallow. I am held down, held tightly here. God calls me, and yet I feel myself bound to my nest. Bound by whom? by God himself. This is the discrepancy in my nature. These birds are happy; they emigrate in families. We, almost always, one by one, make a solitary migration towards the other life. In life we were together, but we start out alone on the unknown journey. Age brings fear and sadness to those who

love. I hope, believe and trust. I shall die only to live
again. But, alas! if in that second life I should not see
my beloved!

" Do you wish to know more of my melancholy? I
am sad at being still so imperfect. He calls me his sanctuary, and how little do I deserve the name! I had
wished to retain for him the true purity of childhood,
a virgin treasure of wisdom, a place of repose which
should be the paradise of his heart. I had wished to
pluck a thorn each day from this garden of his, and
add to it a flower. This culture has resulted poorly,
and I am no longer capable of anything."

These are her dilemmas, the questions and the answers that she imagines, while walking up and down,
such the misgivings which at this moment have wrinkled
her beautiful brow—a brow so pure that time respects
it, and dares not touch it yet.

Is this really all? Is this sadness explained solely by
these thoughts of the future, these high aspirations towards supreme perfection? I, who know you, Madame,
having seen you when you were yet very young, dare
to say that your heart contains a secret and keeps it.
You seem afraid of saddening your husband? Or might
we believe that a woman always retains, even late in
life, a little timidity at confessing certain things?

" You will have it then?" she replies. " Frankly, the
thought that so saddens and weighs me down is that to-
morrow I shall be old. . . . . .

" I am not a fool, to revolt against God's will. What
should I care for growing old, if I were alone? But I
love, and am still loved. Love is a double mystery. It
is not of the mind alone; something else is needed. Is

not the happiness conferred upon me by a faithfu., loving, and inexhaustibly youthful husband, an embarrassing
thing when I feel the progress of time? It is for his
sake that I would retain some portion of that which first
pleased him. He has always had in me (he said so himself) a renewing of the heart, a feast of life. His illusion
continues, not mine. I dare not tell him my thoughts,
my uneasiness. If I keep silent, if I continue to receive
the adoration of which I am so little worthy, I shall be
vexed with, and accuse, myself of being vain and false.
His love and admiration humiliate me; it seems to me
that his transports are for another, not for me."

"You may rest assured, Madame, that the touching
humility, the solicitude, the emotional and graceful tenderness which desires to bestow without stint, is a stimulus to love. The older one grows, the more he sees that
the most truly charming woman is she who feels most,
who gives herself up without reservation, and is unhappy
because she has nothing more to give.

"It is this, too, which accounts for that ardent constancy that so astonishes you. Who would not love a
modest, simple woman, who is ignorant of her own goodness, who sees nothing of her own merits, and always
imagines that she is tolerated and excused? What a
happiness is it for the man to deny this; and who would
not feel the necessity of constantly reassuring her?

"What do you regret? The beauty of complexion
and feature that you received by the chance of birth,
like a reflection from your mother—the happy accident
of that period through which we all pass? But the rare
and peculiar beauty that you possess in yourself, your
visible soul, you have created by a pure life, a noble

and unbroken harmony. It is the light of love, like the soft and faithful lamp, in transparent alabaster, which watches over us by night."

When will man learn that he is his own sculptor? It is his task to make himself beautiful. Socrates was born as ugly as a satyr; but by his deep thought, by the sculpture of reason, virtue, and self-sacrifice, he so reconstructed his face, that at last a god saw himself therein, and the Phaedon shone with him.

I have seen a second instance of this phenomenon in one of my most illustrious friends, the first linguist of this century. When a boy, he had all the mean ugliness of a little Norman peasant; but his powerful will, his immense labor and ingenious research, traced in his face lines of exquisite delicacy. All Persian refinements hovered about his lips with the subtle turns of Western criticism, while the genius of India expanded itself in the luminous beauty of his grand forehead, capacious enough to hold the world.

Madame, permit me to tell you frankly that you were only pretty, you were not beautiful at first, but you are now. And why? Because you have loved.

Others allow themselves to be loved; but you have loved, and always sculptured your love in kindness, purity, fidelity, and sacrifice. In return, it has made you beautiful.

The best of us, both men and women, are born with a certain fresh and rugged vigor, if I may so express it, or else with a something of dryness and barrenness. Children, through ignorance or otherwise, are cruel in their nature. Young people of both sexes, if they are

not cruel, are at least colder-hearted than they them
selves believe. Desire to them seems love. The ardor
of the blood and of the temperament they call tender.
ness. But ever their rude, abrupt, violent deportment,
their frivolous or ironical speeches, their vain or contemptuous expressions of countenance give the lie to all grace,
and say plainly : "The heart is not yet touched."

Time, trials, sorrows bravely endured, and love, faith.
ful love, are required to give grace of heart, and what
is its exact equivalent, grace of speech and ways, in
gesture and in bearing.

This is the true, the charming youth, which, however,
begins late.

You were not young, Madame; but you are going to
become so.

It has been scarcely observed, I think, that a number
of pretty and graceful—hence youthful—things are impossible to youth.

The young girl, a semi-captive, captive to a single
thought, awaiting a change of situation, thinks but of
love and marriage—that is to say, of herself; she has
neither the sentiment nor the grace of charity. As a
young wife, while nursing her children, or at least assiduous in her attentions to them, all her mind is in the
cradle; and if she gives to the poor, she says: "Pray
for my son."

To her whose heart is more free from this concentration, every suffering creature is as her own child. She
is radiant with kindliness and active charity. She cur
tails all her expenses to be able to dispense free hospital
ity in her house; and at her simple but abundant table

she would like to seat all the kingdom of God. She goes out in search of the poor, gives them money, and best of all, comforts them. She weeps with those who are in affliction. And then how beautiful she is! How I should like to kiss her hands!

Her husband frequently catches her in the very act of charity. A convalescent invalid, or a woman recovered from confinement, enters accidentally and betrays her secret. She is embarrassed—their mal-à-propos benedictions disclosing her concealed goodness, that bashfulness of charity which dared not confess its weakness. He smiles and says: "Ah! so I have caught you at it again, have I!"

Some day he finds her blushing. Why? A young servant girl has committed a fault, and the wife, fearing that she will be too severely scolded, tacitly intercedes for her with a supplicating look.

But the occasion on which every man would be captivated by her, is when, surrounded by a party of young people of both sexes, she makes such kind and skilful exertions to set off the young girls to the best advantage. She draws something graceful out of these poor, dumb things, emancipating them by a sign or an apt word. She is very far from being jealous. She loves them, and by her own love evokes love from hearts which would have been the last to be roused. The one who is too timid to either move or speak, she draws towards her, makes a sort of pet dove of her, embraces and kisses her. Then that young creature appears charming. . . . And as for the wife, heaven is in her eyes!

VI.

IS UNITY SECURED?

WE have brought to light something which had not previously been felt:

That the advance of time, the succession of years, which was thought to be fatal to love, is its natural and necessary development; each additional year strengthens it, and after its manner, confirms and secures the bond, sustains and strengthens it. It was but a gossamer before,· but in the end it becomes a cable that will defy a tempest.

———

Love has then won the victory. Time is his servant, and works for him. We may then close up this book.

No, not yet. The last difficulty is now to be approached. It is that this conqueror of conquerors has nevertheless an obstacle to encounter—in himself.

An insurmountable obstacle perhaps, since it is in the very essence of love.

How shall we unite if we are one? To unite *we must remain two.*

As long as life lasts, in the completest union, there will be necessarily a shade of separation. *She* will always be a woman, and she will be loved the more on that account. She will have, however thoughtful she may be, approaches to childish innocence; and for these she will be adored.

She would suppress this distinction entirely. I see

her (and it is a touching sight) examining herself, asking herself what more she can do to please him, to agree
still better with him, to form a closer union with him?
There is but one obstacle to this: she is a woman.

There will always be a difference between them—a
difference which is diminished by age, by the will, and
by increase of love, but has nevertheless not yet disappeared.

Woman is beauty—much tenderness, a little weakness, modesty, timidity, changefulness, a confiding trust
in the future, innumerable delightful turns (of style and
movement as well as of form); in short, she is all beauty
and grace. All this is the very opposite to that right
line of precision and strict justice which is the proper
walk of man.

Woman is always either above or below justice. Of
love, holiness, chivalry, magnanimity, and honor, she
has a marvellous appreciation; but for law, that comes
last of all.

Nevertheless, law and justice are the sovereign principles of modern life; exalted and complete principles
too; for impartial and kind justice (as justice ought to
be, to be justice at all) has the effect of love—that loftier
love which embraces the community.

If woman, in former times, ever rose to an appreciation of this, it was by an extraordinary effort. As her
great mission here below is to bring forth children, to
incarnate individuals, she takes everything individually,
and nothing by masses. Woman's charity consists in
bestowing alms upon whoever asks—in giving bread to
the hungry; and man's charity in those laws which
assure to all the action of all their powers; which make

all men free and strong, capable of providing for them
selves, and living with dignity.

Let us look into details. Let us see how slowly
woman enters into the spirit of the age.

Whose heart is more tender than that of a woman?
Her kindness embraces all nature. Everything that
suffers and is weak, among men or animals, is loved and
protected by her. Her gentleness towards her servants
is extreme ; and—what is new, and not of former times—
she never utters a command without giving her reason
for it, an explanation, with a touching consideration
which I may call the modesty of equality. But her
natural equals, whom she does not have to protect, who
never ask more than simple justice, are less agreeable to her. Her delicacy, not aristocratic, but that
which every refined and elegant woman has, suffers from
their rude contact. The great word of this new age,
"Fraternity," she spells, but cannot yet read.

She seems at times above the other virtues of our age:
She is more than just—chivalrous, and profusely generous. But justice, carried to excess, is no longer justice.

Her husband, who usually tells her everything, has
been very agitated—has passed a sleepless night, and
hesitates to disclose the cause of his uneasiness. There
are, in our struggling lives, many harsh and painful
things of which we are tempted to spare woman the
sad knowledge. She is all love, gentleness, and thank-
fulness. You can tell her of the love of the good ; but
how of the hatred of the bad ?—the hostile necessities of
justice and honor? the sacred wrath of justice? It
would make her heart ache to tell her all that.

This silence never alarms her. She is patient all night, hoping and waiting. At last, when morning comes, taking his hand in hers, she cautiously asks if he is not ill. He speaks out then, and no longer conceals the struggle he has undergone, the moral duel to which he is now challenged. He is compelled, this morning, either to ruin a competitor or succumb himself. He has a deadly weapon in reserve for his adversary—a secret, the revelation of which will effectually decide the matter between them. He can put this man down, and it is his duty to do so; for he is a factious man, an enemy to the public good.

"Yes, but he is your enemy," she answers. "That is what deterred me," he says. "And yet what can I do? If I sacrifice myself, I also disregard law and justice."

"Ah! my love, how I regret that I am no longer young and beautiful, no longer what I was that morning when I had the happiness to conceive a child from you. I love you so much! Alas! why have I not the same power over you! I swear to you that I would have clasped you so tightly, guarded you so closely, that you would never have been able to go out this morning."

"What would you have me do? In an hour all must be decided. By my absence I lose everything. I condemn myself. I yield the victory to injustice."

"But you are sparing your enemy. Be noble and good, for my sake. Make this beautiful sacrifice for me, and I will still believe myself young."

He is touched. She is so humble, so charming in her modesty and generosity! She who never asked anything for her own sake, is now all self-forgetful and self-sacri ficing, for the first time asking a favor. It is hard to refuse, to be unable to prove to her how much you sympathize with her feelings, how you respect and love her. She weeps and seems mortified. This is too strong a temptation. Yet justice claims him—his coun· try, and the right.

O Love! Love! you do not yet know what justice is!

---•---

VII.

DEATH AND AFFLICTION.

As age advances, my thought, journeying on, a per· severing traveller, through life and history, has at last reached the summits of two hills, where it gladly rests, and whence it can see all the world. These hills are Death and Love.

From these two, the earth seems a very little thing. Its extent is as nothing; and even the duration and the difference of ages grow dim. Our ignorance causes us to exaggerate all diversities. From this elevated seat, under different costumes I see the eternal man.

This does not deter me from descending to the plain beneath, and reaping my harvest on the fields of His· tory and Natural History. But I do like the Swiss. In winter I work below; when my work is done, I ascend again to those solitary summits which console me, by permitting me to embrace, in a grand simplicity, all the seeming combats of things, and to recognise the profound harmony in all that seems discordant.

This book set out from death, to which it now returns.

In the first pages we saw it; there death, violent death, revealed to us woman (and through her love) in the organic mystery from which everything proceeds.

, Death, the invisible yet ever-present companion of this book, has appeared but twice in it, and both times without striking a blow. And this has sufficed to tighten the bond of love, with a nervous strength that it never had before. Death threatened to appear in the drama of Confinement. It again showed itself on the lark day of Illness; and such is its potent charm in uniting hearts, that, at its second appearance, an everlasting jet of flame burst forth; and this I called the *Rejuvenescence of Love.*

But Death is not done yet. It contends that Life, which is believed to be the sole condition and the means of being, yet prevents the existence of certain other things. It asserts that if there still remain a distinction between the two souls—if the woman remain ever devoted to Grace, and the man to Justice, without the possibility of blending, it is the fault of Life. Death says that it alone can remove this last difference, and that Love, which is unable to do away with it, will obtain through his sombre sister the effectual union.

Well, Death, if it must be so, I ought not to object. I cannot defend these two children of my brain against you, though I have created, nourished, caressed, united, and counselled them for the twenty years that I was meditating this book of Love, and the two years that I have been writing it; I have loved them, I regret to part from them. But what can I do, if it is Life itself which prevents Love from attaining its consummation?

It is for the man to die and for the woman to mourn.

So we generally see it. The feeble woman, from grief to grief, from tears to tears, lives on, and is left a widow.

It is beautiful in man to die in his strength, to die young, at least in full vigor. He is so much the more regretted. Let us not pity him, but her.

If the man should survive, being occupied and diverted by work, he would perhaps feel this great affliction less, or at least not for so long a time. But for her—alas! how deep will Death's shaft strike! We hardly dare to think of that.

I remember, as if it were yesterday, that, on the day after my grandfather was buried, it having rained that night, my grandmother said, in a tone which brings the tears to my eyes, for all these forty years: " Mon Dieu! it is raining on him!"

We cannot change that; it is the voice of nature. That will be said over and over again, by all men and all women—perhaps whispered, and inwardly stifled—but thought certainly.

When we are cool, and love but little, we are more exalted and prouder. We have no idea of burying our heart in the grave. We imagine beautiful wings for it. But when the anguish of bereavement really holds us in its clutches, takes us by the throat as it were, it becomes invincible, and we say "It is raining on him!"

Is this a simple vesture, a garment, as it is said to be? This body which day by day received the alluvium of life, which in its indestructible bones bears traces of all its activity and passion, which for a thousand years will retain those admired teeth, that living silk of hair which you have so often caressed—all is so blended with the creature herself that his heart is to be pardoned for confounding them, for seeing in them her who is no longer there, for saying, "It is raining on her."

* * * * * * * * * *

It is December. A cold sun lights up the frost with which the fields are whitened. The house, once noisy, now silent, shivers in the winter blast. The fireplace, which formerly shed its light upon the complete family circle, now desolate itself, hardly serves to warm the widow who crouches over it. In a corner of the room two chairs wait—and will wait for ever: the armchair which, as he entered, he drew up to her side, to talk over the events of the day, and his projects for the morrow—and near it, the little low chair in which the child slipped between father and mother, and, interrupting them with his prattle, forced them to smile.

Of her what remains? a shadow. Her beautiful hair, now arranged in white bands, covers her thin temples. She is yet elegant, and looks even grand, with her still young and slender form, as she walks with downcast eyes through the deserted rooms. She no longer recalls the charming face, the eyes which once unsettled hearts, and were for one faithful heart a destiny; she conceals all that she can conceal of them. But, nevertheless, two things remain which the young would envy her. One is the admirable attribute of purity which God grants as a consolation to the innocent woman who passes through life without touching it. The complexion in which no trouble is ever visible, gains in transparency; it passes from the rosiness of youth to a rosy pearliness, with delicate shadings.

The other attribute which adorns our widow in spite of herself, which even lends her perhaps, under her mourning and her black veil, a mysterious éclat that was wanting in her days of triumph, is her gentle yet penetrating look. The eye is the true beauty, the lasting beauty which time itself is forced to respect, age even to augment. Trials and sufferings may have impaired the rest; but the eye, like the heart, is embellished by suffering.

She leaves the half-extinguished fire, and, approaching the window, happy to see the close of day, looks out upon the dreariness of winter, with her hands clasped over her heart, to whose voice she listens. Soon the northern sky is studded with bright stars. Death, Old Age, Winter, which, in these bright nights, sharpens his piercing shafts—all these combine against the poor heart and chill its everlasting flame.

"The world, youth, and distinction," she says, "were but partial slumbers, troubled dreams, from which my love never derived its clearness. Now, all thine, I watch!"

VIII.

OF LOVE BEYOND THE GRAVE.

But, dear one, this is watching and weeping too long. The light of the stars grows dim, and in a moment it will be morning. Take some repose now. Your other half, whose absence so afflicts you, and whom you seek in vain in your empty rooms and in your widow's couch, will talk to you in your dreams:

"Oh! how much I had to say! and how little, while alive, did I say! At the first word, God took me away from you. I had hardly time enough to say: I LOVE. To pour out my heart to you I require eternity.

"A sweet concert, sanctifying earth, had commenced between us. Of our double heart the celestial harmonist had just made a divine instrument; he was playing the prelude. If the string has snapped, if death, which seems to us such a shrieking discord, has hushed this lyre, do not think, my love, that it is hushed for ever, nor that God has thrown it aside. No, the hymn is suspended, to be resumed in a more sonorous sphere, in sovereign liberty, enfranchised from this lower world.

"You know, not a morsel, not an atom of the body in which my soul was clothed, is lost. Of the elements which constituted it, each one will surely find its fellow, and return to its affinities. How much more then should the soul itself, the harmonic power which constituted the unity of this body, survive and last! It does survive, but as one. Unity is its nature. It remains, and is

14

more and more what it was, a centre of attraction. All
that revolved about it in its first life, by the analogies
of nature, and the assimilation of love, irresistibly returns
to it. I am incomplete, and await you; the need of union
that my soul carried away with it, makes it ever aspire
towards the possession of its dearest half, which your
world still keeps from it.

———

"It had to be thus. Recall to your mind our torments of love—the effort, always made but never satisfied, to interchange our souls—the impotence of pleasure
even, the trace of melancholy in our happiness. Words,
looks, and the most ardent transports, still left a barrier
between us. What it was we knew not. The heart
always said: "By and by," and "That is not it." In
generation even, where Nature herself pauses, Love went
on. Its natural regret was that, itself proceeding from
light, being the sole and exclusive love of the beloved
object, it should so soon be blinded and left in utter
darkness, that in this profound obscuring personality
should disappear and be swallowed up; that in her it
no longer knew at that moment, it was she. . . . Hence
came sadness, and doubt, and the bitterness of saying
"What is this thing, always incomplete and uncertain,
which only attains its *desire* by undefining it, by losing
all idea of it?—In this impulse of soul to soul, all has
vani..ned; and I cannot tell whether the union was a
u:..on, or a momentary death, in a flash of pleasure.

"So that with these burning transports an unexpected
third was mingled—the idea of death. Not frightful,
but melancholy, and not without a certain charm. Death
said: 'Fear not, but hope. A false death has made you

feel that you will progress but little here below. It is
elsewhere, it is by me and through my deliverance that,
ascending the ladder of luminous worlds, yourselves par
ticipating in the freedom of light, you may penetrate
each other, and, without losing for a moment the clearness of love, blend together in one emanation of
light!'

———

"We will ascend thus. But by what means, and at
what cost? Seek the simplest means, and it will be that
of God. For, though human art gropes its way by complicated and painful circuits, that of God goes on the
straight road, quickly and easily. Mentally, as physically, like seeks like, and instinctively they come together. Otherwise infinite strength would be lost in
dispersion. This machine of the universe—so visibly
harmonic in palpable things, would be in things invisible
just the opposite—a discordance, far beneath the failures
of the most unskilful of workmen.

"Did we on earth obtain an assimilation and a perfect resemblance? Our essays thereto were vain. The
blindness of my desire, the abandonment of your sacrifice, bringing us always back to the same effort, left beyond our reach a hundred accessible doors of the soul
by which we might have joined each other. You knew
but a single man in me; and yet I contained several.
The quiet of widowhood, and the strength of your
memory, will bring them back to you gradually, and in
the world of a soul which belongs to you, which is
always your property, you will make more than one
happy discovery. Gather up this strength and these
thoughts, which were myself. Taken into your heart

and brooded over by your love, they will be to you as a
new impregnation, got from the world of spirits.

"I suffer at seeing you suffer. But yet you must not
recover. Such a posthumous assimilation as ours is
only effected by pain, a bleeding wound. This wound
will swallow up my soul, and, fusion thus effected, you
can no longer remain down there. An irresistible attraction, taking you some morning, there where your
heart is not, will bring you, like an arrow, here where it
is, where I am. It will be no more difficult than it is for
a spring, which has been kept down by a heavy weight,
the weight removed, to rebound and leap up again,
returning to its nature. Now, I am your nature and
your natural life; the obstacle removed, you return to me.

"This obstacle is the difference which is still between
us. Oh! I implore you, become myself, and you will
be mine entirely!

"Sorrow is all your present existence. I would have
you filled with an active sorrow. Do not remain seated
at that cold marble sepulchre. Wear a great affliction,
really worthy of me, with noble tears, which should enlarge all hearts.

"I see those poor creatures, my friends, distracted, not
feeling my spirit among them. I see the lost flock running wildly away, as if I were really in the tomb. Your
work be it not to permit them to despair or forget.
Yours the duty to say: 'He still lives!'

"If you affirm this, they will believe it. My house,
which was their house, will call them back and maintain
their fraternity. In their uncertainties, and painful fluc-
tuations, they will wish to see my hearth again, to warm
themselves by its fire: that fire burns in you.

"Tl ere you will preserve my soul, and perhaps extend its dominion. Through you it will vegetate and put forth new roots. More than one whom I could not gain over, in the roughness of my masculine manners, may come to me when he finds me under the touching figure of a woman, beautiful in her sorrow and hei hope.

"This circle of friendships, which was my glory, has in you its unity, the flame which will prolong my life to it. Keep this loved group together; maintain among them so thoroughly my thought, that, assimilated to me, I may see you some day all arriving together in my new sojourn—that I may see you again as formerly, when young and so charming, as you entered the room and cut short my work, saying with your dawn-like smile: 'Be joyful, for here are your friends!'"

Such the widow, and such the widowhood. It is the delayed soul of the husband, who, in his faithful half, still manifests himself here, and, as memory and presentiment, affects the transition between two worlds.

A great and sacred position this, to have one foot already in the higher path, ready and eager to ascend towards the superior life! So, in approaching this woman, we all perceive a sacred thing in her, the gentle influence of the dead, who have no battles here on earth, and only wish to do here what good they can. I should like to dwell on this; this priesthood of the widow is a touching feature in the Religion of the Future. But enough for the present.

So I do not follow her in those friendships of the past of which she forms the connecting bond, nor in those new friendships that she makes with the one who is no more, in transmitting his soul under that form of maternal love which is called instruction.

If the husband has left no works to answer for him, simply acts which are still discussed, if he had especially worn out his days in the struggles of public life, then, then above all, will he require to have his other and surviving self watch over his memory, to preserve and defend it from misconstruction, to secure to him the heart of posterity, a resurrection of glory.

This always comes to whosoever awaits it in the person of a patient watcher. Some morning a light breaks; and the widow, long thrust into the shade, as if buried with him, sees (as saw the Seven Sleepers of the legend) the banner he had followed, hung out upon the walls of the temples, bright and clear in the splendor of the dawn.

And she has then, in her old age, the charming surprise of hearing people say, as if HE were still alive: "This is a just man!"

From all sides, children, whom he did not know, come to her, all claiming such a father. They regret that they are young, because they could not see him. They interrogate curiously her who had the happiness of being an eye-witness of his life. Lo! he is already one of the ancients. She sees him receiving the homage of posterity.

Such is the effect of the legend, his memory, upon all. How much more, then, upon her who has beheld so near loved, touched the lamented object, and who now sees him through the vistas of tradition, transfigured with light!

The shrine of the departed just remains for new

generations, an object of religion. No youth approaches it without honoring the widow. He finds a pleasing woman, who is far from recalling the long ago from which the legend comes. What preserves this grace, is the love that fills her heart, her kindness towards all, her gentle resignation, her sympathy with the young and her wishes for their happiness.

She is still beautiful in her love, and beautiful in the broad shade which adorns and enfolds her. More than one, at twenty, sorry to have been born so late, returns to her in spite of himself, and leaves her with regret, cursing time, which delights in separating us thus, and saying from the bottom of his heart . " **O woman, whom I could have loved !**"

Notes and Explanations.

Notes and Explanations.

———o———

1. *What Love has been* in ancient and modern society.

2. *What it might be now*, in our present condition, taking it as a means of moral reform, which alone can render social reforms possible.

3. Finally, *what it will become*, in a world of justice and intelligence, such as we some day shall have.

Such is the subject in its completeness. At present I deal with the *second* part only.

The first and the third are necessarily complicated by an endless number of religious, social, and political questions, which I must postpone.

The second part, which I give, is *love in itself*, concentred on what appears an individual object; love followed in a progress usually deemed solitary. But nothing in morals is thus isolated.

Here it creates the home, and creates it solidly, because it makes of it a living, expanding, and progressive thing. The fire dies out if it is left alone; the tree dies if it does not vegetate.

Proceeding in its true spirit, free from the vain agitation which enervates and renders it barren, Love will have that natural progress which it so often has had, that powerful radiation from which so often, in history, societies have sprung.

————

My peculiar regret, in leaving this book so brief and imperfect, is that I have not been able this time to develope the chapters which might rightly be called those on *culture and education*, or moral discipline, those being substantially practical chapters, into which I have put (according to my limited capability) the germs of a new art—ne w, but how necessary! For the family nowadays, being so little upheld by the Church and the community, is each day obliged to ask of Love the aliment of its moral life, to draw continually from its profound depths.

How can we talk to woman at the sacred moments which precede and follow marriage? How can we take her always in those hours of perfect faith when she listens, and believes everything beforehand? And how, also, may we call her back when, long after, her heart wavers, when, weary and sad, it lies at the mercy of caprice? This is what I should have wished to develope at length.

In the chapters on *Fecundation* and *Moral Incubation*, I should have wished to give some examples of the true culture of love. I have at least marked a very essential point, where the education of woman is distinguished from our own by the necessity of observing the rhythm of her life, and the manner in which nature measures out her time.

In the chapters on *Temptation* and *Medication of the Heart*, I would have multiplied the often very simple recipes by which love is diverted from its course, evaded or cured. Oftenest the beloved object counts for but little in the passion ; it is the occasion which does everything: the person who loves has need of loving. She is but slightly smitten, perhaps in love with love itself. The love of a child, the love of an idea, of a new place, of a serious affair, would suffice to calm it. Often, too, a woman who has seen but little of life becomes prejudiced in favor of a man of inferior merit of whom she constructs an ideal. Her good sense would return to her if you should bring her face to face with true superiority. One who was infatuated with a brilliant provincial talker needed nothing more, to cure her, than to go and see Béranger.

Again: I should have wished to develope those main and important chapters where the woman, having obtained all her legitimate ascendency, being a tender loving wife, is also like a young mother to the man, regulating and repairing his expenditure of life ; often calming his blind fury, often restoring him his brilliancy of mind ; at one time imparting pleasure, at another power, but always—always happiness. (Book V chapters ii. and iii.)

It is here that the agreement of the moral and physiological sciences will create the most fertile of all arts, diametrically opposed to the morbid influence of the old casuistic laws —*the art of vivifying by love.*

We have paused on the threshold of this delicate subject, although we know very well that the hypocritical modesty which has here drawn the curtain and left all to caprice, has purified nothing, rendered nothing more moral than before. In relinquishing the task of informing us as to the internal affinities of marriage, it has made of it the obscure sphere of a prosaic physical life, which men have thought they could safely despise. It has been decided that love is nothing but enervation, not knowing that in it resides the stimulus to infinite strength.

Not long ago a brilliant surgeon, the oracle of students, was lecturing them, in accordance with the doctrines of a great and harsh master, on the inferiority of woman and the royalty of man, the vanity of love, etc. He thought to emancipate them, and make them despise pleasure. An illustrious physiologist, a friend of mine, who was present, said to him: "Take care, sir! take care! They will adopt the brutality of love with only too great facility; but not its gravity, not the masculine tenderness which it conceals in the heart of the family. They will not understand this bitter censor, who would strike too hard to produce an impression. I tell you, as a physician, that this contemptuous talk about women is very dangerous; it does not induce abstinence; on the contrary, it makes the man wander wretchedly about, and leads him straight into enervation."

To return to the gaps in this book. I should have wished to guide the woman in the interior culture that she can give herself. Her husband, who upheld her when she was young—later, in the press of business, and in the cares of life, returns home at night fatigued, and often disheartened. But it is her task to create in her own heart that paradise wherein revivifying sources will abound to reanimate him. She will find this in her love, in the innocent voices of Nature, which translate to her God's word. "A Rose for a Counsellor" is a great deal. I should have liked to let that rose speak often, for a long time, continually. It has much to say to the woman of these days. And the latter can readily understand it, being herself so delicate in heart and ear.

That great adept in harmony, Nature, in the name of God, will advise either the woman or the flower to harmonize with the strong stalk which supports her, and not to bloom by herself. And of what use would it be to shine separately for a few moments in the peril of a bouquet? This stem must not be disdained. Neither disdain this man. If he is not the contemplative genius of a past age, if he is not the handsome warrior, the hero of antiquity, remember, my dear girl, that to offset this, he has one very superior aspect—he is the strong workman, he is the powerful creator of an immense world of science, of industry, and of riches, which yesterday arose from his energy and activity. He has changed all things. By the side of Nature, he has built another nature, of his genius and his strength. You lollers (we must say it of the richer classes), you beautiful indolence, look on and enjoy this.

"But how can that be? My husband is a merchant, a tradesman, a workman." Then he is a creator of riches. "A writer? a painter?" A creator in works of art. And you may go as low as you please; for all trade is art nowadays.

This universal effort, ideas, works, and productions, piling rapidly one above the other, all rise up to an enormous height. "Such means are prosaic," you say. But the result is so grand! Your husband, the man of modern times, found nothing done, and has done everything. If our fathers could return to earth, they would be frightened, and go down on their knees before their terrible sons. Look upon this martyr of labor with respect, with love, and with pity also. Do not be so puerile as to observe a little dust which your glorious Prometheus may have on his garments. Look at that pale forehead. In the aureole which irradiates it you see the sweat stand out, often a sweat of blood.

He, also, has a duty. It is not to let himself be so carried away in the fury of work that he shall be swallowed up in it, that he shall see but his own narrow road, and nothing but its details. There are no little things, I know. To succeed, minutiæ are necessary; without this, without precision, no result is possible. But the workman must remain greater than his work; he must prevail over it. It can only be strongly embraced when he is above it. If he retains the highest thought of it, he will have in that, day by day, a power over the woman, a hold upon her which he will never lose. She is faithful and loving to whosoever is great and strong. Now, in the lowest occupation, he who feels the life thereof, its affinities with art, reveals himself with grandeur.

I might have written more in this quiet retreat of Pornic, before this tranquil sea, which sympathized with this book, and whose deep rhymes have served it as an accompaniment. But here is a little girl— six or seven years old, I should judge—who unwittingly warns me that I have done enough. On the beach they were drawing sea water in buckets for bathing purposes. The child, a fisherman's daughter, stopped in her play to look on. "What are you thinking about?" I asked. "Sir," she answered, "the sea is a very strange thing. You may keep taking out as much as you please, but it always stays just as full."

This is just what I was thinking at that very moment, but of an other sea.

I have drawn what I could from this subject, bottomless and shore less ; but it is never exhausted.

My historical materials would make two volumes. My physiological notes one, or more. I cannot tell how many it would take to give even the extracts, the letters, the revelations and the actual facts by which I have profited.

This little sea, drawn from the great ocean of Love, sufficed to drown me. I was submerged in the multitude of my notes. I shall put them off now, and content myself with these.

NOTE 1.

A Glance at the Ensemble of this Book.

If towards the close of this volume we have not completely lost sight of the beginning, we should remember one of love's singulari- ties that at each of its stages it has imagined itself at the end, and thought itself sure of the infinite. Then every one laughed and said it was mad.

Not so much so as it seemed. Several times has it occupied and mastered the everlastingness of the soul, but, you will understand, of the

soul as it could only be at that time, in the narrow limits in which ı
is at first contained.

When love's flower, at twenty, said so impulsively, "I give myself
up to you, take me entirely!" it was not a lie; but what did she give ?
as yet but little. She gave what she had, not what she still lacked.
(Book II.)

When fecundation impregnated her so profoundly and changed her
being; when a blond and silken down, which came to deck her lip,
revealed her transformation; when her voice, gait, and so many involuntary signs seemed to say, "*He* is all in me," undoubtedly the consummation was attained. Attained, yes, inevitably; not the free consummation of the soul. (Book III.)

But, finally, the cravings of this imperfect liberty, which capriciously
protested, having conquered themselves, the momentary disagreement
of the mental and physical maladies (Book IV.) having given way to
harmony, the two souls found themselves in the most loving unity
they had ever yet obtained. With a more effusive joy, Love tri-
umphed this time, and said to itself, "I possess the infinite."

One thing, which woman only really attains in her second youth,
was wanting: that by an effort of the heart she should leave behind
her the passive state in which she nearly always lived, to take upon
her activity and movement, to make herself *him*; not by the dull fatality of impregnation, but by active will, by love (Book V.). Until then,
work separated them, and the woman had her own hours; now all hours
of the day and night are hers. In everything he feels that she is useful and charming, he cannot get on without her. She is the cherished
young companion in whom he finds seriousness, pleasure, whatsoever
he wills, ever ready to transform itself for him. She is his Viola, his
Rosalind, a loving friend in the morning, a wife in the evening, an
angel at all times.

Though obedient, she has, if need be, the upper hand; she knows
how to plan and to act. And, when the man, either in business or
thought, is weak and hesitates, in the agitated night especially, when his
troubled soul seeks and finds nothing, and seems as though bewildered,
she is there and smiles. The evil enchantment disappearing, he
laughs at himself. A kiss restores to him his wings.

Have we not here obtained what we sought, the absolute interchange
of being? Has not love now attained the infinite? Now that the

feeble woman has received, so completely taken, the soul of man, that she can, if necessary, give it back to him, and that in the failure of his manly genius she gives him what she has not, the generating spark—does not this seem the miracle of unity?

No, this may still be intensified one degree more: when both their minds meet in a kindly project, when both are softened by the surprise of finding that they have the same heart to such a degree, when love and pity blended melt in silent tears; this is the moment of fusion, when invincible love triumphs, when the soul renews its sense, when, often more ardently than in youth, returns the incentive to desire.

What a great thing is goodness! Everything else is secondary to it; grace, wit, intelligence, are worth nothing when not accompanied by it. Even alone, it is all-powerful. It is not a rare thing for a man to desire a woman because she is good, and for no other reason. Profound harmony of our being! It goes by the senses to the heart; it tends, by physical union, to attain and possess the moral suavity which is there. God is felt in it. This is why we wish to be united.

Love is a thing of the brain. All desire was first an idea.

Often a very confused idea—an idea that a state of the body (heat, intoxication, plethora) has seconded and inflamed, but not preceded. Of the two extremities of nervous life, the inferior one, that of sex, has little initiative power. It awaits the sign from above.

Recall your souvenirs. In the pleasure which seemed to you altogether instinctive, and not at all a matter of forethought, you will find, by thinking it over, that an occasion, an incident, or some new circumstance had previously awakened the mind.

If the circumstance was piquant, the idea new and lively, then your pleasure was great.

The renewing of desire is rendered inexhaustible by the fertility of the mind, the originality of ideas, the art of seeing and finding new mental aspects—in short, by the *optics of love.*

The simple changing of surroundings, climate, habitation, often suffices to change everything. The man who wearies of his wife in the lowlands, would love her on the Alps. Rousseau says that he was made virtuous by the sight of the Pont du Gard. And such a man would feel himself in love again at seeing the Lago Maggiore, Coliseum, or Vesuvius. This is no pleasantry. Do better. Transport these wearied ones to America: put them where a foreign language is spoken, amid new manners and customs, on the borders of the great forests; they will find it very nice to be together, to be to each other both native land and universe. The dear wife of his youth will find herself young again, desired as on the first day, and fruitful; she will be so without doubt. In the new world, new loves.

How much more vigorously would love be awakened, if to one or the other of the married pair there should come one of those joys of the mind which so add to beauty!—a heroic act, a triumph of opinion, anything for example. One of my friends, whose plays are very successful, finds at home, at each success, a recompense—he sees himself very much beloved. He who performs a noble, daring act, who saves a life, let us suppose, by risking his own, is never an old husband to his wife, but always a young lover. Love, in these circumstances, acquires immense strength, becomes a torrent of poetic life, which had never been looked for.

NOTE 2.

Is the Author Excusable for Believing that we can still Love?

As I have said, the subject of this book has recurred to me on many occasions: in 1836 through history; in 1844 through my sympathy for those young people whose life is a suicide; in 1849 through social tumults. I felt that *here* was the evil and the remedy. My discouraged mind brought up the public morals against me, and asked: "What is the use?"

Yet the terrible official statistics, of undoubted accuracy, which came to me at times, seemed to sound in my ears like a funeral knell—that the race even, the physical basis of this people, was compromised. For instance, the young men unfit for military service, dwarfed, hump backed, lame, in the seven years, 1831—1837, numbered only 460,000, and in the following seven years they increased 31,000, etc. Marriages have diminished to a fearful degree, in certain years; in 1851 *nine thousand less* than in the year preceding; in 1852 *seven thousand less* than in 1851 (that is 16,000 less than in 1850), etc. The official statistics of 1856 show that the population is diminishing or remains stationary. Widowers marry again, but widows do not. Add the enormous num ber of women who have committed suicide, or died miserably. As to the Morgue, see the *Annals of Hygiene and Forensic Medicine*, vols. II., VII., XVII, XLIV., XLV., XLVI., XLVIII., L., and VII. of the second series.

Neither do I see that the rest of Europe is less diseased than France.

Mark, that the life of Europe, so far, is the life of the world. If it dies, the world dies. America, flooded from Ireland, and by a hundred troublous elements, is urged on, by her adopted barbarity, to the conquest of the Catholic and uncivilized world, which threatens to destroy whatever youth she still retains, and to blast the hope of possible rejuvenescence that she might offer to the rest of the human race.'

I know that Europe has already undergone a sort of eclipse in the fall of the Roman Empire. But the situation was different, and even opposite in one point. That political event was preceded by an extraordinary enfeeblement of the mind. Now, on the contrary, the progress of inventive genius, accelerated in the last three centuries (which have done the work of ten thousand years), is in a brilliant *crescendo*. The miracle of miracles is not far from being accomplished; and truly, the greatest event that has occurred on this planet is that through the electric wire, becoming conscious of thought, the planet every moment obtains a sort of identity and personality.

·Whence come these miraculous applications? They are things sent down to us from the lofty tower reared by all the sciences. Babel? No, but a marvellous harmony. The short-sighted man calls it Babel, because when he has one stone under his eye, he does not see the next one, far less the whole edifice. But the sublime and master structure may laugh at that, for its base. is in Mathematics and its head in the Milky Way!

An incalculable power is this, not of intelligence only, but of life and its force. There can be no intellectual truth which does not bear upon actions.

In this great enlightenment, how can you die—with this, with such a perfect knowledge of the world and of yourself? When the Roman empire foundered, it went down in utter darkness. Before death, came night.

If the moral sense has declined, it is not a failure of the mind. The brain is not directly attacked, but it floats and fluctuates, through the enervation of the inferior organs. We have enormous strength but it is sadly scattered and wasted.

This whole book has its end in this:

Either concentrate yourself, or die.—The concentration of the vital forces supposes, first of all, the stability of the home.

We must not despise ourselves, and idly fold our arms. If we do, all is lost.

We are corrupted, it is true; but tainted water may again become good to drink. Our heroic fathers were not saints. The Idea, when it came, found them tramping about wofully in a bog. Now they look towards heaven, and inspired with the eternal beauty, they no longer know each other; wings have sprung from their shoulders!

Are the people of to-day worth less, on the whole, than those of my childhood? I see it to be the contrary. Of those former times there remains to me a sense of terrible barrenness. Who would support in these days the mortal dreariness of the *Martyrs?* The Abbé Geoffroy, Messrs. De Jouy, Baour held the reins of the press. No natural sentiment then. But few birds; not a flower. I saw them appear one by one: the hydrangea at forty years of age, the dahlia at thirty, etc. Nowadays, every hut has a rose-bush at the door, every seventh-story garret a flower on its window sill. The flag-man on the railroad, who cannot leave his sentry-box, takes advantage of the time between two trains to make himself a garden.

In my sixty years of life, I have seen the commencement and growth of one of the most serious manifestations of the human soul— the religion of the dead, the adornment of the grave. I was twelve years old in 1810, and my memories of that time are very clear. I distinctly remember that a cemetery then was an Arabian desert, where hardly any one ever came. Now it is a garden full of monuments and flowers. The progress of wealth has undoubtedly much to do with this; but so also has the progress of the heart. The cemetery is visited now; even the poorest find means to carry to it garlands and souvenirs. At the easiest season of the year, the wife of the poorest workman economizes a few pence from the family bread in order to buy flowers for the dead.

Death is the sister of Love. These two religions are related—indestructible, eternal. And if Death live on, why may not Love also?

I did not imagine, in the winter of 1856, that the cold public would hear a certain bird-song, an impatient robin-redbreast who flew away before the snow was fairly melted. But he was listened to. I then doubted that the noise of an ant-hill would be heard. But that also was listened to, and, some persons, they say, were much affected by it. How could this dark-working world of imperceptible creatures, having not the winged grace of the bird, make an impression? Because Love, which circulates in all things, was recognised there.

So I hoped on, *in spite of everything*. The excess even of evils gave me courage. Must not these follies and squanderings cease some time, through impotency at least? Ennui is also visible. Do the husband and wife gain anything by the practical divorce which is the custom nowadays? The wife, only too thoroughly feels the truth laid down by George Sand: "The lover is just as tiresome as the husband." On the other hand the poor husband does not reap complete enjoyment. There are no longer *filles de joie;* there are *filles de marbre* and women of sadness.

Besides, if *society* will not reform itself, there are thirty millions of French, a hundred or two hundred millions of Europeans, who are not at all in *society*, know nothing about the Bourse, nor fast balls, nor kept women. If there still remain two hundred millions of men to love, it will suffice.

Love cannot d e. It will re-make everything. It will re-make you, young man of twenty-nine years (this is the marrying age in Paris), young man though already not old enough, already fatigued. You think of settling down, but you dare not, in fear of the ruinous course of life to-day. If you are a practical man, read this book. Whatever the style may be, you will find in it several very practical things. You need, in your struggles here on earth, in the quicksands of the world, an earnest partner. You will not find her ready made, but this book will teach you how to make her. The mother cannot know beforehand what the sphere of action of her married daughter will be, nor prepare her for it Everything nowadays has become personal. Marriage varies infinitely, according to the husband. In certain occupations, the wife is a co-laborer with her husband, as, for instance—in trade. In others, as in the arts, she assists and inspires, *associates herself in his thought.* Finally, in the more laborious occupations, the lives of men

ℳ ιction and of public affairs, she is the natural confidante, and the only possible supporter and consoler of the mind. If you do not neglect ner, if you keep her conversant with your concerns, if you establish a complete communion with her, you will see how the person who in certain professions is considered useless, nevertheless brings thereto material force. In a world where everything is changing, you must have a fixed point on which you can rely for support. Now, this point is a home. The hearth is not a stone, as it is often called, it is a heart, and the heart of a woman.

— -

NOTE 3.

WOMAN REINSTATED AND PROCLAIMED INNOCENT BY SCIENCE.

SCIENCE is mistress of the world. It reigns without ever needing to command. The Church and the Law have to inform themselves of its decrees, and reform themselves according to its teachings.

Now, heretofore, the greater part of religious and civil laws in regard to woman could be summed up in one sentence : " *She is considered a thing, and yet punished as a person.*"

As the physiology, so the legislation. The Legislative inconsistencies came originally from the senseless physiology of barbarous ages They said at the same time : "Woman is an *impure thing,—and a esponsible person.*"

A thing *so impure*, that Moses pronounced death against the man who approached her at a certain period of the month.

A person *so responsible*, that her first fault sufficed to pervert for aver the will of the human race.

Christianity follows Moses. All the old Fathers condemn her, and make her the servant of the man, who is the superior being, and relatively pure. Her last and most terrible enemy is the metaphysician Saint Thomas, who reduces their thought to a formula ; he goes so far as to say, that the woman, being an *accidental* and *defective* creature. ought not to have entered into the primal creation.

What a fearful proposition ! God was mistaken, and made his work *defective !*

But, *defective* in what? Certainly not in beauty. They can bring forward nothing but the childish ideas of barbarians, about the physique. *She is impure.* Pope Innocent III. expressed it strongly: " *Offen-sive odors* and *uncleannesses* always accompany her."

This doctrine is not yet abandoned. A physician of Lyons, a stubborn defender of all the errors of the Middle Ages, declares and prints, in 1858, "that the menstrual blood is impure."

Now, let us state the facts:

1. *The woman is as pure as the man.* Our first Chemists, Messrs. Bouchardat, Denis, and others, have analysed this blood and found it to be the same as elsewhere in the organization.

2. *Is the woman responsible?* Undoubtedly, she is a person; but she is a *sick* person, or, to state it more exactly, a person *wounded* every month, who suffers almost constantly from that wound and from its healing. This has been admirably proved by the ovologists (Baër Négrier, Pouchet, Coste) between 1827 and 1847.

When an invalid is in question, if the law wishes to be just, it ought always to take into consideration, in every punishable act, this extenu-ating circumstance. To impose upon her the same punishment as upon the well person (I mean the man), is not an impartiality of justice, but a partiality and an injustice.

The law will modify itself, I have no doubt. But the first modifica-tion should take place in jurisprudence and legal practice. The magistrates will feel, as I have said, that, to decide and punish what there is *free* in the acts of woman, they must take into account the involuntariness which is associated therewith by illness. The continual presence of a medical jury in our courts of justice is indis-pensable. I have contended elsewhere that the death-punishment is wholly inapplicable to women. And there is hardly any article in the Code which can be applied to them without modification, espe-cially when they are pregnant. A woman takes something which does not belong to her. What can you do? She has had an insur-mountable *desire* for it. If you arrest her, you will do her a great injury. If you put her in prison, you will kill her. "Property is sacred," you say; I know it, because it is the fruit of labor. But there is in this case a superior *labor* which must be respected, and the fruit that she bears in her womb is the property of the human race. So that to have yours, which is perhaps worth two pence, back again you are going to risk two murders! I would much rather have you, when the thing taken is worth but a trifle, permit yourself to be robbed with a good grace, and abstain from arresting her. The ancient German laws expressly permit her to take a little fruit, without being subject to arrest.

With these thoughts of humanity is connected what I have said about the union of the two branches of science, *the science of justice, the science of nature.* What is most wanting in these is the sense of their analogies. In many points they are one and the same. *Justice must become Medicine,* informing itself from the physiological sciences, appreciating the degree of fatality which is connected with free actions, in short curing, not to punish solely, but to cure *Medicine must become Justice* and Morality. That is to say, that the physician, an intelligent judge of internal life, should enter into an examination of the moral causes which produce physical illness, and dare to go to the root of the evil, to reform the habits from which the malady proceeds. There is no malady which is not derived from our whole life. All attempts at cure are made in the dark, if not based upon a perfect knowledge of the patient, and his complete confession.

NOTE 4.

OF THE SOURCES OF THIS BOOK OF LOVE, AND OF THE SUPPORT THAT PHYSIOLOGY HEREIN LENDS MORALITY.

THE richest source from which I have drawn materials for this book, is, as I have said, the confidence with which my friends and many other persons have revealed to me their interior life. They were so sure of my sympathy that they often made me acquainted with more than one delicate particular which they concealed even from their own families. I have profited by everything, of course, without indicating anyone by too precise signs. But here, once for all, I can assure the reader that the ground upon which he walks is solid, and based upon realities. Such and such a sentence, which might be taken as a bit of literary filling in, is, in reality, an anecdote or a fact from everyday life.

Nevertheless—these rich materials, so precious in the study of human morality, would have been of but little use to me, if I had not had for my advantage the sure starting point which physiology has recently given us. I have drawn largely upon the works of physicians, and their infinitely instructive verbal communications.

Not having this instruction, the literary men who have treated the same subject before me, have floated about at the mercy of chance, and said many vague and contradictory things.

It will be readily understood why I do not examine the more recent works, despite my esteem and respect for the genius of their authors. As for the more ancient, two works have occupied the public mind: the serious book of Senancour (the 1st and 2nd editions, not the 3rd); and the jesting one of Balzac. These books are in every way opposed to each other. The man of 1800 utters the severest condemnations against adultery. And the man of 1830 begins and ends his book with the well known phrase, "Adultery is merely the affair of a sofa." Balzac confesses that he intended to write a serious work, but could not succeed. Besides, there is absolutely *nothing* in his book, either serious or comic. That of Senancour, on the contrary, if we except two or three pages inspired by the times in which he lived, is very beautiful, very forcible, and full of ideas. His bitter sadness is very eloquent. "O woman, whom I could have loved!" etc. I have stolen this line from him, it is the last one of my book.

To return to the physicians, we may say that they have done themselves injustice by their exteriors. They cannot surely be accused of hypocrisy. With an ostentation of brutality that they get from the lecture-room and the hospital and the handling of the scalpel, they have none the less laid down truly humane doctrines. Rough and cynical in appearance, they have nevertheless founded what may be called the *creed of mercy*.

They think themselves materialists. They are not so much so as they would appear to be. Their discoveries in material things have lent admirable confirmation to the voice of the heart. Natural History

15

has spoken like Philosophy itself. Nature has u.tered the words of the soul.

Nothing is purer and higher than this revolution. .t is the victory of the Mind.

Hence three capital results :

1. The low and material ideas that were entertained of the periodi- .cal crisis of woman are now elevated, purified, spiritualized.

2. The material and brutal decisions, so often unjust, that were passed upon the maiden, are reduced to naught, and marriage brought back to the confidence, the harmony of two hearts.

3. But at the same time it receives a serious consecration from Nature herself. So forcible and decisive is the first marriage, that its physical effects continue in the second.

In the very brief chapter on the Wedding, I have summed up, under a simple form, and with a regard for propriety, the numerous facts for which I am indebted to the confidences of medical men. I have there set forth, in accordance with their instructions, the insignificance of a proof which proves nothing—nowadays especially, in the refined and nervous classes, often sickly and thin-blooded Ancient barbarism, continued in a so-called spiritual age, began the union by distrust, exacted pain, and often visited a poor innocent girl with eternal sorrow and humiliation. Debased and cruel materialism! Her whom you esteem sufficiently to confide to her your entire life and future, you should place confidence in at once for all her past life. How would it be, if she should dare to ask you about yours? And when she has had a *misfortune*, a weakness even, you are sure that she will love him who adopts her much more than the cruel ingrate whose love was but an outrage.

Medicine has here made matter subordinate, laid down the fact that this bodily accident is entirely secondary. The rights of the soul are reëstablished. Marriage henceforward is but love. Far from exacting that this day, which is one of bliss to one, should be a day of tears to the other, the mother and the husband have been advised of the precautions which diminish pain. (Fabre, I., 3, 19 ; Menville, II., 103 ; Raciborski, 133 ; etc.)

On the grave question of the supposed impurity of woman, her periodical suffering, we find the same material barbarity among these pretended spiritual'sts. On the other hand, physicians, purifying this phenoltenon, have proved its touching and elevated character. What you call a purgation, you fools, is the sacred wound of love in which your mothers conceived you.

This ovarium, always torn and always healing, is nothing less than a continual accouchement. From 1821 to 1826, two Englishmen, Power and Girwood, it is said, suspected this law. But their works remained unknown, even in England. It was from wholly new and personal observations that the German, Baër, in 1827, established the existence of the ovum in woman, and the Frenchman, Négrier, in 1831 and in 1858, showed that each month the ovum matures, ruptures its envelope, and makes its way from the ovary to the matrix.

Pouchet's great work (*Spontaneous Ovulation*, 1842, 1847) establishes, on a systematic basis, the law of generation, showing by analogous facts, observed in all races of animals, not only that this law is such in the human race, but that it could not be otherwise.

The law laid down by Pouchet, and the modifications added by Négrier and Raciborski (in a report approved by the *Academy of Sciences*), and the unpublished observations of M. Coste, prove that conception only takes place when the discharge announces the appearance of the ovum ; that is to say, that it occurs during the courses, as well as a little before or a little after. Hence, there is barrenness during a part of the month.

These truths, endorsed by the opinion of the *Academy of Sciences*, and the teachings of the *College of France*, have appeared in all their glory from the labors of Messrs. Coste and Gerbe. In ten years' observations on women who have committed suicide, they have, by a practical book of admirable clearness, by an atlas (which will remain an immortal chef d'œuvre), effectually confirmed this law.

The history of human ovology is summed up in a most satisfactory manner in an excellent work, full of new and original matter, the Physiology of Messrs. Robin and Béraud. Already this anatomist, our first microscopist (Robin), had shed strong light upon the science of generation, both by his description of the uterine mucus, and his Report on the male ovum, which from the female to the male, from animals to vegetables, discloses the uniformity of nature's process.

In 1847, the same year in which M. Coste published the results of his numerous dissections, and decided the ovology of woman, Dr

Lucas published a work on *Physical Transmission*, two volumes oc
tavo. This is an important and capital work, which in spite of cer
tain cloudy abstractions, called attention to its author, previously
unknown, as a man of superior and excellent mind. The press took
but little notice of it. I do not know what has become of the author
I have sought for him in vain. If he is still living, I beg that he will
here receive the assurance of my gratitude and admiration.

In Vol. II., Chapter IV., pages 53–65, M. Lucas brings together a
great number of facts, which prove that, from the lowest to the highest in the scale of life, from the least of the insects to birds, to mammalia, and even to the human species, fecundation extends far beyond
its actual moment; that the act of generation does not give a single
result, but that it has many and enduring effects, and often continues
long into the future.

The plant-louse is impregnated at one time for forty successive generations (Bonnet); others reduce this number, but without denying the
fact. The caterpillar is impregnated for three or four generations
(Bernouilli). The bee for a year (Réaumur). The hen for her whole
brood (Harvey).

As to the mammalia, the most accurate observations are derived from
the skilful and persevering English breeders. The pedigree of race-
norses, their marriages, their *mésalliances*, recorded for the last two
hundred years in their stud-book, with as much care as any royal gene-
alogy, have put science on the right track. We have learned how to
observe and experiment. It has been found that the Arabian mare,
who has, though only on one occasion, had a caprice for an ass, presents nothing but asses to the illustrious lovers she may afterwards
entertain (Edward Home); or, at best, mixed colts, which sadly
remind you, by their hides or their forms, that their mother has stooped
from her station. Our Poitou breeders understand this perfectly, and
do all they can to guard against it (Magne). But in Africa, where the
mares are but little watched, the colts they have, even from the purest
Arabians, often betray, by their scrawny and awkward appearance, the
inferiority of the first love.

It is the same with the bitch; the first dog impresses her more than
twenty that may follow; he marks their offspring with a resemblance
to himself (Stark, Burdach); a thing very commonly observed by our
peasants in the south of France. The domestic sow, surprised by the

wild boar, retains his fierceness, and bears to his peaceat e s. ocessors, bristling pigs (Meckel). This law, which plainly devotes the female to her first love, and protests against those which follow, appears to be universal among the superior animals.

Is it the same in the human species? Analogous to the other mammalia in the development of the ovum and the periodical crisis (*Veterinary Journal*, 1846), are they so also in the enduring character of the first impregnation? Do the first love and the first child determine those of the future? And does the father of that child extend his paternity to those which the woman may have by a lover, or by a second husband?

There is no doubt that in us, whose mind and will interfere so powerfully in the functions of physical life, the immutability of general laws has to contend with the reactions of freedom and of individual passion, which cannot be calculated upon.

Nevertheless, the facts seem to attest that nature usually resists such reactions, and imparts a durable character to the first fecundation (Lucas, Vol. II., 60). The old-time physicians, Fienus and Aldovrand, observed that adulterous women often had, from the lover, children resembling the husband. In their day, it was an adage that "The son of adultery pleads for his mother." It was supposed that the woman, in this stolen act, had thought of him whom she feared, and that this fear marked her offspring with his features. But this explanation will not do for the females of the lower animals. It is not fear which makes them reproduce the likeness of the first male in the young they bear to the second and his successors.

Besides, we have seen widows, impregnated in their first marriage, afterwards have, by a second, and a dearly beloved husband, children who resembled the first husband, long dead, and but little regretted. Here, neither fear nor love had any influence. It was the physical result of a modification of the organism. The first fecundation influenced the succeeding for several years in advance—perhaps for life.

If it were always thus; if the first impregnation infallibly modified the woman for ever, adultery would be impossible (at least in its results). The possession of the husband being unalterable, the only one deceived would be the lover.

This transformation of the woman does not appear alone in the process of generation, but virtually in everything. The wife, even when very young, after a year or two of marriage, wears on her lip a light down, imperceptible in blondes, but very noticeable in brunoetts. The voice and gait become less feminine, and proclaim a new cond. hou. But what is surprising, a thing I have often observed, is, that her handwriting changes: that of the wife gradually grows more like that of the husband.

Some ancient physicians, Bartholin, Perrault, Sturm, and, later Grasmoyer, have thought that, even without fecundation, the marriage relation suffices, after a time, to masculize woman. My friend, Doctor Robin, so profound an observer of the microscopic world, without admitting the rasher theory of these authors, for different reasons believes in this transformation.

The principle of permanent impregnation, prolonged into the future, saddens one at the first glance like a fate. But, on the other hand, it lights up to a great moral depth the dark crisis of love, and spiritual izes it. It reveals itself in all creatures; at this moment, most clearly in man, in a soaring towards the infinite, a flight into eternity.

What goes on then, with the greatest and the smallest, resembles so little the ordinary phenomena of matter, that we are tempted to say, in regarding the lowest of all created things, Here nothing is matter; all is mind.

One phrase resounds, always the same, along the scale of life, whether you go up or down—a single phrase (Love knows but one)—"I wish for something beyond myself. I wish for too much—all! always!"

The blind impulse of desire in inferior beings is a gross infinity of strength, which, creating an infinity of *numbers*, guarantees an infinity of succession. The superior longing, in ascending, is for an infinity of the beautiful, of the good—an infinity of *quality*. Desire, then, cre-ates concentrated and powerful beings, if not capable of feeling, at least capable of conceiving of, the infinite.

So Love ascends, and always will ascend, without reaching its sum-mit. It would have nothing that is not absolute, endless, without margin or limit. In its profound instinct, it desires itself—like Love Eternal. It penetrates itself with light, feels itself God, but dazzles itself. . . . . Darkness closes around it. . . . . The Infinite has appeared —disappeared. . . . .

"Alas!" it says, "I had so many things to say to it!"

www.ingramcontent.com/pod-product-compliance
Lightning Source LLC
Chambersburg PA
CBHW022149010726
47493CB00002B/404